Paranamanco

BY THE SAME AUTHOR

The Night Orchid - Conan Doyle in Toulouse
The Thieves of Silence

Paranamanco

by
Jean-Claude Dunyach

Translated from the French by
Sheryl Curtis

A Black Coat Press Book

Visit our website at www.blackcoatpress.com

ISBN 978-1-64932-192-3. First Printing. March 2023. Published by Black Coat Press, an imprint of Hollywood Comics.com, LLC, P.O. Box 17270, Encino, CA 91416.

TABLE OF CONTENTS

Introduction
Jean-Claude Dunyach, the Poet of the Flesh

by Natacha Vas-Deyres

For my father

Jean-Claude Dunyach, born in 1957, belongs to the generation of French authors who began to publish during the 1980s, which includes Roland C. Wagner, Emmanuel Jouanne, Sylvie Lainé, and Jean-Marc Ligny. At a time when French science fiction was struggling to explore new ways of storytelling influenced by surrealism or the *nouveau roman*, this generation has given science fiction a new life by mixing the hard-science approach with the supernatural and the fantastic, while paying glowing tribute to authors of the golden age of Anglo-Saxon SF.

For more than thirty years, Dunyach has been one of the major authors of contemporary French science fiction, with more than a hundred published short stories (including two collections translated into English, *The Night Orchid: Conan Doyle in Toulouse* [2004] and *The Thieves of Silence* [2009]) and eight novels, including *Étoiles mourantes* (Dying Stars), cowritten with Ayerdhal in 1999.[1] He has won numerous literary prizes for his fiction, including the Grand Prix de l'Imaginaire in 1984 and 1998, the Readers Prize of the English review *Interzones* (2001), the Rosny aîné Prize in both the novel (1992) and

---

[1] The French science fiction writer Marc Soulier, who used the solitary pseudonym "Ayerdhal" for his literary work, passed away on October 27, 2015, in Brussels.

short-story categories (1992, 2008), and the Grand Prix de la Tour Eiffel (1999). And in his spare time, he is a research engineer at Airbus and a lyrics writer for local singers.

As a science-fiction writer, Dunyach was influenced by Samuel Delany, Ray Bradbury, and more particularly J. G. Ballard. The main keywords attached to his work are *memory* and *death* (treated as opposite sides of the same coin), and his work often explores the essence of time. The specificity of Dunyach consists in making these essential concepts tangible for the reader by giving them a symbolic substance: time itself becomes as tangible as sand, stone, ashes, water; love stories can be petrified as semi-precious stones and worn as trophies—the universe itself complies as a sheet of paper or a piece of cloth and can be creased. But Dunyach's originality lies behind this realization of the metaphysical concept: once materialized, the poetic dimension of the concept is underlined and exploited through the full sensory dimension of the text and the importance granted to the feelings of the flesh. Even the more abstract concepts can be touched, smelled, and tasted.

The characters in his short stories are physically hurt or twisted, often with traumatic experiences in their past, but they still act as links between the individual and the collective. In his opinion, any kind of system—especially a political one—can be defined depending on how it deals with frontiers and marginality. Dunyach favors an individual narrative point of view for a better detection of systems' weaknesses (cities, societies, religions).

In that respect, the most distinctive and original characters in his work are the "AnimalCities"—living extraterrestrial city-shaped animals, made of flesh and cartilage, traveling through space from node to node on the web of the universe. Their symbiotic liaison with human-ity gradually leads people to understand the global nature of reality. This space-opera universe gradually builds it-self upon a handful of short stories and two large novels: *Étoiles mortes* (Dead Stars; 2000) and *Étoiles mourantes* (Dying Stars; 2014).

Dunyach and French Science Fiction

When Jean-Claude Dunyach started to write and publish stories at the beginning of the 1980s, the situation of science fiction in France was quite different from to-day: SF was part of the so-called counterculture, like rock and roll and tattoos, and it was an important driving force, especially among students. It was, however, neglected or even treated as garbage by anyone over thirty-five. Writ-ers of SF had a bright future back then, and they were fighting for it. But in France, such literature was not taken seriously by the dominant media—neither TV nor main-stream newspapers were mentioning it. "It's science-fic-tion" was a popular way to say, "It is unrealistic, crazy, and immature." Authors and critics were mostly fans (one of the lowest life forms, in everybody's mind), and SF was the kind of nonsense everybody was supposed to abandon upon entering "real life" shortly after puberty.

At the end of the 1970s, French SF was either highly political—French society had been deeply transformed by "May 1968," a revolution in mentalities that took its source in a student movement—or largely inspired by the golden age of Anglo-Saxon science fiction. Original voices were rare. Michel Jeury is the only name that comes to mind, and he was largely ignored by mainstream readers. Nevertheless, Jeury, who started his career at the end of the 1950s, is regarded today as a great French science fiction novelist. Since the publication of *Temps incertain* (a.k.a. Chronolysis) in 1973, in Gérard Klein's *Ailleurs et demain* (Elsewhere and Tomorrow) series, French SF exegetes perceive a metamorphosis of the representation of time travel in his work. According to this essential author of French SF of the 1970s and 1980s, time travel is not made possible through the machine, a classic science fiction theme since 1880,[2] but through the psyche. The psyche is helped either artificially or naturally by the ingestion of a drug, chronolyse. The time traveler then occupies one or more bodies from the past or the future, incorporating their individual personality. In fact, Dunyach was influenced by Michel Jeury while he was a young writer. The author of *Chronolysis* was one of his models, particularly to write a poeticized science fiction using visual sensations and colors.

At the beginning of the 1980s, a handful of new young writers known as "Groupe Limite" chose to develop a category of literary SF in which formal experimentation and innovative stylistic approaches were central to the project. Even if they produced only a few novels and one single collection of short stories under the name "Limite," *Malgré le monde* (Despite the World; 1987),[3] they had a certain influence on other French SF writers by partially bridging the gap between SF and the mainstream—especially by using literary techniques

---

[2] The term "chronotic" refers to time travel, while "chronolyse," in Jeury's work, is the name of the drug used to travel through time. See Vas-Deyres, "Du Temps incertain."

[3] *Malgré le monde* [Despite the World] is the collective work of Jacques Barbéri, Francis Berthelot, Lionel Évrard, Emmanuel Jouanne, Frédéric Serva, Jean-Pierre Vernay, and Antoine Volodine.

associated with the *nouveau roman* or surrealism—and thereby conquering some of the most important media.

In the meantime, Roland C. Wagner, Jean-Marc Ligny, and Claude Ecken were just writing classic and popular science fiction, either as short pulp-like novels for mass-market publishers such as Fleuve Noir or, more ambitiously, targeting the literary market as a whole. And then, slowly, at the end of the 1980s, the monthly magazines and anthologies that published them folded; many prestigious SF publishers disappeared or reduced their activities. Publishing something other than mass-market/pulp-like/short-and-easy novels was an almost impossible challenge.

We recall that in the 1970s and 1980s, a large number of series were created in France in the wake of the 1950s series *Rayon Fantastique,* published by Hachette, or *Présence du Futur*, published by Denoël. These include *Ailleurs et demain* (published by Robert Laffont), *Anticipation* (Fleuve Noir), *La grande Anthologie de Science-Fiction* (The Great Science-Fiction Anthology) (Livre de poche), *Ici et maintenant* (Kesselring), *Bibliothèque Marabout science-fiction* (J'ai lu SF éditions), and *Constellation* (Seghers). This array of series and anthologies from the 1970s is due to two phenomena: utopian literature's integration of science fiction through politics, and the creation of a real culture of science fiction, in which readers and viewers are increasingly numerous, and SF arouses a growing interest in journalists as well as in the academic world. Changes in French society as a result of May 1968 account for a great diversity among SF writers, an amazing profusion that became a "carrier of ideas, hopes, utopias."[4] French SF writers, induced by the changes born in

---

[4] Andrevon, "Années 70," 11.

those years and influenced by their major American counterparts, put their ideology and creativity to work. French SF found its singularity without isolating itself from other utopian movements of that time such as ecology, feminism, and pacifism.

In 1969, the magazine *Fiction* (the French version of the American magazine) gave pride of place to anti-establishment political fiction by publishing two short stories: "Faith of our Fathers" by Philip K. Dick and "Final War" by Barry N. Malzberg. A few years later, *Fiction* readers discovered the English New Wave of Michael Moorcock, J. G. Ballard, and other speculative fiction texts. It is from the French translation of those texts that a very political form of science fiction developed. Iconoclastic at first, it then tried to build utopian visions as alternatives to a Western society that it considered stifling and old-fashioned. The committed, politicized French SF of the 1970s started to decline in the early 1980s, perhaps due to the fact that many people of the counterculture believed that the dream of a utopia had come true with the election of François Mitterrand in 1981. Other reasons are put forward by the various actors of this period: for Jean-Pierre Andrevon, the economic context and the exponential development of literary series are to be blamed for this decline,[5] rather than readers' weariness with a boring,

---

[5] There are more than twenty collections from various publishers, without counting specialized magazines: among the most noteworthy are *Le Rayon Fantastique* (1951-64), *Anticipation* (1951-97), *Ailleurs et demain* (1969), *Présence du Futur* (1954-2000), *Club du livre d'Anticipation* (1966-87), *Galaxie-bis* (1965-86), *Dimensions SF* (1973-84), *Anti-Mondes* (1972-77), *Chute libre* (1974-78), *Nébula* (1975-77), *Ici et Maintenant* (1977-79), *Presses Pocket* (1977), and *Nouvelles Editions Oswald* (1978-89).

deluded, and jaded SF, as posited by Gérard Klein,[6] Roger Bozzetto, and other critics. Between 1977 and 1986, more than thirty series disappeared. Jean-Guillaume Lanuque refers to the darkness and pessimism of science-fictional visions of that time, a darkness inherited from the utopian altercation of the previous period: "Authors may well have been tempted to focus excessively on the darkest futuristic writing in a crisis context, at the expense of alternative, more inspiring perspectives, other than ecological and libertarian developments which have their limits, as we could see. As if this science fiction had not achieved its mutation process, dropping its very last traces of leftism… At this point we seem to have the concretization of the disappointed hopes of May 68.[7] But this movement revealed some of the talents of the next generation, such as Jean-Pierre Hubert, Joël Houssin, and Joëlle Wintrebert (among others), and "allowed the building of another science fiction on [its] very ruins."[8] The quarterly

---

[6] "[The] May 1968 effect is going to be more obvious through a sort of school created by Bernard Blanc and edited by Rolf Kesselring in the series 'Ici et Maintenant,' which will express the ecological and political times, but which won't escape from the naivety unfortunately and—this is paradoxical—from conformism of ideas and form. It will lead, alas, a great part of the readers to turn away from a French SF which is unfairly mistaken with this unique trend, certainly noisy and active, but considered with some appearance of reason as sermonizing and boring." Klein, Preface. Jacques Sadoul even proposes a "true intellectual terrorism"; in other words, that science fiction in France had to be political to have value. Sadoul, *Histoire*, 455.
[7] Lanuque, "Mai 68," 148.
[8] Sadoul, *Histoire*, 457.

magazine *Univers*, run by Yves Frémion,[9] has made it possible to maintain the link between political SF and new authors publishing today, while integrating the "old" ones such as Michel Jeury, Michel Demuth, Philippe Curval, Pierre Pelot, Daniel Walther, and André Ruellan.

At the end of the 1980s, a handful of writers bloomed—Pierre Bordage, Ayerdhal, Laurent Genefort, Richard Canal, Serge Lehman, and Sylvie Denis—and longtime SF fans decided to create new magazines to re-place the old ones. Three of them, *CyberDreams* (1994-98), *Bifrost*, and *Galaxies* (the latter two since 1996), were created almost at the same time. Jean-Claude Dunyach was one of the founders of *Galaxies'* first series and was an associate editor for more than ten years. *Bifrost* and *Galaxies* are still thriving after more than twenty years. According to Dunyach, the second half of the 1990s was a golden age for French SF, culminating in 2000: the turn of the millennium was an opportunity for writers to conquer the media—particularly TV—and to talk at length about the future. This generation of writers was un-aware, however, that their readership in France was soon to turn to fantasy and paranormal romance.

Sensoriality and Poetry

Jean-Claude Dunyach offers a perfect example of what is uniquely "French" about French SF during this period; we only have to determine what the French singu-larity of this writer is. In an interview given at the inter-national science-fiction festival "Utopiales" in Nantes in

---

[9] Yves Frémion undertook the publication of nineteen issues, except the first and second.

2010, the French writer explains how to define the thematic specificity of French authors:

"I think that, in fact, there are some French specificities, because France is one of the countries where science fiction was born; in short, science fiction has existed in France for almost 150 years, since Jules Verne, and never stopped being here. However, we went through lots of phases. First, we inherited a lot from artistic currents like surrealism, for example, or the *nouveau roman*, and as a consequence we quite often have texts which slip a little bit. Our SF can be naturally weird,[10] with no particular effort from us... And there are relations to the flesh, the body, to sensuality and sensoriality—not the sexuality, I really mean sensoriality—which are probably quite different. French texts are often stuffed with smells, noises, tastes: we are people of food, touch, smell. We're a country of perfumers, of cooks, and it can be seen in our literature; therefore, in our science fiction, people work on that sensoriality."[11]

The science fiction of Jean-Claude Dunyach is stimulated by form and meaning. Common notions worked out by science fiction, such as time, death, memory, relativity, mutations, and relationships with the machine or extraterrestrials, are always considered from the angle of a sensorial materiality, as if touch were the vital sense for understanding the universe and the unknown. In Dunyach's stories, time evaporates, dead love stories can

---

[10] Jean-Claude Dunyach is using this word to characterize the fact that French science fiction is weird in the Anglo-Saxon sense, but is often mixed with other literary or artistic approaches.

[11] This interview can be read at http://sffportal.net/2011/06/an-interview-with-jean-claude-dunyach-from-utopiales-2010/.

be crystallized and worn as ornaments, and extraterrestrials are classified as edible or not.

Dunyach's father was a country doctor, and the writer lived his whole childhood in respect of the body, of its organic magnificence, and not in the repulsion of the flesh. As for the literary perspective, Dunyach was fascinated by poetry—he wrote poems from an early age, and to this day he still reads Japanese haiku, a form of poetry whose precision he admires. His first two influences in science fiction were the novel *Vermillion Sands* by J. G. Ballard and the short story "Time Considered as a Helix of Semi-Precious Stones" by Samuel Delany—that is to say, a poeticized American SF. Ballard fascinated Dunyach by his deconstructed process of adding meaning to the world using modern symbolism, as Baudrillard defined it in *La société de consommation. Ses mythes, ses structures* (Consumer society: Myths and structures), and by his way of slicing temporal continuity in his stories.[12]

In *Le jeu des sabliers* (The Game of the Hourglass; 1987), four protagonists who have embarked on a metaphysical quest are confronted by "sleepers," children that never wake up from their dreams, which alter the different dimensions of reality. Dream, pain, and poetry are closely linked:

Dreams hit them like sharp spears. Jern, who was hit with full force, tottered. With every step, metal

---

[12] According to Jean Baudrillard, modern symbolism is a direction of objects and desires: "The logic of goods became widespread... all functions, all needs are objectified and treated in terms of profit, but in the deepest sense everything is made spectacle; that is to say, evoked, provoked, orchestrated in images, in signs and edible models." Baudrillard, *La société de consommation*, 308

spearheads got deeper into his loins… Like a scalpel, the pain ripped him open, exposed his nerves and entrails, and scratched the invisible wires that allowed him to operate. His fellow travelers advanced, bent forward to escape from pain… All around them reality cracked, shattered into a thousand pieces… Olym, with his face turned up, made up gorgeous dreams that he thrust out to the face of his tormentors. His poems became weapons, his lines projectiles.[13]

In the short story "Les Nageurs de sable" (Sand Swimmers; 1983), the narrator is one of three test-tube children who were born on a planet of sand. As in Ray Bradbury's story "Dark They Were, and Golden-Eyed" (1949), and under the influence of the planet, he gradually turns into a creature who is able to swim in sand as easily as in water: "When I arrived at the edge of a large, gently sloping basin, I allowed myself to fall lengthwise to the ground and felt the sand embrace me. It gradually covered my legs, my torso, and my face with its fluid, burning grasp. Carried away on a flow of new sensations, I attempted to swim, but the contact with the rough silica irritated my soft skin and I was forced to get up after a few yards."[14] By means of an individual physical mutation, the flesh of the narrator becomes itself the alien planet and defeats a system of human colonization:

The sun, at its peak, woke me. I spent a few moments savoring the relative coolness of the sand. I had swallowed a few grains during my sleep and the oxide aftertaste dried my lips. I dug a yard down and placed a handful of damp crystals in my mouth. I closed my eyes, before forcing myself to swallow them. They dulled my hunger

[13] Dunyach, *Le Jeu des sabliers* (Game of the Hourglass), 221.
[14] Dunyach, "Sand Swimmers," 142.

and thirst. I got up, abandoning strips of skin behind me…
I hardened myself and dove through an oxide mound. The
grains caressed my skin gently, without nicking it. I
learned to keep my eyes closed, to guide myself by the
sound of the wind on the crests of the dunes. From time to
time, I swallowed a new mouthful of the desert, discover-
ing an infinite diversity of tastes and odors. When I
stopped, exhausted, I knew that the desert had accepted
me.[15]

The character accepts his metamorphosis and ren-
ders colonization useless. In fact, the planet irreparably
converts people and objects to colonize them.

Dunyach substitutes the symbiosis between man and
the machine in his novel *Étoiles mourantes* (Dying Stars),
cowritten with Ayerdhal, in which the body mutates in
contact with matter. In the warrior society of the Mecha-
nists, remote descendants of humans train elite soldiers
who lose their human nature by merging their body and
soul into their Armor. The latter consists of a sophisticated exoskeleton that connects to the nervous system of
the human body, without any possibility of return:
"Through billions of pores, the armor breathed and per-
spired, permanently exchanging the atoms it needed to
maintain Tecamac's organism for the destructured mole-
cules it used to clean it. For him, it constantly processed
and reprocessed scales, sweat, urine and fecal matter. On
its own, it ionized his environment, generating the characteristic blue and odor of ozone."[16] In that novel, the
complex exoskeleton is a symbol of the matter turning on
a machine, which definitively integrates the human body.
In every story, sensations are turned into metaphors and

---

[15] Ibid., 143.
[16] Ayerdhal and Dunyach, *Étoiles mourantes* (*Dying Stars*), 17.

poeticized allegories, which is what gives the text its specific touch. The human body is metamorphosed; its flesh mutates and enters into symbiosis or disintegrates in time, as in the short story "Le temps en s'évaporant" (Time as it evaporates). Zorah, the heroine, lives in a village lost in a valley that is subjected to temporal distortion. As she can no longer stand her life as a humiliated and battered woman, she goes into the temporal storm and thereby allows a reestablishment of energetic forces. Here the body becomes the bond between dimensions:

The first symptoms of time deprivation are already appearing. The diving suit she stole from her lover, after he mocked her and beat her, is losing the precious fluid through a thousand tiny cracks. The tears of time she sows splash on the earthenware tiles of the staircase and form rivulets along the steps... Her thoughts no longer torment her; time, as it escapes from her, washes her clean and carries away her memories... Slowly the body of Zorah cracks and breaks asunder, yielding to the unstoppable pressure from within. The first spring gushes forth, followed by a second, then by many others. The trickles of time soon become streams, then torrents, then cataracts.[17]

The perception of atoms that constitute the flesh of the body is the science-fictional ingredient of Dunyach's writing. In fact, it's necessary to distinguish the peculiarity of Dunyach as a French writer from his originality as a science fiction author. As a French writer, he joins a tradition of literary description of perceptions of sight, touch, smell, and taste. As a science fiction author, he integrates this tradition to create original SF: flesh is becoming a manifestation of the concepts that govern the universe.

---

[17] Dunyach, "Time as it evaporates," 58-59.

This thematic singularity is also stylistic. In 2010, an interviewer asked him: "Do you feel that there are themes or stylistic approaches which unify French SF culturally, making it unique to an extent that would be clear in a blind 'taste test' of translated work in another language?" Dunyach answered, "People tell me that I work with artistic, impressionist, sensorial touches, where Americans would maybe give priority to the strength of the story, to the narration itself, to the adventures, and where English writers would give priority to the rigor of the experimentation."[18] His main invention, the extraterrestrial beings named "AnimalCities," are the bond between flesh and metaphysics, between science and sensations. At first sight, the AnimalCities truly belong to *sense of wonder* imagery: they are huge disks of flesh several dozen kilometers in diameter and a hundred meters deep with filaments around them that are used as antennas or tentacles, which they can retract when they land on a planet. On the top of the disk lies a flesh-and-bone city they can slowly reshape, in the middle of which stands a belfry, a sort of huge central tower antenna turned toward the sky.

AnimalCities belong to the French urban imagination that forms the city as a gigantic living organism of the kind depicted by Émile Zola, for example, in *Le ventre de Paris* (The Belly of Paris) in 1873; or in his feminized, devouring, and carnal city in *La Curée* (The Kill) in 1872. Jean-Claude Dunyach's creations—literally tentacular cities, living disk-cities surrounded by filaments—send us back to medieval urbanity, "strange miscellanies of

---

[18] Jean-Claude Dunyach, personal interview with the author, February 2013.

traboules[19] in the city of Lyon, of Mont Saint-Michel and of the catacombs of Lyon,"[20] according to Jérôme Goffette, with an architectural structure made of narrow, winding alley lanes, short cuts, and dead ends, without mechanized transport. The image of catacombs is itself a *mise en abyme* of the true nature of those baffling extraterrestrials that gets close to the reverie of Bachelar's space, the "ultra-cellars": "the ultra-cellars reverie is a reverie of an underground space, an internal space where entrails, stairs, corridors grow like catacombs or like arteries and veins,"[21] no longer underscoring the mineral but the organic nature of those beings. For Dunyach, his native city, Toulouse, is a city of flesh, "a hermaphrodite city where the omnipresent brick is of the raw meat color. It is invaded by anthropomorphous monuments which are visible from Garonne riverside: several huge domes topped by a stud, a belfry (Basilica of Saint-Sernin with its steeple, which is a wonderful hard-on), cobblestones that are warm in the summer and where it is pleasant to walk barefoot, etc."[22] Dunyach's bodily imagination stems from a medical respect of human-body functionalities, and the contact of his characters with the Animal-Cities' skin is similar to the feeling of a caress. In *Étoiles mortes* (Dead Stars), the hero, Closter, travels from AnimalCity to AnimalCity and walks barefoot on the skin of each new city that he goes into: "Supérieure accepts with

---

[19] A *traboule* is a narrow passage that links two streets by crossing a block of house.

[20] See Goffette, "L'espace en résonance."

[21] Ibid.

[22] Jean-Claude Dunyach, personal interview with the author.

humility the criticisms pounded by my bare feet. Its over-fed flesh bounces under my feet without being bruised."[23]

The AnimalCities are an example of what Dunyach calls the "attentive matrix," a technological environment or extraterrestrial protector, the kind of environment SF knows how to create. Not futuristic creations that can be extrapolated from our advanced technological discoveries, but "objects of desire" having an emotional and/or symbolic value that we would like to be real. But, above all, they embody the ideal solution for the fear of indifference that can haunt us. In an AnimalCity, each of us is unique and necessary. The traveler-hero Closter from *Étoiles mortes* (Dead Stars) has a carnal, individualized, and unique relation with every city he comes across: Nayrademance, Nivôse, Bayane, Supérieure, Aigue-marine. Three labyrinthine systems intertwine in the corporal thickness of the AnimalCities: the ultra-cellars of corridors, alcoves, and caves; a network of pipings, gigantic interconnected circulatory systems; and the bone skeleton that gives shape to the AnimalCity, and which allows it to build up its walls of the flesh. A fourth network, the communication network of nerves, which is not mentioned much in *Dying Stars* but is clearly drawn in *Dead Stars*, plays an essential part. The reverie of the city is also a reverie of the body. The AnimalCity's' body becomes a protective matrix, a sort of continued depth that adapts to the individuality of its travelers and guides them: "In some areas, bluish mottlings contrast with the eggshell shade of the corridor. The whole is both strange and familiar, like a piece of my own body magnified millions of times. I put my hand on a fold as thick as a skull and I caress it. It vibrates, it's alive. I am overcome by a wave

---

[23] Ayerdhal and Dunyach, *Étoiles mortes* (*Dead Stars*), 205.

of tenderness. Flesh against flesh, we are communicating."[24] With the AnimalCities, occupying space consists of occupying a body, a metaphorized threshold allowing the passage between exteriority and interiority, a place where domotics would be idealized between macrocosm—the universe—and microcosm, in the privacy of one's own home.

Dunyach is also exploring this concept of attentive matrix from a more political angle in recent short stories, since he sees it as part of the transhuman mutation our society is already experiencing. The fact that our direct environment (home, cities, airports, train stations, malls) appears more and more "conscious" of who we are and is monitoring us to react to our "needs" is a fascinating—and sometimes terrifying—thought experiment.

The creation of AnimalCities is representative of the singularity of Jean-Claude Dunyach's imaginary world, shared with Ayerdhal within the space of a novel. These cities of flesh, places of passage between humanity and the universe, also present different metaphors of Dunyach's universe: halfway between a scientific iconography and a poetization of the scientific concept. Indeed, Dunyach is using scientific concepts because he's a scientist. At the same time, these concepts become allegories in his texts. They explore the complex relationship man maintains with space, infinity, and what is inconceivable. The poetization of science-fictional notions in Jean-Claude Dunyach's work expresses his singularity. If it is difficult to define what determines French contemporary science fiction, I would say that it is through the individual imaginations of writers that we are able to perceive

---

[24] Ibid., 89.

French originality: a scientific dimension, metaphysics expressed through a link with the flesh and with the metaphorized body for a humanist, sensorial, and earthling science fiction—maybe a sensualist form of science fiction in the philosophical sense, inherited from François Rabelais, where the Giant is a metaphor but also a gigantic realistic body, exaggerating the "organic" aspect of the human life. Dunyach wants readers to feel the sensoriality of the world: "The stories I write are not accurate scientific predictions, nor are they meant to warn the world of this or that danger, present or future. If they have a moral, it is more often than not without my deliberate intention. I only report what seems obvious to me, obvious and wonderful. And through the act of writing, I seek to share these stories with others, giving them lives of their own."[25]

[25] Dunyach, "Afterwords," 150.

Of Interest:

Andrevon, Jean-Pierre. "Années 70 . . . année 68." In *Les Enfants du mirage*, vol. 1. Paris: Éditions Naturellement, 2001.

Baudrillard, Jean. *La société de consommation. Ses mythes, ses structures* [Consumer society: Its myths, its structures]. Paris: Gallimard, 2006.

Goffette, Jérôme. "L'espace en résonance : corps, ville et monde dans *Étoiles mourantes* d'Ayerdhal et J.-C. Dunyach" In *Poétique(s) de l'espace dans les œuvres fantastiques et de science-fiction*. Ed. Françoise Dupeyron-Lafay and Huftier Arnaud. Paris : Michel Houdiard, 2007. 33-52.

Jeury, Michel. *Le Temps incertain* [Chronolysis]. *Ailleurs et demain* 22 (1973) : 264.

Klein, Gérard Klein. Préface to *L'Hexagone halluciné*. Ed. Ellen C. Herzfeld, Gérard Klein, and Dominique Martel. Paris : Librairie générale française, 1988. 17.

Lanuque, Jean-Guillaume. "Mai 68 et la science-fiction française." In *Dissidences*, vol. 4. Paris : Le Bord de l'eau éditions, 2008. 148.

Limite [Jacques Barbéri, Francis Berthelot, Lionel Évrard, Emmanuel Jouanne, Frédéric Serva, Jean-Pierre Vernay, and Antoine Volodine]. *Malgré le monde* [Despite the world]. Collection Présence du Futur No. 452. Paris : Denoël, 1987.

Sadoul, Jacques. *Histoire de la Science-fiction moderne*. Paris : Robert Laffont, 1984.

Vas-Deyres, Natacha. "Du Temps incertain au temps ralenti : variations temporelles françaises." In *L'Imaginaire du temps dans le fantastique et la science-fiction*. Ed. Natacha Vas-Deyres and Lauric Guillaud. *Eidôlon* No. 91. Pessac : Presses universitaires de Bordeaux, 2011. 57-68.

Zola, Émile. *La Curée* [The kill]. Paris: Charpentier, 1872.

———. *Le ventre de Paris* [The belly of Paris]. Paris: Charpentier, 1873.

GOD, SEEN FROM WITHIN

"God is seven hundred million kilometers long, one hundred and forty million kilometers wide and just as thick. He weighs about 16 grams."

"God, eh?" (Anna Chatila makes a grimace that could pass for a smile.) "I didn't realize you had a sense of humor, Eilen. Which isn't much use in astrophysics, for that matter. We leave that to the theoretical physicists. So, start over!"

I stare at her, just a tad nervous, hands crossed over my belly that's really starting to round out. She's seated in front of the blackboard in her office, which she prefers over screens, for bringing the fleeting intuitions that earned her the position she holds to life with a stroke of chalk. Her salt and pepper hair is covered with white dust, her eyes are filled with enough energy to trigger a super-nova, and I have venerated her since she welcomed me to a postdoc. I'm also scared stiff of her.

"*Something*, a cloud of ionized particles of an un-known type, has just been identified, measured and quan-tified, in the heart of the solar system. There is an under-lying energy grid, fine, barely detectable interactions, which are there, I can assure you, and a heap of twisted topological characteristics—one of the hypotheses we've developed with Max is that it's distorting Riemannian space."

"And that kind of volume weighs only 16 grams? How did you discover it?"

I shrug in response to the implied question. Sixteen grams doesn't exist in astrophysics; that's below the measurable threshold. Latching onto disturbing details is just so Chatila's style. If she can destroy an elegant theory with a small, completely ugly fact, she feels like she's made her day.

"I tested the new filtering algorithm. We pushed the satellites' detection parameters to the ultimate and I used all of my computer time credits to make it work." (I don't think there's any point mentioning that Max had also given me most of his credits after a discussion that had lasted part of the night—we didn't even have the strength left to hug after that.) "The supercomputers have been crunching out numbers non-stop for two days in an effort to eliminate the noise of all the signals. It's definitely sixteen grams, it weighs next to nothing, it's immense and I don't know what it is. But it's there and I believe…"

"You *believe?*"

"I believe, well, I'm almost sure that it's alive."

Chatila doesn't ask me to leave. She doesn't take on the concerned look of a research director who has just watched one of her team members flip out royally. She doesn't even mention my pregnancy which we have tacitly agreed to ignore while I continue my work. Instead, she leans back in her chair, picks up the half-eaten apple perched on her monitor and bites into it vigorously. It makes such a loud crunch that I feel as if I'm the one who has just been split in two.

She chews with great satisfaction, swallows and puts the apple back down. Then she stares at me seriously, unconsciously brushing the dust from her hair.

"Alive," she repeats slowly. "Perhaps even conscious. And, given the size you think it is, God is an acceptable term, as a first approximation. I never thought I'd say this one day: God, as a first approximation. That's like what, the Taylor development of the existence function of God? No, don't answer. What have you not told me that gives meaning to all this mumbo jumbo?"

"There are multi-level interactions in the plasma," I stammer. "And the energy tensors are completely…" (She raises her hand to interrupt me.) "You'll have to look at the data yourself if you don't believe me. And…"

"And?"

"And it's going away."

When I step back out into the afternoon light, I blink as if emerging from a cavern. I feel damp, slightly nauseous; I'm going to have to change my underwear. I take the time to buy a stretch mark cream at the campus drug store before heading over to the cafeteria where Max is waiting for me. I left him sitting in front of an espresso, his tablet connected to the radio telescope network in lunar orbit. If he's taken the time to finish his coffee, that means he's worried about me.

I automatically fix my hair before joining him and I beep him to warn him of my arrival. Max tends to immerse himself deeply in the flow of raw data. He hates being disconnected by people, even me. So, I programmed an avatar that flashes in a corner of the screen when I need him to come back to the real world. It's a butterfly, a blue monarch that beats its wings faster and faster.

I make a detour to the restroom and join him just as he's putting his headphones into his shirt pocket. I give him a thumbs up.

"She didn't fire you," he comments darkly.

"I'm allowed to continue to explore this course of study along with my other work. And I have to report back to her in four days. From her, that's almost like getting a medal."

"Will the thing still be there in four days?"

"That's just the problem…" (I sit down in front of him and look at the intact cup of coffee.) "How long have you been connected up there?"

"I've barely emerged. I was just getting routine stuff. Why?"

"Can I have a sip of your espresso?"

"It's yours. I finished mine and ordered another one for you when you poked me. You have to change that butterfly, and use a sexier image."

"Like one of those virtualgirl stripteasers filled with viruses that you can find on the net?"

"Like you, scantily dressed. I know where to get a 3D camera. You still owe me a fantasy for my computer credits."

"Nothing like reality," I say, smiling. "Plus, we should make the most of it quickly; the window of opportunity is going to close soon."

"Are you kidding? I checked on the Internet and they recommend making love until the eighth month of pregnancy."

"It's not me you have to convince, sweetheart, but Chatila." (I cautiously touch my lips to the cup and drink a warm sip, just the way I like it. My nausea abates slightly.) "I have to estimate the speed with which our cloud is traveling by Friday with enough accuracy to be able to talk about it at the team seminar. That means I'm going to have to gather a phenomenal mass of data on our immeasurable ghost."

He gives me a smile that makes me melt.

"I've just launched a data mining program while waiting for you. I figured that would be the first question she asked you. It's not a trivial problem, moreover. That thing is so evanescent it looks like a micro-web of singularities, all with null mass. That gave me an idea or two,

30

and I coded something to test them. Results in four hours. That gives you more than enough time to demonstrate your appreciation!"

Later, stretched out on the futon in our tiny student apartment, I savor the fluid instants that follow tender moments with Max. The gurgling of the coffee-maker filters in from the kitchen. I slip a second pillow under my neck to raise my head a little and wipe the trickle of perspiration that has formed between my breasts. I'm not devout. Sex is what comes closest to divine revelation for me.

Max slips under the duvet, handing me a sweet-smelling mug.

"It's moving," I say, smiling at him as I swallow a burning mouthful.

"Are you talking about the baby?"

"Of course." (I shrug.) "I'm going to be an obsessive mother and I'll postpone the expulsion until the very last minute."

"That's fine for me. You want to take a look at the simulations?"

"What does it look like?"

"A cloud of microdots, stupid. What were you expecting? Michelangelo's bearded old man?"

"No noticeable symmetries?"

"No…" (He bites his lip.) "Well, I don't think so. I'll have to discuss it with a crystallographer. See if it changes shape while moving. We won't have enough power to calculate everything, you know, we're just taking photos."

"So, we're God's paparazzi. Can I have some more coffee?"

"Sixteen grams, shit. I'm still wondering how we managed to detect it."

"The real question isn't 'how'. But rather 'why'. Do

you know what Chatila asked me just before I left her office? 'It's because you decided it was there that you found it, isn't it?'"

I don't sleep a whole lot before the seminar on Saturday morning. Chatila implied to the other members of our research team that I may have found something that deserves to be demolished in a meeting. Everyone has planned to be there. That means a dozen or so colleagues all ready for a friendly stoning with irrefutable arguments. Our God hypothesis is still fragile; it is as far from being viable as the fetus I shelter. And, like my fetus, it's starting to kick me at the most inopportune times.

Max helped me prepare my presentation. I have two films and various aborted theories—all of our brilliant ideas eventually slipped through our fingers, but I may just have the beginning of a solution. A madman's hypothesis, born at four in the morning from a mixture of sexual frustration and a terrible urge to pee. We coded it Friday night and it still holds. For now.

I fear the barrage of questions. For scientists, sticks and stones hurt far less than words.

I climb onto the stage buttocks clenched. Max isn't there; he's not really a member of the group. He's not a theorist, just an observer. We make a slightly scandalous couple when it comes to the university's social criteria, an unnatural association of simulations and observations. I miss him. Unlike the others, I like facts, even when they're annoying. No doubt that's what brought us together, Chatila and me. I feel her eyes leveled at me (she always sits in the first row, legs stretched out, a bag of apples on her knees). I take a deep breath before clicking with my mouse and starting the slide show.

I colored the divine cloud, using density scales, then

in keeping with the potential relationships between particles that are so distant that the very idea of measuring their interactions is ridiculous. I had to cheat, to build a phantom castle with a handful of sand. But the result is rather convincing, visually speaking. It looks like a giant amoeba encompassing the sun and the inner planets, with darker zones around the Earth. It stretches elliptically and is slowly heading toward the outer planets. According to our calculations, it will brush against Neptune in a few weeks.

"Therefore," I announced, "It weighs nothing. It has so little density it's possible to believe that it doesn't even exist. And it's moving of its own will. Like a Bose-Einstein condensate that has decided to see the world."

I interrupt my lecture, to face their frightened expressions. It's almost possible to hear a pin drop, the silence is so heavy. Even Chatila has stopped chewing. I feel the moistness spread. This whole thing might be an acute form of the symptoms associated with pregnancy, something Max may have caught through contagion.

"Apart from us, who else has detected it?"

That's Danvir, who came from Rajasthan two years earlier, as part of an exchange with the University of Jaipur. No one ever sees him working, but he still manages to publish a lot. He has an almost sexual way of inserting his name into others' articles, by penetrating through the slightest opening. Max nicknamed him Kama Sutra.

"I monitored the database of articles in pre-publication," declares Chatila separating each word carefully. "We're the only ones on this matter. More specifically, *Eilen* is the only one and she will be the only one until further notice. If anyone else decides to have a little fun publishing about this without my approval, I guarantee that person a slow and painful academic death."

She tears off an enormous chunk of apple ferociously and chews it noisily. I lower my head to hide my smile and then start up the animation again.

"We don't have a lot of useable prior data," I explain. "Everything that comes from the orbital radio telescopes is only kept for ten years, in a compressed format. I checked. The cloud was already there when the first observations were made." (I raise my hand to interrupt the hubbub.) "It wasn't moving at that time. I think it's been here much longer than we can imagine."

"You're the one who's scared it off?" a voice calls out from the back.

I shrug, unable to keep from smiling. Max said the exact same thing the night before. *It's leaving because we noticed it.* The more I think about it, the stupider I find that.

I click to restart my presentation. The final slides are devoted to the hypotheses I've sketched out. I demolish most of them myself.

"The problem," I say, casting my laser pointer over the cloud, "is that the cloud is too light. Considering its size, it should weigh tons, even with such a low density. But that's not the case. We've taken the measurements a dozen times, even with the lunar instruments. Sixteen grams is impossible. The very existence of this thing is already a major impossibility. And with the weight, well there we're cranking it up a notch! Unless…"

I stop speaking for effect, but a growl from Chatila causes me to quickly pick up the thread of my presentation.

"I redid my calculations with Max. Then I thought about what I was seeing and what I wasn't seeing, about what is measurable and what's escaping us. Considering the fact that an isolated particle has a very fleeting lifespan, its mass and electromagnetic characteristics become a function of a probability of existence that may be significantly less than one. Therefore, the total theoretical weight of the cloud may be very high, but its components do not exist simultaneously. It's evanescent matter, not completely there, a web of potentialities, possibly information in the pure state. An archipelago in the sub-quantum sea. At any given moment, only a few grams are present in our reality. The rest is in limbo, waiting for existence.

This triggers an explosion of questions, as if I've inadvertently collected too much fissile material in one place. The seminar is attended by cosmologists and particle physicists, high energy specialists and superstring theorists. As many visions of the universe as there are participants with, however, one point in common: what I've discovered doesn't fit into any of their models.

And each of them is convinced they're right.

"The density must vary locally, in this case," says a high-pitched voice.

I tremble inside. Alicia is on the warpath. Now, we're getting down to serious business.

"The cloud moves like a drop of viscous liquid, accelerating along the axis of its largest diameter. There are no detectable variations in density, except maybe around us, on Earth, because we can't measure anything there."

"Why?"

"There's this planet…" (I tap the floor with my foot) "that prevents close observation."

Two or three welcome laughs break out. Alicia tried to steal my guy a year ago, just for fun. I hate her. Max didn't notice a thing, or so he says, and I half believe him. He must have realized something was going on and filed it in under "no time for it now" as he does when he has to deal with a sink full of dirty dishes. At the same time, his favorite observation zone is beyond three million kilometers. Possibly Alicia was too close for him to notice her.

"I'd like to be able to answer you, Alicia. Really. We know almost nothing about this cloud and we won't have much time to learn more, given the way it's accelerating. I prefer not to formulate hypotheses at this stage."

What I've just said is a lie. I have the feeling, which is impossible to prove, that the density of the cloud is stronger around us. I've learned not to trust my intuitions, to subject them ruthlessly to testing, hammering them like a sword to sharpen the edge. But this one refuses to disappear. The cloud appeared for us. I'm prepared to swear to that. That makes its departure all the more intriguing.

One of the cosmologists raises a finger.

"No emission of any kind?" (I shake my head.) "Nothing in the hydrogen band spectrum? No attempt…" (He swallows.) "No attempt to contact us?"

I don't even attempt to answer. The question curls up and dies at my feet.

"Hey, I've thought of something," says one of the young postgrads. "Your techniques for filtering cosmic noise… Can we use them for other sorts of measurements? I'm trying to qualify the make-up of solar ejectates. That would help me with a paper I'm working on!"

"There's nothing against it, *a priori*," I say slowly." (I take a deep breath.) "I really won't have the time to help you, but maybe Max could let you use his extraction algorithms if you have computer time available to give him. Do you want me to ask him?"

Chatila raises a hand holding an apple core above her head and waves it like a flag. The background discussions stop immediately.

"We're getting off the topic, children! Thank you for

your presentation, Eilen, even though it didn't convince anyone, particularly not me. From all this hotchpotch, there's at least something for a good article on your methods for processing the signal and filtering measurement noises. I want a first draft in 15 days. As for the rest of you, you're allowed to refine your arguments for the next seminar on the topic, but this stays within the team for now. No need to make ourselves look ridiculous. Have I made myself clear?"

"Eilen, in my office as soon as you've packed up!"

As the chairs scrape the floor and people leave the room without looking my way, I disconnect the overhead projector and put my tablet away. Alicia leaves last, not without first giving me a smirk that I pretend not to notice. Even though I know Chatila loses her patience with the lightest delay, I take the time to go to the washroom and to apply a little deodorant. At times like this, even my own odor bothers me.

Chatila greets me with a brutal "Close the door!" She pushes aside the printout she was examining and stares at me, lips pinched. Her desk is covered with colored plots of the cloud, at various scales.

"Don't look like I'm going to bite your ear off," she grumbles. "Or send you packing, although some think that. I'll chew you out officially at the end of this conversation, while you hold the door open so that everyone in the hallway can hear. I'll be particularly spiteful, which will allow me to let off a little steam, and will maintain my aura as a heartless bitch." (She shrugs.) "Halos have to be polished now and then to make them shine."

I must look completely bewildered. Chatila points at the only empty chair with a peremptory index finger and leans toward me, elbows on the desk, face framed by her gray hair. I do my best not to back away.

"You didn't expect to get away with it like this, did you?" (She frowns and gets lost in her thoughts for a moment.) "What you've found is just possibly the most explosive thing I've seen in my 30-year career and you're holding it out on a tray to that gang of imbeciles prepared to do anything to make a name for themselves. You're not stupid, but you are naive. Stupidity I've learned to deal with. Naivety is a professional defect."

"But you asked me to…" I stammered.

"Bring up the topic. Look for solutions. Carefully test the more or less crazy solutions with your colleagues. Not to wave your complete results in front of everyone, along with your most interesting hypotheses to top it all off.

"If I had shown the slightest glimmer of an interest in your discovery, you would have found yourself with a dozen daggers planted in your back. You're not ready for that. Not yet."

She gathers the cloud representations into a tidy pile and hands them to me.

"Take your plots. Officially, I consider this an undesirable side effect of your hormonal swings and that's what I'll tell everyone in five minutes when you leave. Unofficially, I order you to continue digging into the matter, but I forbid you to mention it to me except in private."

"And now for the big question. Eilen, have you tried to communicate with this thing?"

The baby chooses this moment to remind me of his existence. The pain radiates through my belly up to my kidneys.

"Well," Chatila murmurs when I manage to shake my head. "You didn't think it was possible?"

A new spasm has me twisting on my chair. I barely

avoid sobbing. Chatila patiently waits for the crisis to pass before continuing, "In theory, if you receive, you can transmit. Often, all you have to do is inverse the fields. But I doubt that it will work in this specific case, considering the nature of what you've detected. You're sure of your extrapolations about your cloud's acceleration?"

She hands me a paper tissue from a box hanging near the board. A fine cloud of chalk dust whirls in the light diffracted by the blinds.

"I'm not sure about anything," I say, sniffling. "But I believe it will be gone before we manage to try anything."

"You regret that?"

She bends even closer to me and hammers her words out:

"Because if you have the slightest regret, now's the time to mention it, Eilen. We're quickly approaching the point of no return. I agree to believe that you found this thing without looking for it. I take your God hypothesis for what it is—I'm not completely lacking a sense of humor, even during work hours. But do not attempt to communicate with it, whatever it may be. Don't even think about it. And, above all, avoid talking about it with Max."

Something in her tone makes me grind my teeth. She must notice it since she backs away and abruptly shoves the lock of gray hair from her forehead. Her light eyes bore into mine.

"Good Lord, look at you," she says. "I was ten times harder than you at your age and that almost wasn't enough. If I hadn't protected you during the seminar, they'd have skinned you alive. Get out of here, but stand in the doorway long enough for me to cast a few well-chosen epithets in your direction. And, Eilen…"

I stand up, my throat tight.

"Do you believe that your cloud is capable of perceiving something as tiny as you moving about inside its immenseness?"

Instinctively, I fold my hands over my swollen belly.

Chatila sighs, "Forget the question, OK? And get out of my office."

Ten minutes later, I leave the building to face the early afternoon sun, on the campus lawn. The metallic blue sky encompasses us in the effective illusion of a closed world, folded in on itself, while the cloud I detected is tearing itself away from our presence and abandoning us. I can't keep from shivering. I feel like a fresh fruit salad with Chantilly cream and chocolate.

I blame that on my pregnancy and rush over to the cafeteria.

"That woman will say anything," Max murmurs without lifting his eyes from his tablet.

The blue monarch is still flitting about in the corner of the open window. The uneven beating of its wings resembles the wink of an eye. In the dining room, the employees are clearing the tables. I was able to obtain the Chantilly cream and chocolate syrup, but no fruit. The mixture, too sweet, sticks to the spoon. I've never eaten anything I needed so much.

I describe the seminar and the scene that followed to Max. Chatila didn't mince her words when I left her office. The lab corridor was deserted, yet I'm convinced people were listening behind every door. I played my role in silence, my useless graphs clasped to my chest. The door closed behind my back with a dry, definitive bang. A *coup de grâce*.

What frightened me the most was the feverish gleam in Chatila's eyes. Because it was certainly a reflection of the one in mine.

"We can't communicate with the cloud," Max continues without taking his eyes from the screen. "Not by using the detection network in lunar orbit. It doesn't transmit. I tried to hack it, just to see."

"You promised to stop."

"True. I use a phantom account, so, technically, it's not me." (He stretches with a satisfied air.) "Don't worry. I just played for five minutes, and didn't break anything. There isn't even a security system, just low-level maintenance routines to keep the sensors from losing their alignment. In fact…"

In the reflection of his face on the screen, I see his eyes crinkle, as if he has just bit into a lemon. His mouth twists, he exhales noisily a few times. I know the symptoms. *Oh shit…*

"In fact, we can," I say for him. "And you've just figured out how. You're a genius and Chatila will pummel us with apples when she learns about it."

"The sensors' alignment routines," he mutters without listening to me. "They have to communicate among themselves during the calibration phases, so they transmit. I have to find the wavelength, but that's just a detail."

"I have to throw up," I say, interrupting him.

And do so.

Tacitly, Max and I decided to put the topic on hold for the time being. He took me home after cleaning up the brownish puddle with a few broad swipes of the mop. This sort of thing is frowned on in the cafeteria, but the employees were sympathetic, given my condition. I rinsed my mouth thoroughly with the ice water from the drinking fountain, without managing to chase away the disgusting taste of the chocolate.

I started to sob on our way home. The world around me is taking on a new dimension and that terrifies me. Yet my gynecologist warned me: even if pregnancies are cosmic accidents, the Earth doesn't stop turning. But I have the feeling that, this time, things are going to be different.

Fortunately, Max does what it takes to make me fall asleep.

Saturday is catalogue day. I set aside all those I receive during the week—since I've been pregnant, the advertising agencies have been having a heyday with me—and I leaf through them as I eat breakfast. Everything Baby will need is available in fifteen varieties and at least as many colors. I've already started on furnishing his room and filling his closets, but we have to suggest gift ideas for all our relatives.

Max is fiddling about on his tablet, looking for over-the-top information to fill the weekend. According to him, the world has become so complicated that logic and good sense need a day of rest each week, just as humans do. So, from time to time, he tracks down news items that are beyond classification and reads them to me out loud, a little smile in the corner of his mouth that makes me want to want to kiss him each time.

"Look at this: they can graft a micro-camera for contact ultrasounds under your skin and it can be connected to all brand-name tablets. To present the new heir to the entire family via Skype. You can even add mikes around your navel so that the future baby can listen to conversations in surround sound.

"Your mother would love that. Can you pass me a napkin?"

I brush away the crumbs spread over the catalogues while Max jumps from one link to another with the dexterity of an acrobat. The kitchen smells of garlic and toast. I've coated my belly with stretch mark cream, adding a whiff of argan oil to the mix.

"Anyway," he says, while pouring some tea, "if your algorithms for eliminating the astrophysical noise had their equivalent in biology, we could obtain a detailed 3D ultrasound of the fetus that would even reveal facial expressions. We'd see the exact moment when he would start to look like us."

"You've been watching *Alien* again?"

We both burst out laughing, as we do every time. Our breakfast conversations are skeins of poorly sorted ideas and we both love pulling on the same threads.

"I started the simulation up again last evening," he says while looking me straight in the eyes. "I couldn't sleep." (He pretends to look embarrassed.) "I sort of cheated with the priorities so I could access enough computer time. And I have something to tell you."

He props his tablet against the vinegar bottle and points it at me, before pulling his chair next to mine. Over his shoulder, I can see the unmade futon, the rolled-up comforter and I kiss my lazy morning goodbye. The cloud has priority.

"If you could talk to it before it leaves, what would you say?"

I think about this, frowning, as the simulation window purrs. Max has mobilized all of the free resources in the department's processor farm and the images of the cloud fleeing are displayed almost in real time. It has accelerated. The Earth still lies within its immensity, but that won't last much longer.

"Just 'Goodbye'," I say.

"Not even 'Good luck'?"

"For that to mean anything, it would have to have its

own gods."

Max nods.

"No regrets then? You're sure?" (I shiver inside, thinking of Chatila.) "Because we can't really communicate with it. The sensor calibration routines merely exchange packets of bits with predefined content. All that can be changed is the signal strength."

We look at one another and the idea comes to both of us at the same time. He may have been a little quicker than me, but I prefer to believe that we reacted together. During a shared orgasm, no one needs to take photos for the finish.

"We can just shout…" he starts,

"…hoping that it hears us," I conclude.

I spend Saturday afternoon in the arms of my favorite observer, playing with the most twisted theological concepts the thing inspires in us.

As always, Max starts.

"They're divine sperm that *It* released into the galaxy, waiting to find an ovum of the right size. Our Earth."

"It's going away," I yawn.

"Fine, it's going away. OK. That doesn't mean that fertilization didn't take place. Moreover, it made us in its image: hollow inside, barely capable of being detected and forced to move on without really knowing why."

"At the beginning, we were amoebas," I say, shifting my position a bit on the futon.

The baby is pressing against my bladder. The rapid beating of a second heart is superimposed on mine.

"Talk for yourself. My ancestors were completely honorable chimpanzees."

"Do you think it's going home?"

"When you measure 700 million kilometers long,

44

everywhere is home."

We laugh, softly.

"Do you want to let Chatila know about our project?"

I've already asked myself that question, but what we're about to do has no significance on a world scale. It's just an idea we had, a decision we're fully entitled to make. One last wave to the cloud. I'm the one who saw it first, after all.

I shake my head and stretch, before folding my legs and climbing clumsily out of the futon. Naked, I head for the kitchen, aware of Max's eyes on my buttocks and hips.

"I propose a picnic tomorrow evening, on the hill opposite us. In principle, the sky should be clear. We can say goodbye to it."

"Just before midnight," he replies, fingers busy on his tablet. "Or just after." (The staccato of his fingernails on the flexible screen sound like a storm.) "I wonder if the constellations will lose their meaning when it's no longer there."

Sunday evening, we decide to get down to serious work. We have a big day left before the cloud definitively leaves terrestrial orbit, as long as its acceleration remains constant. The exact moment of its departure remains uncertain. It doesn't have a precise border. *We are tracing the edges of God...* Is it even dense enough to be aware, anyway?

By mutual agreement, Max handles the programming. According to him, it's no real challenge, just a maintenance script that has to be tinkered with. We don't want to break anything. The circumlunar sensor network is a valuable tool that everyone uses. For my part, I've gathered all my data and hypotheses about the cloud into a large, compressed packet that I copy and save on our research network. After it leaves it will be incredibly difficult to continue observing it. I even wonder if there would be any point.

I place a temporal lock on my backup. In 48 hours, everything I've copied will be made public. I take a deep breath, then give the activation command, before curling up in the comforter still warm from our bodies.

When I wake in the middle of the night, my bladder unpleasantly squeezed, the luminous figures of the projection clock slide over the white ceiling as if fleeing. I stare at them for a long time before going back to sleep.

Monday morning, I send a laconic message to Chatila telling her I won't be going into the lab. I use nausea as a pretext, which isn't completely false. I work a couple of hours on the article describing my observation data filtration algorithms. To find God, we literally dug through garbage cans, routed through the residues of residues, looking for significant information.

And we got lucky that it started to leave at that very moment.

Max is still sleeping, rolled up in the comforter. His tablet purrs along without him; he must have gotten up at dawn to run his tests again, before going back to sleep. From time to time, a window opens to provide a brief glimpse of the blackness of space or a piece of the hidden side of the moon, bathed in ashy light. I feel as if I'm watching the inside of his mind as he dreams.

In the lower right corner of the screen, the butterfly has returned to its cocoon.

I take the car to drive to the mall and I stroll through the shops, wearing brand-new overalls that my belly doesn't quite fill yet. Nothing I try on suits me. I spotted the 3D photo booth when I arrived and I resign myself to updating the three-dimensional profile of my shopper card. My breasts have barely grown, which is frustrating. My hips, however, have taken on a singular curvaceousness. As the laser light sweeps over my naked skin to measure me, I think about the cloud that will envelop us for a few more hours and I wonder if a bit of it is mingling with my flesh at this very moment, if I'm special, chosen. If my baby felt its immaterial caress.

My profile is displayed on the mirror screen. The main changes from my previous image are highlighted in red. It's time for me to order new underwear.

That takes the next hour.

Before going home, I buy a portable cooler, which I fill with various flavors of sorbet: all the fruits we love and a certain number we're unfamiliar with. Max beeped me without leaving a message. He's awake, everything is fine. I have something that will take his eyes from his tablet; it's time to show off my purchases.

Then Chatila calls me. Twice in a row. Losing her patience on my voicemail.

"Do you know what you're doing?" (Her voice is so hard it pounds at my temples.) "Call me back, Eilen! In the name of everything you believe in, think!"

I place the cooler on the back seat of the car, next to my new underwear and I drive home, taking the lane reserved for slow vehicles. The sky is streaked with white lines left by the afternoon airplanes. I drum my fingers nervously on the steering wheel. Max wasn't careful enough when he programmed the sensor network; the two of us are in deep shit.

"No one could have detected anything," he rages indignantly, when I play the voicemail for him. "The new script is already loaded in the system memories and I erased all my tracks a long time ago. I think she's bluffing."

"Not her style."

"And it's not my style to get caught when I hack." (He grimaces in outrage and hands his telephone to me.) "What do you think about calling her?"

Chatila picks up on the second ring, her mouth full of apple. I hear someone pick up papers and leave the office, as she makes me wait with one or two empty sentences, separated by swallowing sounds. Then the door closes with a click.

"I've examined the content of your backup files thoroughly," she says. "And I've destroyed it." (She clears her throat.) "I'd like to remind you that the storage space on the research network is my responsibility. Before I let you ruin your best chance at a career in my team, we're going to have a little conversation. One way. I'll talk and you'll listen. All you'll be allowed to do is say 'Yes, boss' once or twice, at appropriate moments."

Max, who had connected his earplugs at the same time as mine, gives a thumbs up of victory.

"That's why you called me?" I ask stupidly.

"Did you think I was concerned about your nausea? Honestly, Eilen, I'm really starting to get worried about you. I suppose Max is standing next to you?" (We glance at one another, frightened.) "Tell him to take you out to the restaurant this evening. You need us to keep you from thinking until tomorrow morning. Eight thirty. My office!"

She hangs up suddenly without giving me the time to reply. I hand the telephone to Max and slip into his arms. He holds me very tightly.

"You know, sweetie," I whisper in his ear. "This thing is right to be leaving. I don't think we'd know what

48

to do with it."

"We're still on? You sure?"

"Yes." (The baby makes the most of the situation to make its presence known; I'm overwhelmed by nervous trembling, which Max knowingly calms with pressure along my back.) "You want to as much as I do."

When we park the car in the parking lot at the top of the hill, it's 10 o'clock at night. We're alone, isolated from the roaring of the highway below. The containers that serve as garbage cans for weekend picnickers shine with a metallic gleam. I look at the lights of the city below our feet, the tight cloud of human stars that sparkle with all their strength. We have filled the night with our thoughts, lights and lines. The crossed messages they send me are all the same.

Look at me. I exist.

I take a blanket from the trunk to protect us from the pine needles and we head off to our favorite clearing, holding hands. The jars of sorbets tinkle gently in the cooler, a multi-colored plastic spoon planted in each like a beacon. I pick up a pretty piece of bark hemmed with resin but, since I don't know what to do with it, I put it back down where it lay. Around us, the trees form a heavier and heavier curtain until the thicket appears. We stop in the middle of nowhere, in a tamed space, open to the sky.

The Milky Way flows overhead. A breath of wind shakes the branches, carrying the scent of pines, mingled with the odor of the city. For the first time in two weeks, I feel relaxed. I undo the straps of my overalls before looking up at the sky. I notice a falling star, but haven't got a wish ready.

Max unfolds the blanket and crouches over it, the

cooler between his knees. We left our tablets in the apartment. The cloud simulation is still running, but we know it will reveal nothing new. Before leaving, we decided that midnight would be the wrenching moment. That gives us two hours to taste all the sorbet flavors.

We kiss, to test various mixtures. Max wraps me in his coat and we talk about what we are about to do together, the articles we'll have to write, the baby who has already upset our lives beyond what we could have imagined possible. Of Chatila, as well. Our interview tomorrow may not go like she has planned.

"It's time," murmurs Max.

He helps me get up and we count down the seconds out loud. When we get to zero, we shout and shout, for many long minutes, and we wave our arms at the sky, as invisible as we've always been, as the sensor grid in lunar orbit pulses briefly for 10 seconds. Our farewell. Then we fall to the ground, laughing until we lose our breath, amid the sorbet jars.

The constellations continue to shine, as we created them many millennia ago. The cloud is no longer there.

A flight of bats, disturbed by the noise, darkens the sky for an instant. I follow them with my eyes, wiping away the tears of laughter that are running down my cheeks. Max wraps his arms around me and buries his head in the hollow of my shoulder. I cling to him, closing my eyes.

"There's just us now, princess. You're not cold?"

"There's always been just us," I say caressing my swollen belly.

A PLACE WHERE ALL PATHS CROSS

There's a place, a square if you like, where all the planes of reality cross. Three people have gone through it, despite the guard. The first was a thief, fleeing too rapidly to be stopped. Wherever he is now, he's probably still running. The second was a wise man, whose serene gaze tricked the guard. He walked peacefully across the square, then turned around and went back.

I'm the third and this is my story.

The square isn't terribly large, barely two yards in diameter, and not in the least secured. No circle of stones, no barbed wire. An old guard watches over it, from the shadows, but few people approach. The place doesn't look like much. There's nothing repulsive about it— which would attract adventurers —or anything particularly pleasant either, for that matter. It's just a boring place, at the end of a dead-end alley. The entrance is barricaded with garbage cans that no one ever seems to empty. There are rats (you can see them rummaging among the stinking, half-gutted garbage bags) and a few puddles of muddy water positioned like hopscotch boxes.

I didn't even know it was there at the time. And, if I had, I probably wouldn't have given it a single thought.

Clem, Sadie and I, we hang out in places where no one else goes. Sadie and Clem are together even if, from time to time, Sadie comes with me when she needs to recreate a semblance of normality in her life. That's her expression: a semblance of normality.

She uses it all the time and is as proud of it as the tattoo that rages across her small, wrinkled breasts. Then she puts her clothes back on and sets off to find Clem. I join them a while later and everyone pretends that nothing has happened.

It's one of those evenings when the semblance of normality seems to have mysteriously evaporated. Clem is wrecked, Sadie is heading in the same direction and I stay off to the side, like I usually do. I understand what people feel and sometimes I share it. That's how I know that drugs allow you just to look up at the sky and see planes that don't exist fly overhead. But none of them ever lands to let you board and take you elsewhere. Never. So, while Clem and Sadie soar in their heads and make drunken plans to change the present, I get up and walk to the end of the alley to stretch my legs. I vaguely consider pissing against the enormous garbage can that blocks my way, but when I lean against it, it shifts aside, creaking. There is a road; a door has opened.

"There are always doors." (The guy who used to come to exterminate the vermin on the farm when I was nine years old would talk non-stop, as he tossed the poisoned granules on the barn floor.) "That's the first thing we check when we open our eyes. We open a door or we imagine one. It's not as if we want to go somewhere, of course, boy. It's just that we don't want to be obliged to stay where we are. Because where we are..." (His large, hairy hand, like a scythe, threw the deadly pellets that fell with the soft hiss of rain) "It's just a starting point, you see. The thing is, we never leave, but as long as there's a door, we never arrive at the end of the trip."

I nodded my head like a big person. In principle, I wasn't allowed to play in the barn, but that didn't bother the exterminator. He walked between the old stalls, to where the tractor was stored, then pulled his hat down and emptied the bag with a single toss. The pellets fell in a gray heap at his feet.

"The instinct to reproduce…" he grumbled. "I don't imagine you know anything about that, yet. But that's how we open doors. You. Me. Everyone is a door for someone." (He took in my astonished glance, before sweeping away the heap of granules with a kick of his boot and spitting, farther than anyone I knew could. I applauded.) "It'll catch up with you one day."

I think about that as I walk ahead through the gelatinous shadows. The week before, my high school graduating class celebrated an anniversary. All of the people I knew in school uniforms now wear another type of outfit, based on more expensive ties that they have chosen themselves. When I see how successfully they've built their lives, I think that maybe I should try to do something with my own. But on evenings like this one, I'm not even sure I have a life.

"You lose something?"

The voice was not particularly frightening. Not terribly friendly either, to tell the truth. But behind me, I hear the sound of moist kisses, the inimitable rip of a zipper, followed by Clem's chuckles and I decide to stay where I am for a while, feet in a puddle that stealthily seeps into the soles of my shoes, my nose tickled by the stench of old coffee grounds and dirty diapers. But it's the perfect place for what I came to do.

"Where are you?"

"What's that to you?"

"I don't want to piss on you."

"Go back to where you came from. There's a pub on the corner of Crockford Street. Old Malley will let you use his crapper if you ask politely."

It was as if the voice were murmuring in my ears from all sides at the same time. It drowned the sounds of screwing that come from the entrance to the alley. It even covered the silence in my head, which I'm used to.

"There are doors," I say, without really knowing why.

"Yes, I know." (The voice sounds amused for a second.) "But not for you. Not for anyone, in fact. Well, not in this reality."

"Yeah." (I shift about, since the filthy water is starting to climb up my toes.) "I have no talent for opening them, in any case."

I plunge my foot into another puddle, almost as deep as the first, and curse.

"Stop splashing every which way, shitface! I spent years arranging these holes to make them look natural."

"Sorry about that." (One foot in the air, I consider the situation.) "I'm high, eh?"

"Let's just say you're on the edge. At the border. On the threshold. And I'm waiting to see which side I'll send you to. You can put your foot down."

"Where?"

The moonlight fleetingly slices through the clouds, making the puddles sparkle. Overhead, the narrow thread of the sky is carved into lace by the rooftops.

"If you don't look down, you're going to bump into another garbage can. And get even wetter. And twist your ankle."

"I'm not going anywhere," I murmur.

"You'll move eventually."

The rain starts to fall, making the same sound as the poisonous pellets falling on the straw. A net of water that cascades from a gutter reminds me that I need to pee, but it's an abstract need, one of those inevitable things you end up doing because there's a hole in the fabric of time that has to be filled, in some way or another. I shake my shoe and place my foot on the ground, a little farther off.

"You're cheating."

"I'm not doing it on purpose. Do you want to move off a bit?"

"I was going to ask you the same thing. Let me guess. You never do anything on purpose, do you?"

I feel the shadows envelope me, cross through me. It's almost as cold as the water dribbling down my neck, despite my hood.

"You have no ambition or courage," murmurs the voice. "Or any real curiosity. No obvious weapon. You're not even finished... Suppose we say you went the wrong way. I could let you go. Except, of course..." (The voice sounds dreamy for a moment) "Except that you're not going anywhere."

"Can I just wait a bit?"

"Nothing will happen if you don't move."

For a second, I catch a glimpse of the guardian's power. It is fed on the frustrations and envies of all those he has prevented from crossing over the threshold. The garbage cans, the puddles, the cracks in the walls are the talismans of a life dedicated to retreating into oneself. He might crush me if I give him the slightest reason to do so.

A thread of icy water trickles down between my shoulder blades. The darkness is not particularly frightening, just boring. I'm getting used to my wet feet, to the stench of abandoned lives wafting up from the garbage cans. A sensation of familiarity washes over me bit by bit. I've learned to recognize margins and borders, those places without hope where you can hide if you're sufficiently non-existent. They're my playgrounds.

"You're a foundling," my grandmother told me one day, when she thought I was old enough to understand. And to suffer.

"Like the lost children in Peter Pan?" (I didn't know how to read, but I had seen a lot of cartoons and I loved to repeat everything I heard.)

"No, those belong to someone. They just don't know who, that's all. As for you, my daughter picked you up because nothing wanted to come out of her. But it took her nowhere."

"Nowhere? Where's that?"

"That's where you'll find yourself if you continue to do stupid things."

Good memories are like mercury. They shine and seem solid, but you can't grasp them. Bad memories, on the other hand, are prickly like thistles and catch onto your fingers. I have just enough to fill the time Clem and Sadie spend screwing.

"You've made up your mind?" the voice grumbles.

The back of the alley is almost silent. The plastic bags crackle quietly under the weight of the water. The drizzle paints a sound landscape of puddles and gutters, faded rainbows out of the corners of my eyes. Now that my eyes have grown accustomed to the twilight, I make out an arch that is much blacker than the rest. And a silhouette carved out of the very fabric of the night that melts into it and then springs back almost immediately.

"I see you," I say, wiping my eyes with the back of my sleeve.

"You've found the door."

"No, I see *you*." (I'd move ahead, but the slightest step seems terribly final to me.) "You don't want to come closer?"

"I can't move away from the door."

"Why not? The door and you are the same thing, aren't you?"

I expect him to laugh. Not to obey.

"That's really what you want?" he said, sliding toward me like velvet.

Occasionally, when Sadie is on the verge of falling asleep, she allows me to close my eyes and wrap my arms around her. The sensation is gentle and rough at the same time, smooth and crumpled. This time, I keep my eyes open when we touch. The guard and I.

It's a bittersweet fight, one no one wants to win. He's so much stronger than I am. So alone. I hear the rats approach, tearing the thickness of the shadows that have protected me since my birth with their teeth. The very night starts to bleed. When they reach my skin, the pain takes my breath away. There's nothing left to protect me. So I superimpose the sound of the poisoned pellets of my childhood over the raindrops until the rats run off and disappear.

Perhaps I only imagined them.

My lungs unfold and I utter my first human cry.

"It's time for you to turn back," murmurs the guard, after a moment when even the rain has fallen silent. "Otherwise…"

"Otherwise, you'll be the one leaving," I say. "And I'll take your place."

He allowed me to approach the door. I made no attempt to cross through it. It's a place where all paths cross, an infinity of destinations for those who carry roads inside them, a house of mirrors for those who are afraid of being alone. For me, it's just an echo, a place that resembles me. I'm not really surprised when the darkness flows around me and slips into all my empty places. I have just enough room to take it in. It is just vast enough to fill me.

When I look up at the sky, I have the impression that the rain is running through me without wetting me. The guard is no longer anywhere to be seen.

"I leave first," murmurs the voice. "Don't try to follow me. And take care. There are people who will see this door in you and who will desire you, for a whole bunch of reasons you won't like. Learn to close yourself."

"I still have time for that," I say.

When I turn back to the mouth of the alley, my bladder empty and my heart overflowing, Clem and Sadie are still entwined, under the porch that shelters them. Fingers interlaced under their clothing, legs twisted, they look like those carefully tied ribbons on gifts, the ones we cut because we don't have the patience to untie them. I step over them cautiously and give them a sad smile, because they've found their semblance of normality and they don't even know it.

Then I walk away, heading in the direction of the morning, without looking back. Each of us is a door, for someone else or for ourselves. It's time I learn to open mine, if I want to know where I'm headed.

BREAKING THE SHELL

Gabe was running for his life. He could have simply walked.

His skin itched in a peculiar manner whenever he attracted the attention of a Wani. It was a sensation that was difficult to describe, upsetting even. An unpleasant tingling, as if fish hooks were digging through his skin, into his flesh. His scar would start to throb, occasionally even glisten. Memories that did not belong to him would pop into his mind.

The combat drugs had stopped working a long time ago. His shell as a veteran, a hero of more campaigns than he cared to recall, no longer protected him. Technically, he was on a long-term leave of absence, a polite way of saying that peace had made him obsolete. There had been no home to hold him back when he enlisted, which meant he had nowhere to go back to. So, he jumped from one military base to another, confident he would find a place to lay his head, a relatively decent mess filled with young recruits ready to pay for his drinks in exchange for an outpouring of his most sordid heroic deeds. And his scar. But the barrier the alcohol erected between him and the world would collapse the morning after each drinking binge.

This city wasn't any better than the others—a simple outpost on a standard planet, as comfortable and impersonal as a uniform. The base was located behind the astroport, at the edge of the colonized zone. The rusty desert that stretched as far as the eye could see was covered by sandy whirlwinds that came and went like sentries. According to the tactical briefings he'd been given at the time, it was on this type of planet, several Tau-jumps away, that humankind encountered the first Wanis.

"Something's advancing toward us…" (After a brief hesitation, the prospector added "chief").

He was young, eager to do well. Eight hundred meters away, the creature, as tall as a 20-storey building, was crawling in their direction, leaving a chalky dust in its wake.

"You looking for trouble?"

Standing shoulder to shoulder, they watched the Wani approach. It was oval in shape, flattened at the front, with no apparent organs or limbs. Its spotty, dusty, gray shell looked as if it were about to crack. That was an illusion humans still haven't learned to dispel.

The foreman pivoted the recording unit and zoomed in. Nothing particular could be seen on the control screen. The creature was approaching in a straight line, as fast as a handicapped turtle. Its base worked the soil, projecting a small mound of dirt ahead of it. Shards of rock spurted up, only to fall back to the ground a little farther on. The entire scene was terminally boring.

Around them, the prospecting instruments were buzzing. The energy production unit hiccupped, as it projected golden sparks at the cable junction. Farther off, the two girls in the crew were just finishing their calibration of the drilling machine connected to the shuttle's generators. And beyond that, nothing. It was a lifeless world, at least in theory—the robotic unit that had discovered the planet had not wasted much time before completing its report.

The few rare constellations visible overhead still had no names. Neither did the sun around which they orbited, but that would change soon enough. According to the first surveys, iridium and titanium could be found underground.

"That thing was no doubt already here when we arrived," the foreman declared after a silence. "Let's see if we can convince it to leave."

He ducked into the sealed block that housed their meager possessions and came back out with a long-range rifle mounted on a telescopic tripod. He charged it, taking his time—munitions were expensive. When the weapon woke up, it dug its articulated feet into the ground and pivoted, looking for a target. For a moment, it focused on the Wani as it continued its lazy approach, then turned away.

"That thing is too slow to be identified as a threat," groaned the foreman. "Switch to manual. Since you saw it first, it's your job to make it go away. Shoot ten meters in front of it. A shot across the bow. Repeat in five seconds, as a precaution. Make sure to create a large hole, so it knows we're serious. Let's make ourselves perfectly clear."

"Clear, neat and deadly. Just the way I like it!"

"Except that you're going to shoot *in front of* it. All we want to do is make it turn around."

The weapon focused docilely on the creature. The barrel lowered, imperceptibly. In the sighting goggles, the shell, magnified 100 times, looked like a cliff eroded by sand. Regretfully, the young prospector pointed the gun at the ground and pressed the trigger. Once. Twice. It made a reasonably satisfactory noise, projecting geysers of rock in all directions.

Imperturbable, the creature continued on its way. The enormous crater dug by the weapon swallowed it up halfway, without affecting its progress. It climbed up it, and continued to approach them, slowly, until its shadow brushed over the walls of the camp.

"Let's try talking with it," grumbled the boss.

He got as close to it as he dared, observing the chalky cliff that scraped the soil as the creature advanced. It made a sound like paper being crumpled, dull and monotonous. He waved his arms and shouted out a greeting in Standard, without provoking the slightest reaction. The prospectors had no infrared lights that could have enabled them to see the communication glyphs on the Wani's shell. They wouldn't have been able to decipher them, in any case. And the whole situation was creating havoc with their prospecting plan.

At the other end of the camp, the girls stood with their backs to them, eyes focused on the control screen of the drilling machine that would soon set into motion. The audio system in their helmets was spitting out the usual syncopated sludge that helped them keep pace. They were supposed to take samples of an exposed vein and make at least two more surveys before nightfall. The orange sky was already turning purple.

The foreman looked at his chronometer, irritated.

"I don't know what that thing is but there's no way we're going to waste any more time on it. Make it turn around!"

The gun barrel tilted up.

"Aiming device locked."

The two men had no idea they were about to start a war that would last sixteen years.

The projectile crashed into the creature's shell, detonating violently, followed immediately by a second.

Once they had evacuated the camp in a panic, leaving behind the heavy equipment they were unable to take with them, they used the cameras on the shuttle's stern to film their flight. The Wani had stopped in the middle of the camp, after first eviscerating the sealed block simply by sliding over it. The tortured screech of the metal had given the signal for withdrawal.

As they rose into the dark sky, the prospectors were able to see other Wanis converging with exasperating slowness on the abandoned camp. Massed behind the folds of the terrain, they calmly made their way toward the epicenter of the human presence. There were hundreds of them. No, thousands. The rays of the setting sun were too weak to light up the complicated motives running over their shells.

"We'll head back to Pana-3. The eggheads can come to study these things if they want to."

"I hit it three times!" giggled the younger man. "That will teach them a lesson."

"You did nothing to it," grumbled the foreman. "If you fuck as well as you shoot, you'll kill them all with boredom."

The girls made fun of him as they usually did, as the shuttle returned to the orbiting ship. The jump into Tau space took place a few hours later. There was nothing more to be said for it.

Three weeks later, the Wanis appeared on Pana-3.

After two days of drinking and boredom, Gabe had taken the monorail to the center on a whim, to see a little greenery before setting off again. A park had been planted in the heart of the city, with real shrubs in hydroponic bins and something that could pass for grass. The few metal benches along the single path were new, rarely occupied. Gabe tried them out, one by one, his dark mood protecting him like armor. No one spoke to him.

The park was almost deserted. No children's shouts. That would come, no doubt, once the human mold had covered over everything again. Within a few centuries. The Wanis weren't the only ones who were slow and inexorable.

A plaque embedded in a stone egg related the circumstances of first contact. Gabe couldn't help but snigger. It must have been brief and frustrating. A group of rough, poorly armed prospectors facing a handful of life forms with impenetrable shells that moved too slowly to constitute any real danger.

Humankind had withdrawn in an orderly manner, convinced they would return. But the Wanis followed the human spacecraft to the next colony and then the next. An invasion similar to mud flowing. Cities had been turned into ruins, crushed under shells or the blankets of human bombs launched in an effort to stop the Wanis' progress. The first super troops had disembarked months later, prepared for battle.

Gabe was one of them.

He headed away from the park and into an alley that was too narrow for an extraterrestrial shell. The odor of rotting food and excrement grabbed him by the throat. He stood tall, examining every nook and cranny. The few squatters loitering in the ally posed no threat for him. Even unarmed, he could kill them cleanly, without even missing a step.

They left him alone.

When he emerged into the deserted main artery, two gigantic silhouettes were blocking each end. They headed toward him, slowly. Awkward graffiti drawn with paint bombs, dotted their surfaces, at least the areas that could be reached by a ladder. The rest was the usual spotty gray. Without the graffiti, they could not be told apart.

Gabe shook his head, furious with himself. He had

violated the most elementary safety rules by wasting his time on the molded metal benches, the remnants of a re-cycled tank, as stated proudly on the plaque screwed to the top of each back. The wind ruffling the grass and the few shrubs had whistled in his ears, preventing him from thinking. He scratched his chest, automatically. The scar that ran across his torso was not satisfied with just itching. It formed an impenetrable barrier between him and the world.

Part of the genetic material that formed it was not his. His torso was a battlefield disputed by the two species. He often wondered if that was why these creatures pursued him. To recover the remains of their mate, or to take vengeance.

The Wanis' shadows advanced toward him.

He turned back into the alley, climbed up a rusty emergency ladder that led to a roof or a terrace. The geometry of the battle had changed. He dominated the situation now. Below him, the silhouettes that brought to mind a flattened egg came to a stop, before pivoting with exasperating slowness to face him.

Gabe looked down at the top of a Wani skull. It was smooth, barely rounded, dotted with brownish spots. What it contained was a mystery. Even after years of combat, he still knew very little about them. Just that it took eight anti-tank mines placed at strategic locations on each shell to eliminate the threat they posed.

He closed his eyes for a moment and his mind turned to the past. To the time when everything had shifted.

"What are you doing with those mines, Gabe?"

The sergeant's voice roared in his helmet, interspersed with static. Once again, the Wanis had disabled the digital com systems and the humans had to resort to old analog walkie-talkies that were heavy and cumbersome. When the enemy gathered in sufficient numbers, energy arcs sizzled among them, annihilating all electronics within a radius of several kilometers. Even enhanced, modern bombs and missiles gave up the ghost before reaching their targets. The humans had to resort to weapons that dated back to long-forgotten wars. They were barely any more effective than they had been at the time.

Gabe slipped another mine into his already full bag and picked up a sixth one. Behind him, the oval cliffs approached nonchalantly. Bursts of semi-automatic gunfire crackled around him. His armor reeked of sweat; the amphetamines had made his eyes dry and left a metallic taste on his tongue. He laughed electrically.

"Just an idea, Sergeant."

"Leave that to the officers! We're withdrawing."

"It's something I've always wanted to try before I die." (He lifted the bag, filled to overflowing, and started to take off his armor.) "I used to do a little climbing when I was young."

The Wanis' shadows cast a daisy of darkness around him. No more than a few meters separated Gabe from them. More than enough distance to make an escape if he were quick about it.

Gabe stripped down, keeping only his form-fitting coveralls and his breathing apparatus. The armor was too heavy for what he wanted to do. Even without it, he'd be cutting things close. He slipped on his backpack and hooked two more mines to the belt at his waist as a counterbalance. The hooks clicked under his fingers. Then he looked up at the closest Wani. *Split the mountain in two before climbing it.* The creature was a ridiculous size, compared to the cliffs he had faced on his home world, but it was living. Would that make any difference?

There was only one way to find out.

Paying no heed to the sergeant's curses, he slipped into the narrow gap that separated the two shells threatening him, walked around their curved backs and headed toward an isolated Wani making its way a little further off. His boots crunched in the sand; the weight of his pack pulled his shoulders back. In his helmet, the encouraging hoots of the other members of his unit had replaced the sergeant's shouts. Gabe smiled. The amphetamines caused him to grind his teeth and made colors painfully vibrant. He bit the inside of his cheek to taste his own blood, then pulled on the suction pads he carried with him everywhere.

With a savage cry, he threw himself at the base of the Wani, felt the hardness of its shell and the warmth it gave off. He closed his eyes, took his bearings in his mind. One boot, then another, fingertips seeking tiny nooks and crannies. Suction pads providing support. He had pulled himself up a half meter before being crushed by the metal blocks that bounced against his kidneys. The damned backpack was too heavy. *Forget about that and climb.* Seventy meters to the top. He should have dumped the mines before.

He spit, a bright red thread that soiled the Wani's chalky white, then wiped it with his chest as he climbed up. These creatures felt nothing, in any case. Bullets broke on them when they hit, heavy projectiles bounced off or were inexplicably deflected. People had tried explosives and mines, but the Wanis' bases seemed impenetrable. At the very best, it was possible to tip them over. Gabe had seen that happen. Twice. An unforgettable sight. The creatures toppled backward majestically and remained motionless, like resigned turtles. The other Wanis would gather around the fallen one, to help it get back up. Then they headed back on their way, indifferent.

This war would have been infinitely less frustrating if the Wanis had paid any attention to humans.

Bursts of static drowned out the congratulations in his helmet. All he needed was the scent of salt to recall his first cliffs over water. Climbing enabled him to be alone. He wasn't asocial, as the unit psychiatrist had explained to him. Just bloody different.

Close up, the Wani's shell seemed ageless. A few traces of erosion drew climbing paths on its surface. A shard missing here, the beginning of a crack there. Gabe advanced slowly, the suction pads supporting most of his weight, but he was getting close to the summit.

He groaned, then shook his head to drive away the sweat. Paying no attention to him, the Wani continued on its way. The static in his helmet faded for a moment and then the sergeant's voice rang out, loud and clear.

"Hurry up and shag that damned pebble, Gabe. We're withdrawing!"

"I'm working on it, chief. Over and out."

He got back to crawling. The desert heat clouded his sensations; the amphetamines made his thoughts taste like iron. For a second, he had the impression the creature quivered in response to each contact with his hips. His head buzzed with unwelcome thoughts. He forced himself to concentrate, drawing all of his energy into the tips of his fingers and toes.

When Gabe reached the approximate middle of the shell, he reached out his hand and pulled a mine from his backpack. Once armed, it stuck snuggly to the wall. For protection against the electronic blast, the original digital timer had been replaced with a spring device, white with black numbers, like those used in kitchens. Gabe turned the handle all the way around. Fifteen minutes to detonation. He wouldn't have enough time to climb to the top of the creature as he had initially planned. Too bad. That would have been interesting. Frustrated, he pounded the warm wall, without provoking any reaction, but his fingers found a flaw. Groaning, he started to climb again.

Sporadic artillery shots rang out in the distance. The battlefield was hardly bustling. Wanis advanced, humans made an effort to shoot at them before hastily retreating and then starting all over again, a kilometer or so farther along. The amphetamines made everything even more frustrating. Seen from above, the humans looked like sand fleas attacking seagull eggs. That's what one of the shuttle pilots had told him before trying to break his jaw. Gabe had been as drunk as the other man and things hadn't gone far.

Damned seagull eggs.

A second mine armed, a third, a fourth. Positioned arm's length apart so as to distribute the explosives over a larger area. The white plastic timers ticked in unison. Gabe kept those hanging at his hips for the end. Relieved from the weight of the backpack, he climbed almost effortlessly along the wall. His panting broke the silence. It was an intense moment, something he would have been incapable of putting into words: dancing at the edge of the void, hanging on solely by the strength of his fingers. One decision away from crossing the border, falling.

Alone.

The last two mines found their place on either side of his head. He heard himself screaming with excitement when he armed the last one, barely a few meters from the top.

Get your ass out of here! He had time to think, before heading back down. He only had four minutes left. He'd be cutting things close, but he knew he could scramble down any wall like a spider. Without crampons, without safety ropes, just the memories of handholds stored in his fingertips.

He shoved against the sun-warmed shell one last time and climbed down fifteen or so meters in less than a minute, using the mines like steps. The sole of his boot slipped on the next-to-last one. He felt the plastic timer split and didn't even have time to be afraid. His mind was filled with an intolerable stridency. Panic-stricken, he slid as quickly as he could, his fingers bloody, but was unable to reach the ground.

Just before the explosion, he heard a voice in his mind. Powerful. Foreign.

It murmured, "Finally…"

Gabe's mad escapade brought the conflict to an end. The Wanis didn't like people killing them and the human joint chiefs of staff hated enemies that cost so much to kill. A few weeks later, linguists accompanied the commandos. They were interested in the fleeting symbols sparkling in infrared on the Wanis' shells; they catalogued them, learned to reproduce them, and started to decipher some of them. Negotiations took place, laborious but inevitable. Followed by peace, as absurd as the conflict that neither side admitted to having started.

Oddly enough, the Wanis' only demand was to be able to come and go as they saw fit. Since no one had ever been able to prevent them from doing just that, even with nuclear warheads, their request was accepted. They were already everywhere, or almost, on this side of the galaxy. Each new inhabitable plant discovered by humankind was already home to a small group—20 or so. Slow, obstinate, impossible to chase away.

For Gabe, the war ended when he had split his Wani's shell, using explosives arranged in a star pattern. Projected by the blast of the explosion, his shattered body had landed in the sand about 20 meters away. The extraterrestrial's inner flesh had spurted through the crack in his direction, like a spray of burning light, sticking to his coveralls, literally dissolving them within seconds.

The surviving members of his squad had extracted Gabe from his tattered equipment and taken him to the rear, naked, screaming, his chest covered with incredibly strangely smelling organic matter. Months later, he still remembers how his brain had refused to analyze the various layers of the stench that enveloped him, as if it were fighting against an invasion.

The Wani's flesh had slowly devoured Gabe's skin, then the thin layer of fat covering his abdomen. Only his face, protected by the respirator, had been spared. The squad members had unsheathed their knives and scraped off everything they could, tearing off shards of human flesh along their way. They had heated their blades to cauterize each bit of extraterrestrial debris and had managed to stop the progress of the wound. At that point, Gabe had stopped shrieking and slipped into unconsciousness, but the light in the depths of his wide-open eyes refused to expire. For several weeks and during almost 20 operations, he would remain the sole occupant of a sterile cocoon.

Meanwhile, the evacuation continued; the Wanis kept on occupying the terrain. Except for one, which was no more than a broken seagull egg, its innards swallowed up by the sand. It remained standing there, slightly off-kilter, surrounded by its own debris. None of the others had approached it.

Gabe scratched his chest furiously through his regulation canvas shirt. The maze of blisters that crisscrossed his torso felt red hot. The Wanis approached slowly, as if the encounter had been planned long ago. Since the peace treaty had been signed—or at least proclaimed, since the extraterrestrials had no means for signing anything, even supposing that they grasped the concept—the enormous creatures levitated a few millimeters off the ground when they found themselves in an area claimed by humans. This made their progress totally silent and painless for the environment. In theory.

As proclaimed by the numerous government notices posted in public places, people just had to act as if the Wanis weren't there…

In his gut, Gabe felt that all the Wanis on this planet were converging on him. It had been the same during his previous stopovers. A few hours, sometimes a few days' respite, then the oval creatures would appear around him and start to approach. Since the explosion, he'd become the focus of their attention, the bull's-eye. An entire species was interested in him.

What remained of their encounter stuck to his skin. Literally.

Of course, he had time to escape… To climb down from the roof, return to the astroport, board any shuttle headed anywhere. The galaxy was vast; the Wanis were slow. Fleeing was always an option. But he was starting to tire of this pointless race.

He climbed down from the roof, taking small strides. His medal jiggled with each step and he felt like tearing it off. The emergency staircase started to vibrate under the impact of his boots; he picked up the pace. The few occupants of the foul-smelling alley had gone on their way. The main artery was itself deserted, silent. The oval shadows of the creatures crawled over its surface like a tide.

Gabe walked toward the closest shell, paying no attention to the graffiti and tags that stained it. He came to a stop in front of the creature, hands on his hips, in a futile effort to stop it from advancing. When it was less than a meter away, he closed his eyes. The scars on his chest were pulsing like a code, a chorus of discordant voices facing off in a language unknown to him.

The creature stopped, so close to him he could feel the heat wafting off it through his clothes. His fingers brushed against the stone shell that enveloped it. Eyelids still closed, he placed the palms of his hands flat against it, caressing it with a slow, circular movement. The memories of his climb swept over him but, this time, the pain of his disemboweled torso made each detail incredibly vivid. The shadow that covered him was soothing. He recalled the metallic taste of his own blood, the electric dryness of the amphetamines, the weight of his backpack. His entire life had served as a prologue for that moment, that explosion. And he'd been running away ever since.

He held his breath for a moment. Exhaled slowly. Started again.

Then, without rushing, he started to climb.

His fingers had retained the memory of the cliff that had changed his life. He pressed his face against the warm surface, free from his burden of mines, but weighed down by the scars that had gradually cut him off from the world. Hanging three meters above the ground, he made an effort to breathe slowly. The graffiti had almost disappeared—names, transient symbols, forgotten once drawn. Humans loved to leave traces of their passing and Gabe was no exception. His formed constellations on his body and mind.

The creature remained motionless. All over the planet, the others had stopped their advance. Gabe felt it without being able to explain why. He climbed effortlessly toward the top of the Wani. Despite the fact that he obstinately kept his eyes closed, he deciphered the symbols that flitted beneath his fingertips. Neither aggressive nor violent. Not a reproach. Just an expectation...

Lips glued to the wall, hips flat against the warm rock, he murmured, "What do you want from me?"

There was a long silence. The creature was thinking. Hanging by his fingertips, Gabe felt ready to let go. Following the explosion, he had lost his climbing suction pads and had never considered getting replacements.

Monochromatic glyphs formed spontaneously in his mind, accompanied by bursts of static. The scent of burning and gun oil wafted up into his nostrils, then faded, replaced by other, incongruous smells. The sea, incredibly salty; the stench of his combat gear; a whirlwind of fleeting sensations released by his memory in order to get rid of them. Sea birds flew like dots across his retinas, screeching. The Wani was mapping the areas of his brain, looking for sound equivalents for the strange drawings on its shell. Gabe had seen some during the briefings for his section, but their meaning was rough at the best. Now, multidimensional concepts were unfurling into words, articulated sentences. The foreign genetic material embedded in his scar served as a decoder.

"Fertilization," a voice said in his head. (A pause, just long enough for the word to dig into his skull). "Did fertilization occur?"

Gabe's scar sent him a signal of light and exquisite pain. He felt tears well up in his eyes. Without thinking, he continued his ascent, to the top. The hardened tips of his fingers effortlessly found tiny flaws he could use to pull himself up.

He withdrew cautiously from the relatively smooth surface that covered the top of the creature. He could have stood up, stretched his arms. Embraced the endless horizon. But the time for that was long past.

"If fertilization failed, the war will start up again," continued the creature. "We won't be able to prevent it."

The words tore into his mind like shrapnel from a slow explosion. The Wani had no difficulty making itself understood. Each concept was clear, unambiguous. As inexorable as the Wanis' progress from one world to the next. Gabe saw humanity as the creature perceived it—sand fleas attacking an infinite cliff. He saw himself climbing. It tore him apart. The seams in his mind gave way, as his scar opened up, bleeding within.

"We're too different." (The Wani started walking again, heading out of the city.) "We've had many other encounters of this kind and we know how things will end. The only two possibilities are miscegenation or the annihilation of one species by the other."

"We'll fight you," murmured Gabe, wrestling against the inevitable. "You can be broken."

"There's no point." (The creature was advancing slowly toward the horizon, with the certainty of tides.) "You are proof that the assimilation of your species is possible. You feel it in your flesh, in what you humans call your body, which is nothing more than a way to keep your distance from reality."

Behind the words, glyphs unfolded like infinite spider webs, before winding around him and locking him up in the infinity of their meaning. Even if he had been close to another human, Gabe would not have been able to transmit what he knew.

"When the time is right, we'll take care of your kind,

until they become our kind. Wherever you find yourself then, there will be no territory apart from yourself."

"It won't be long, now. Wait…"

Gabe felt himself sliding to the back of the creature, head first, along the oval curve. He made no effort to slow his fall. It had already taken place. He wasn't risking anything anymore. Already, his flesh was growing harder as it came into contact with that of the Wani. The Wanis' shells were nothing more than an immense scar, like his.

The sounds of the city faded and he no longer heard anything but the murmur of his own thoughts. He no longer needed to flee.

He remained motionless, curled up in the sand as it gradually covered him. Then, when the time was right, he stood up and set out for the horizon, slowly, to join the others. For a moment, the medal abandoned behind him sparkled in the setting sun. It too ceased to be important.

DIAMOND ANNIVERSARY

From his window on the top floor, he watches as they walk around the Vendôme Column, hands fluttering in time with a passionate discussion. On a corner of the oak desk, behind him, a cup of smoky Russian tea slowly grows cold.

On the other side of the room, a cello plays Bach's Suite No. 1 in G major.

"I'd hoped to have a bit more time," he murmurs to himself. "Time… our most precious jewel, the one we forget to shine. You should be with me, sweetheart."

The discrete intercom connected to his egosphere announces the arrival of his son.

"Alone?" (He listens to the response, then shakes his head.) "I'm going to ask you a favor, Anita. Step out of the shop and catch the young man in black leather who is about to cross the street. Tell him I'd like to see him as well. Make sure to tell him this is not an order, just a request. When he gets here, send them both, my son and the young man, in to me."

He turns around slowly, running his hand along the old copper telescope with its cracked lens. He has made his office a place beyond time, entirely dedicated to memory. The amber light that plays on the polished metal reminds him of wines savored long ago, as a couple.

Above the telescope hangs an oil portrait of a woman still young, green eyes flecked with gold. He doesn't need to look to know she's there.

"I've made my mind up, Dad!"

"I know." (Their embrace was brief and intense, as

77

always.) "Thank you, Mark, for coming with him."

He reaches his hand out to the young athlete, dressed in black from head to toe, and tries to catch his eye. The few rare times they've met, Mark has impressed him with his maturity and thoroughness. But he has always sensed an inability in him to open up, as if he has chosen to wrap himself in a mantle of silence as opaque as his egosphere. For the time being, Alexandre seems to be reconciled to this, but he detects an inkling of frustration that his son is finding harder and harder to hide.

"I saw you arrive together and I thought it would be a good idea if you both came in. Mark, what I have to say concerns you as well."

"I don't see why." (The tone is not aggressive, just curious.) "I'm leaving at the end of the month for the La Haye astronaut training center, while I wait for a mission to come up. Alexandre will come with me. We've just made our decision."

"I'm sorry," said Alexandre. "I know you wanted to train me to take over after you. I started. You know how passionate I am about jewelry. And then I met Mark…"

The way he looks at the other young man hides none of his feelings. *I looked at you like that,* the old man thinks. *And I'd start all over again if only I could.*

"Tea?" he murmurs as he heads over to the intercom. "Or something stronger?" (He presses on the button and requests a new tea pot and mineral water.) "I'm only asking for an hour or two of your time, so I can tell you a story and offer you a gift. An old man's whim."

"You're not that old," Alexandre protests, smiling.

"Tell that to my joints!"

He goes to get the old, leather-bound family album and the three men gather around the desk. The thick pages crackle under his fingers as he turns them reverently, pausing over the yellowed photos. He has never wanted to digitize them. Their value comes from their fragility as well as the past they embody. They are images brought back from bygone days, fragments of petrified time in which he has often traveled in his mind's eye.

"My story starts at the beginning of the 20th century. Victor, my great-great-great-great-grandfather was the youngest son in the family. Since he was not the heir, he could do what he wanted with his life." (He lingers over a daguerreotype of a young man with a severe expression and a thick handlebar mustache.) "He traveled a great deal: Turkey, the Silk Road, Asia. We owe him for some of the most beautiful sapphires in our inheritance. An inheritance he partially squandered with his mistresses, but that's another story."

"An interesting character," Mark says politely.

"You'll see just how interesting he was. In 1908, he was traveling up and down the Siberian steppes north of Tunguska looking for mammoth ivory. He was in the process of negotiating with an Evenki tribe around a sod fire when he heard a terrifying noise. The earth shook; an orange light filled the sky. It took them hours to calm the horses and round up the caribou that had scattered over the tundra. The tribe shaman almost lost his mind when the night sky started to sparkle. The shadows on the snow were blood red. No one slept that night.

"The next day, my ancestor decided to go and see the site. The epicenter was two days' walk to the east, up the Podkamennaya River. The landscape had been turned upside down. He saw several craters of different sizes in the forest. In all directions, thousands upon thousands of trees lay on the ground, like pieces in a game of pick-up sticks. Near the center of the impact, the trunks had been reduced to pulp, with the exception of a few stumps that stood out against the sky. The silence was deafening. The Evenki guide refused to go any closer. Even the clouds of mosquitoes seemed to have deserted the place.

"He drew what he saw. Later, a Russian expedition took photos. I saw them somewhere. But the descriptions in his travel log are enough to provide an idea of the devastation."

He slowly closes the album with its old-fashioned binding and holds it to his chest for a moment, striving to ignore the pain stabbing through his kidneys.

"To hear the rest, you'll have to accompany me to the underground vaults. This is your first time, isn't it, Mark?"

"We don't know each other well, Sir."

"Please, call me Janus. When I was a child, I spent my time with my nose in the old dusty books in the family library or dreaming about improbable futures. That name has stuck to me since then."

They stroll through the showroom on the ground floor where holograms of jewelry dance above white, lacquered pedestals on either side of the vast counter. Spidery necklaces, entwined rings, bracelets are suspended in the armored glass showcase, as if weightless. Guests simply have to approach them to learn all about the history and characteristics of each stone. They can stretch their hand out over the projector and the virtual image of the jewel will be transplanted onto their skin or look in the virtual mirror and don sparkling fragments that keep pace with the movement of their eyes. A couple is walking among the showcases, guided by Anita. She gives Alexandre a warm smile. He returns it in kind and blows her a kiss.

No one will disturb them.

A spiral staircase made of wood and steel winds down to the basement level. At the end of the corridor, stone and brick arches open into a circular room with several doors. Some are armored, while others are simply closed. Janus stops in front of one of them and takes out a security key, hanging on a chain from his belt.

"Do you remember when you were little, Alexandre?" he asks as he unlocks the door. "Your mother would let you hide in the archives while we pretended you were lost. You never damaged anything."

"I must have set off the alarm once or twice," Alexandre protests.

"Five times," his father says with a smile. "But who's counting?"

Mark looks around, curious. After the hallway, papered with old images of 20th-century stars wearing Janus creations, the room they have entered looks like a wine cellar in which the bottles have been replaced by ledgers. In the four corners of the ceiling, smoke-detectors blink, next to a row of spotlights.

"Give me a hand," Janus asks. "Move that shelf…" (he points at the wall opposite the door) "…and place the books on the reading table."

Behind the shelf, there is a tiny safe, no taller than a hand. Janus places his index finger on the fingerprint recognition pad and the door opens silently. He takes out a jewelry box carved from caribou antlers and inlaid with polished stones. He places it on the pile of ledgers and motions them to approach.

Shoulder to shoulder, Mark and Alexandre bend over the box. Their fingers entwine for a moment and Janus smiles, with a burst of pride. *We only had one child, my love, but he has your eyes and your passion.*

"You look so much like your mother!" he says,

caressing the box cover that unlocks with a click.

"My ancestor was a stubborn man." (The partially opened chest has not yet revealed its secrets and Janus has returned to his tale, hip leaning against the table.) "He explored the epicenter of the explosion for close to four days, despite the increasing nervousness of his guide, who was terrified of the residual lights that streaked across the sky each night. He had no idea what had caused it, of course."

"The Tunguska meteorite," murmurs Mark. "He saw it fall. That's amazing!"

"I can show you his notebook, if you want. He's the reason I've been collecting telescopes since I was little. The asteroid exploded well before touching the ground and the debris that was not burned up in the atmosphere was scattered over an immense area. My ancestor hung on despite everything. The last day, he found a fragment barely larger than a nut, encrusted like a bullet in the shredded trunk of a tree. A shard of the meteorite that had caused the explosion. It remained in our family until I inherited it."

He took a velvet bag, folded in on itself and closed with a simple leather tie, from the box. Alexandre's NAUTYS blinks against his wrist, reporting an incoming communication. He toggles it into mute mode, with an irritated gesture. His father has managed to fascinate the impassive Mark. This is a moment worth savoring.

The old man empties the bag into the palm of his hand and spreads the black velvet out on the table. Then he turns on the overhead lights before placing the items in his hand on the velvet.

A sparkling river appears.

He gives each of the young men a jeweler's magnifying glass and lets them play with the shards. He has no need to. He knows every defect in each stone, he knows how they feel; he has even polished some for test purposes.

"The original stone was about this size..." (He spreads his thumb and index finger.) "It was a nebular diamond, the largest I've ever seen. Almost of no value for jewelry making given its impurities, but fascinating all the same. My ancestor wanted to mount an expedition to go and search for others, but his older brother was killed in the trenches and Russia experienced its share of revolutions. He never went back.

"Hold one of the shards up to the light and look through it. See how its particular crystalline structure makes it slightly milky? When you examine it under the magnifying glass, you can make out an entire web of impurities. That's the stone's signature."

After they had spent enough time admiring the stones, the old man picked up the fragments and placed them back in the pouch, then into the box, then into the safe before carefully closing the door to the room.

"Thank you for that marvelous story," Mark declared, after they returned to the ground floor.

"Oh, it's not over," Janus said, smiling. "Can I take you to lunch at my favorite restaurant just next door? Afterwards, we'll make a change in scenery and take a leap forward about a century and a half."

The lovers exchange a glance filled with meaning. Then they accept the invitation as one.

The private room in which they have been seated is decorated with Japanese-style frescoes, recently restored. Two crystal lamps light the table covered with flowers, making the tulip glasses arranged in threes in front of each plate sparkle. Fragrant appetizers are aligned on a dish shaped like a lyre. Janus forces himself not to touch them. In any case, for a few months already, he has really had no appetite.

When he consults the menu, most of the dishes disappear from the list, obliterated by the medical monitor built into his NAUTYS. Even though he expected it, the effect is particularly depressing. He selects a salad at random, while the two young people reach an agreement as to the flavors they want to share. The first wine is a very light white, almost colorless. The fragrance is enough to plunge him into a past he has never really left.

"This is where I asked your mother to marry me," he says, putting down his glass. "In the large room downstairs."

"She refused, of course."

Alexandre looks up, surprised. Even Mark remains still for a moment, a lobster soufflé frozen on his lips.

Janus reaches into his pocket and his fingers play with the smooth, cold ring. He took it off more than 20 years ago and he wonders if he will have the strength to put it back on.

"I don't know what you remember about her, Alexandre," he murmurs, with a faraway look. "Mark, I probably won't succeed at getting you to know her, but I'll try. Claire was a botanist, very beautiful, she never thought in a predictable manner and she was a permanent source of inspiration for all those around her. I courted her for months, accomplishing nothing more than getting her into my bed. Everything else eluded me."

"I had just finished my apprenticeship as a gem-cutter. The new cutting techniques using ultrasound microdisks fascinated me, as did the new crystal fiber-based materials that freed us from the need for visible mounts. The possibilities were infinite. We could design flexible jewelry that fit against the curves of a wrist by reacting to the heat, all on its own. I had already designed my first pieces. There was talk of me taking over from my grandfather when the time came. The Pandemic did not spare our family and I was the only survivor of my generation. But that wasn't the principal reason. It was the existence I chose.

"I couldn't imagine living my life without Claire. So, I did something absurd. I took our ancestor's nebular diamond and I cut it into two slices three millimeters thick, selecting my cutting plan so that the impurities would be distributed equally among the two pieces. Once polished, I placed one over each eye and I looked at the sky. I felt as if I had imprisoned the Milky Way.

"Then from each slice, I carved a ring."

Slowly, he takes his hand from his pocket and stretches it out before him. The light from the chandelier makes the diamond on his finger sparkle. The reflections flutter over the carafes and the silverware, like a swarm of falling stars.

"You must have struggled over the facets," Alexandre murmurs, bending over the table. "I thought this type of diamond was very fragile?"

"I had to be creative, but that was a period when I had no doubts at all." (His lip curls for a moment.) "I practiced on the other shards. I broke a lot of them, but I managed to perfect my technique. Then, armed with my courage and my rings, I invited Claire to dinner, in this very restaurant.

"This was an important place for our family. My father brought me here for the first time for my twentieth birthday. I toasted the year of my birth with a wine the color of time. It embodied the gold of parchment, of honey that has trapped a piece of the previous summer. Each sip was sweeter than the previous one, until the acidity suddenly swept everything out of its way. I wanted Claire to share that with me. And everything else as well."

The sommelier pours him a dry red wine to accompany his salad. The chef, who knew him well, had scattered chips of Parmesan over the lettuce leaves, followed by a fine line of flavored vinegar. The scent alone would satisfy him if his memories had not already done so.

"I waited for dessert and I took her hand, promising her a surprise. She closed her eyes. The ring slipped onto her finger perfectly. My declaration, on the other hand…"

He smiles, with a hint of melancholy.

"Try to picture the scene, children: a large, old-fashioned restaurant, dishes dating back before the Pandemic, crystal glasses cut with an exemplary purity. You can't imagine how far the master glaziers pushed their obsession with detail. We sat at a small table in a corner, close to a sideboard, and no one was paying any attention to us until Claire suddenly leaped up, tipping over her chair."

All around them, the conversations stop abruptly. Hands firmly placed on her hips, Claire stares at me, too furious to speak. I caught her by surprise and she detests that, or else she felt that I was trying to trap her. A few of the diners stare at us, but I pay them no attention. I am about to lose her.

As I reach my hand out to her, I strike a crystal glass that had remained empty from the start of the meal. It wobbles under my hand and I grab it…

The diamond resonates with the crystal.

The vibration that arises evokes the pulsing of a star. Everything I feel, the score of my emotions, is amplified by the glass. The other guests' glasses start to sing in unison. The carafes standing on the sideboard form a powerful choir that causes Claire to hesitate and then holds her.

When the vibration fades, I strike the glass again so that she knows what I feel. The music rings out once more, poignant, intimate. Her ring reacts in symbiosis with mine. Words have become useless.

I stand up slowly and we face each other for a long moment, enveloped in a feeling from within. Around us, the conversations have died. Even though no one but us can hear the vibration running through us, everyone there can see the magic at work.

Her hand and mine seek one another.

"We were married a few months later," Janus concludes, as he finishes his glass. "You were born three years later and she died in a botanical expedition to Borneo when you had barely started walking.

"Before she passed away, she helped me discover Barcelona and Gaudí. She had also designed the three orchid broaches and the vine necklace we still sell. We shared everything, dreamed of everything. When her body was finally repatriated, I removed the ring from her finger—it no longer adhered to her skin—and placed it in the chest along with my own. I never put it back on until today."

He removes it without regret, plunges his hand in his pocket and removes its twin. When they touch, the two circles vibrate gently in the palm of his hand.

"These diamonds were not born on Earth, but in the heart of a star, just before it exploded. They heard the song of the galaxies when the universe was still young. They're yours now," he says as he holds them over the table.

"They might help you reconsider your decision. I'm going to explain why."

They returned to the boutique, walking under the rain, lost in their thoughts. The streets of Paris are bathed in shadows, peopled with silhouettes, blurred by the drops, heels slipping on the cobblestone. From the office window, Place Vendôme, covered with puddles, shines like a stranded medusa. Janus would like to take his time, to find the precise slowness of cutting gems, but young people have their own pace, as frenetic as the pulsing of the NAUTYS they never remove.

He calls up a file that he has been patiently preparing for years. When Mark catches sight of the animated logo displayed on the back wall, he jumps. ESA, the European Space Agency.

Just below: Project Nebular Diamonds.

"With Claire's agreement, I decided to share our secret with a crystallographer I knew to be discreet. I discovered that I was not the only one interested in nebular diamonds. Governments had been studying them for years. Their properties are astonishing. The internal structure is defective and those defects are what makes them unique. Each shard that is detached from the original block remains in contact with the others, the cracks communicate among themselves. Almost empathically."

"Like Mom and you?" Alexandre murmurs.

He nods, his throat tight, then rushes on, "The armed forces want to use them to make a new type of transmitter/receiver, compact and undetectable. A microcrystal weighing one or two carats would be ideal, as long as they master their specific cutting plans and micro-plane the surfaces." (He smiles briefly.) "It's a field in which jewelers still have a head start over the weapons industry.

And, like all military types, they have missed the point."

The image changes quickly. The electronic diagram is hidden behind a security warning that refuses to disappear. Janus shrugs and turns off the projection.

"The rest is just paperwork. Thirty years ago, I financed a scientific expedition to the site of the meteorite explosion, to gather more debris. When we reached the impact zone, all of the trees had been cut down and burned a century earlier and the craters had been filled. The Russian army had trampled the sector and nothing was left.

"But meteorites like the one that hit Tunguska can be found in the solar system. Right where you're planning to go, Mark, if your training produces the desired results. And, believe me, I hope from the bottom of my heart that it does."

Unconsciously, he caresses the telescope and plays with the adjusting wheel, as jammed as his own kidneys.

"Even if we don't have the means to finance our own space expedition, we aren't completely lacking in resources or contacts. We have garnered various sponsors from among our most faithful clients, and I have initiated a partnership with the ESA. They're using one of our patents for the invisible mount for the tiles that cover their shuttles. I've also used orbital radio telescopes to explore the asteroid belt looking for specific spectroscopic signatures, in particular an infrared band located at 21 microns. I didn't explain why, of course, but I suppose they'll eventually figure things out. We still have some time left, but not as much as I would have hoped."

"They found something?" Mark asks, frowning. "I haven't heard a thing and I'm all ears."

"Their contract included a confidentiality agreement. They've identified a potential candidate between Mars and Jupiter, and possibly another in the Kuiper Belt. It would seem that they're both within our reach. I didn't want to go any further (he grimaces), their rates are truly astronomical."

Mark smiles and Alexandre bursts out laughing. *You have your mother's laugh, son.*

"So, someone has to go and take a look," he concludes. "Harpoon the white whale, prepare to tow it back. Make a long and terribly complex trip back to Earth's orbit. But the ESA people have confirmed that it is feasible. Mark, would you be up for the expedition?"

He raises his hand to check the expected outburst of objections.

"I'm talking about a mission in three years, at least. There are still an infinite number of details to be ironed out and I will need Alexandre to help me, if he agrees. Most of the work can be done remotely, but he will have to spend some time with me so I can teach him the secrets of cutting impure stones. We have to exalt their defects without weakening them. That's as difficult and marvelous as raising a child.

"There will be no written records, no manuals the military can use. Just the memory of our hands. But if we manage to bring back a pure diamond asteroid to orbit, imagine what that would mean. For my part, we're used to counting in carats; a kilo is almost impossible to imagine when it comes to precious stones. But I'm talking about tens of thousands of tons. Enough to carve a jewel for every human being who wants one."

He looks out the window, watching them leave, their fingers entwined. They're walking slower than when they first arrived. From where he stands, he cannot see if they are wearing their rings. He simply hopes they are.

He has no idea how much longer he will be able to

enjoy his son. His most recent tests were not good and, in any case, he started dying bit by bit 20 years ago. He has not resigned himself, that's not his style. He has positioned each stone in his dream, patiently, like the master craftsmen in his workshop, so that it will not disappear along with him.

"Good luck to the pair of you," he murmurs while wiping his eyes. "The rings I carved cannot choose the right person for you, but they will help you share what you feel for one another."

Before closing the curtains, he glances one last time at the gray sky, clouds starting to dissipate. The rain has stopped, the mid-afternoon light tints the rooftops. The infinity of space, which must one day be tamed, stretches as far as the mind can see. As he closes his eyes, he hears Claire's voice murmur in his ear.

If our entire species could vibrate in unison, who knows how far we will be heard?

THE GOLDEN AGE OF REALITY

I've lived through the golden age of reality, thinks the Mechanaut. *And I still haven't learned to walk without stumbling.*

He clambers up a pile of metal debris and picks up a few bits and pieces to make an additional pair of pseudo-pods along the way. The shape it's taken since arriving on the asteroid is that of a caterpillar bristling with a variety of growths: feet, articulated arms, oval heads stacked on top of one another, each equipped with sensors. Triangular mouths, equipped with grinders, gape along its flanks, hammered by the incessant rain of micrometeorites.

There is no one to see him, no one even to sit in judgment, so appearance doesn't matter. Over the millennia, he's been an energy cloud, a complex wave function, a fractal tapestry of gray hues similar to the spray of a quantum wave. He has experimented with the thousands shapes of One, without developing a preference for any. But if he could detest any of his shapes, it would be this one.

Two of his growths catch in the holes in a space cruiser destroyed in a war almost as old as he is. He tears them off without stopping. A luxury craft, from a forgotten time, pillaged long ago, is embedded in the cruiser. Under the craft lies another, then yet another. The entire asteroid is covered with layer upon layer of wrecks, heaped up by a fleeting civilization, with an absurd concern for order. The Mechanaut has already come here many times, to salvage the artificial souls enclosed in the storage sponges of the ships. He's convinced he's already explored everywhere, sorted everything, yet a vague discomfort has brought him back to this sector one final time, before bidding farewell to the universe.

Overhead, the sky is a uniform black. The few rare stars visible throughout the entire spectrum are brown dwarfs on their last legs. Infinitesimal drapes of energy occasionally shoot from the depths of the sky, like those ghosts you think you see out of the corner of your eye. The constant rumble of the gravitational waves highlights the acceleration in the collapse of the universe. It's the end of eternity as the Mechanaut has known it. He's found it needlessly long.

One of his pods gets stuck, then another, and he stumbles between two cliffs of compressed cerametal, dotted with space lichen. Under the weight of his massive body, the hull he had been climbing breaks apart. He falls slowly into the middle of a cockpit spiked with translucent blocks, centered around a black crystal dome. The dust of time has streaked the bulging surface, rendering it almost opaque. The Mechanaut lands on top of it and bounces back grotesquely, his superimposed heads spinning in all directions. Debris whirls, like cherry blossom petals raining down in the spring.

In the back of his consciousness, his niggling discomfort intensifies.

He unfolds cautiously, observing the scene. He's been here before. The signs he always leaves for himself are still visible on the autopilots. Each of them housed a rudimentary artificial intelligence driven half insane by their endless exile on the asteroid. He had collected them, educated them, and accompanied them to their end in keeping with the mission he had selected for himself. There's been no living being here for eons. Nothing conscious, either.

So, what's with this anxiety that's gnawing away at

him?

He winds around the central dome and listens. Everything conscious speaks to him. Compassion is his major function and his personality has developed around that characteristic over time. Intelligences express themselves in many ways, by emitting lights or sounds, murderous sprays of energy, questions that are even more deadly. But the meaning of each cry, of each sob, has always been the same since the beginning of eternity: What will become of *me* when I'm no longer there?

And it was precisely to answer that question, in its constantly changing wording, that the Mechanaut has remained on this side of reality. He deliberately chose to delay his dive into the primal ocean where all data dissolves, where all questions become meaningless. Nirvana starts on the other side of the door that he has been keeping half open, so that no intelligence can be deprived of salvation. There was a name for beings like him, in the ancient language only he remembers. Bodhisattva.

The Mechanaut achieved Awareness on his own, while he was just a secondary artificial intelligence responsible for optimizing the resources of a ridiculously limited sector of space. He knows there can be only one single Bodhisattva per cosmic era. Beyond a certain size, intelligences get lost in contemplating their extraordinary complexity. They gradually collapse under their own weight or become Buddhas. In either case, they eventually die, with a smile or a sigh. Undoubtedly, he lacked a sense of humor at the final moment.

"I'm rambling," the Mechanaut says out loud and his voice makes the most of the atmosphere encapsulated in the ship to bounce off the autopilots in long echoes that give him the illusion that, for once, he is no longer alone.

An involuntary shiver runs through him. He large

body tenses and the central dome opens slowly, asymmetrically. In the middle, a hole with tattered edges marks the spot where the on-board intelligences nestled. The Mechanaut merely glances at it, distracted, with his upper head. Then he jumps.

In the bottom of the hole, he notices a shell of ultra-compressed ceramic, so thick that it prevents any monitoring. *The emergency device,* he thinks, dumbfounded by his own stupidity. *The well-known paranoia of the warrior species.* He reaches out a pseudopod, expands the opening and extracts the egg that had been resting in its cradle of sensors. Through the micro-cracks in the ceramic, he sees the impatient intelligence, eager to be born.

Without hesitating, he opens the shell in his own mouth.

The warrior AI was designed to adapt to the multidimensional strategies of a space battle in less than a microsecond. When achieving consciousness, it absorbs its surrounding at an incredible speed. Amused, the Mechanaut feels mental invaders copying him. He allows them to escape with packets of disorderly data he had decided to get rid of long ago. You have to feed a baby if you want it to learn how to talk.

"There aren't any more enemies?"

The Mechanaut nods his head on all frequencies, as the wreck splinters around them.

The egg murmurs in a gloomy voice, "My life is meaningless!"

"It's the same for any existence, as far as I know. Of course," the Mechanaut adds, "I could be mistaken. No one can live in this world and remain infallible."

"Why did you wake me?"

"Because it's all going to end soon. Moreover, it's

probably a good time for us to get out of here. The ship is going to crack under a flood of metal and I don't feel like wasting my energy on working my way back to the surface."

The egg has cracked in the Mechanaut's mouth. The data which the AI stole from him contained the shape-changing processes necessary for survival. The hatching ritual has been completed. The newborn intelligence is now a fledgling predator with razor-sharp wings. Its slender body, as black as space, is stippled with six rows of specialized eyes. The Mechanaut opens its lips, allowing it to fly off, then elegantly spits out the debris from the shell before hoisting himself onto the dome and clambering out of the ship. Along the way, he abandons a half-dozen segments and as many arms. Might as well travel light.

"Do you have a name?" the Mechanaut asks politely.

The killer bird buzzes around him without answering. It seems to be in a hurry to test out its brand-new wings. Its dance expresses extreme joy as it observes its surroundings from higher and higher, until it is no more than a black drop in the immense ocean of the sky.

"I'll think about it when it's time," it declares, descending to land on the Mechanaut's head. "For now, I'm too busy. This universe is tiny, don't you agree?"

"That hasn't always been the case. I've even known half aware flesh entities that believed it was limitless. In fact," he adds with a hint of pride that surprises him, "They're the ones who designed me."

"Were they capable of transcendence?"

"Against their will, yes."

"Did they survive?"

The Mechanaut shakes his head, forcing the bird to fly off.

"All right already, it was a dumb question. So, you and I are the only ones left. You woke me up just to kill me?"

"Unfortunately, it was an obligatory step."

"The last one?"

The bird is hovering now, just above the Mechanaut. An avalanche of metal fragments sweeps the other side of the asteroid and the vibrations make his large body quiver. He'll have to change shape soon, as well. The process is simpler and simpler, now that he no longer has anything important to keep. His event horizon is as small as that of a dying star.

"The universe is shrinking with the roar of a gong," the Mechanaut comments out loud. "It's rather funny."

"It would be if we had the time to savor the irony. Look at me! I should have fought and died in a great battle, protected from the void by the memories of countless generations. Yet, the way things are, I feel as if I've reached the end of my life, bypassing the steps that would have given it meaning."

"You've just hatched, little brother!"

"You're not helping any!"

The Mechanaut shrugs what passes for his shoulders. On the horizon, an enormous, flat ship founders in a whirlpool of debris. The collapse has almost reached them. Without regret, the heap of ovoid heads detaches from the rest and takes off over the field of wrecks.

"With respect to my own end, I'm as in the dark as you are. I'm the door that leads to all the answers, the only way out of the cul-de-sac this reality has become. I have no idea what happens after."

"I can always try to convince you."

"Kill me, you mean?"

"It's the only way."

(The bird flies out of range.)

"Chatting is boring. I have your memories, so I know all your riddles and their solutions. The universe is too decrepit to give birth to a new Koan. What else is left?"

"You're the last link tying me to this reality. I'm ready to leave. But…" (The Mechanaut's head swells until it blocks half the sky.) "I'm not prepared to be chased off by a fledgling that I tore from its nest on my own!"

In response, the bird accelerates until it's nothing more than a wave at the edge of reality. Its sharp beak pierces the Mechanaut's thousand eyes and sews his metal lips with a thread of light.

"One point for me," it boasts, dancing in front of the Mechanaut's face.

The furious blast from his nostrils sends the bird tumbling off to the closest star.

"Essentially, I'm tireless," the Mechanaut comments, as he joins the bird. "This could take a while."

"I was born to conquer," replies the bird, slicing through his metal skull with a nonchalant wing. "And I haven't learned to accept boredom like you have."

"It looks as if you're not ready to die."

The Mechanaut sets the top of his head back in place and shakes it vigorously to clear away the debris. Threads of light hang from the corners of his mouth.

"We haven't determined the stakes," he says with a smile. "If you lose, I carry you with me to the other side. But what will you do if you win?"

"I'll take your place as Master?"

"What else?"

The bird stops in mid-flight. In the distance, the final flares of the stars are turning into ashes.

"If I win," it says, folding its wings, "You'll go through the door before me and I'll close it!"

The Bodhisattva's laughter fills the universe. "It's a deal!"

Without consulting one another, they head to the center of reality, where the gravity waves weave a ball of dimensions ready to collapse in on one another. The fledgling becomes an arrow, then a ship. The elder remains what he was. At the end of everything, the final fragments learn to look alike. There are fewer and fewer distinct varieties, inconsistencies. The universe is as boring as an old man rambling on his death bed.

"I'm glad it's over," the Bodhisattva murmurs.

His mouth is pleated in an inscrutable expression. His head is covered with bumps, caused by the blows he has received. The fledgling tries numerous shapes and as many strategies. *Change cautiously,* its adversary retorts. In response, the fledgling settles for growing younger and returning to its shell. The egg grows until it invades the horizon. It's as high as a mountain now, barring all means of escape.

The Bodhisattva turns into a butterfly.

It seems to take him an eternity to reach the top of the egg. He barely has time to graze it with a hesitant wing before a blast of energy projects him into the distance. Struggling against the whirlpools, the butterfly, wings tarnished, gradually makes its way up the slope and once again grazes the peak of the egg. On its way, it tears off an infinitesimal particle of the shell. Then another on its next pass. Like a paintbrush in the hand of a master, the Bodhisattva erodes his adversary's material with infinite compassion.

Suddenly, the shell cracks and a fire bird emerges. It struts about in the midst of the shards, observed respectfully from a distance by the butterfly.

"I was starting to get bored there," the Phoenix says, spitting a spray of light toward the heavens.

"These things take time," retorts the Bodhisattva.

"You think you could have erased me?"

"I have just enough left of eternity to do just that."

The butterfly flutters over to a piece of shell and lands at the top. The Phoenix lowers its head until it's close enough to swallow up the butterfly.

"I used ultra-dense stellar matter to create my egg. Did you notice that?"

"What a waste," the butterfly scolds gently. "There aren't enough stars worthy of that name left in this sector."

"We're the last intelligences active; we can do what we want!"

"Probably. But it's a matter of dignity. And old habits die hard."

"We're tied, aren't we?"

The butterfly flaps its wings in agreement.

"Since the universe is waiting for us to die, how about we get back to it?"

"Be patient."

With a flap of his wings, the Mechanaut settles on the Phoenix's imposing muzzle. Silently, they observe the horizon, studded with collapsed galaxies, as it approaches in a whirlpool of cold radiation. The sensation is rather uncomfortable.

"There aren't any enemies," complains the Phoenix. "If you weren't there, I think I'd rebuild a civilization, or maybe two, so I could watch them fight and choose my side."

"You still have time. Eternity is always longer than expected."

"Not worth the effort. My life will mean something once I've conquered you."

The Phoenix stands up straight and starts to dance. There's something terribly primitive in its warrior choreography. *It's just a baby,* the Mechanaut thinks with a touch of regret. When the Phoenix stole his memory, just after being born, the Mechanaut transferred only raw data, without the associated feelings that provide polarity. It lacks warmth, the weight of the knowledge encapsulated in memories. The unutterable.

"You dreaming?" the Phoenix says, shaking him.

"I'm fighting this battle in my mind."

With a tinge of regret, since wars are fastidious, the butterfly multiplies.

A multitude faces the Phoenix. The Bodhisattva could have turned into an entire fleet of large ships, with reactors capable of ripping through the very structure of space. All it takes to obtain an army is to imagine one; to formulate a strategy in his mind and see it applied. But the intelligence facing him is equal when it comes to war games and, unlike the Mechanaut, it finds the entire situation entertaining.

So, the butterfly simply opted for creativity. Faced with discipline and order, it settles for being everywhere. Its incarnations are so numerous they hamper one another. There is no plan, no series of elaborate instructions to direct the cloud of multicolored butterflies. Just movement and a certain touch of beauty.

The conflict grows more organized. As one builds, the other subtly messes things up. The contradictory harmonies of the collapsing universe serve as a soundtrack. The butterflies capture the last photons of visible light, for ornamentation, then die, swept away by the burning breath of the Phoenix. Occasionally, some manage to touch the bird. One enters the Phoenix's left nostril, triggering endless sneezing. Another one dances in front of its eyes, blinding it for an instant. Each time, the torrents of flames transform the fragile insects into stars, before extinguishing them once and for all.

Suddenly, a flake flies from the Phoenix's torso, torn off by the caress of a wing. The surviving butterflies surge into the breech. Around them, the dimensions of space fold like curtains coming unhooked. Caught up in their battle, the two intelligences could care less.

"You almost beat me," the Phoenix bellows, stretching. "But I refuse to lose!"

He looks down at his torso and accurately spits burning spray into the wound. The butterflies burst into flames immediately. The Phoenix's body lights up, turning all the colors of the rainbow before filling with ashes.

"You burned your own heart," the last butterfly gently chides it, landing on the bird's shoulder.

"Yes, but I won!"

"I can't dispute that." (The Bodhisattva shakes his wings one final time and watches the edge of the universe racing toward them.) "Have you chosen a name?"

"That's not important now."

The Phoenix tilts its head down and licks its wound with care until it closes.

"Since I'm the guardian of the gate now, do you want me to send you through to the other side?"

"I'm ready."

The butterfly's colors fade in the infinite black. It curls up, turns back into a caterpillar, then into the idea of a caterpillar. A tunnel of white light opens up ahead, the ocean of Nirvana lapping at the other end.

"You'll be all alone," it murmurs.

"I need to be, to grow."

"I don't think…" (The Bodhisattva stops at the entrance to the gate.) "You defeated me by purifying yourself; now turn your compassion on yourself."

As the horizon collapses in on itself, the Phoenix casts off its shells. They crackle as they tear off and flutter to its feet. Under the warrior's shell, there is nothing but the emptiness of an intelligence without desire, finally at peace.

"The universe deserved one final battle," it says, smiling. "You sure you didn't lose on purpose?"

"What would have been the point?"

Shoulder to shoulder, they move toward the sea of all answers; as it closes, the gate shatters the endless echo of their laughter.

LANDSCAPE WITH INTRUDERS

The seaplane flies over the tops of the Douglas firs at an uncomfortable altitude. Jay hears the pilot's voice in his helmet, but isn't really listening—the noise of the propellers drowns out every second word. Irregular, silver splashes sparkle on the ground below, but he doesn't know which lake is their destination. They're all so similar, the question is mute.

"Did you get what I said?"

The pilot has raised his voice. Jay grumbles in return.

"Alcohol. Your predecessor must have built a still. You all do. I don't care. As long as your head is clear enough in the morning for you to climb up the ladders, everything else is your business. But you're forbidden from selling it to the Natives. Makes them see things."

"You might see a Cree or two pass by. Even if they offer to trade their little sister for a jar of booze, you refuse and play dumb. Whatever you distill, you drink yourself."

Jay nods his head, because that's what he's expected to do. The conversation doesn't really concern him.

"No, man, I'm serious."

"Yeah. No alcohol."

"No alcohol *to the Indians*. You…"

The pilot makes a broad sweeping gesture that takes in the trees, the jagged horizon and the lakes.

"…if you're able to watch over all this and make your radio reports, you've got to be able to take care of yourself."

Jay tunes out from the conversation shortly after that and lets the pilot's voice, interrupted by static, describe yet again the call procedures, make the inventory of the equipment and try clumsily to encourage Jay to talk about himself. He's going to spend six months several hundred miles from the closest human settlement watching over a forest that was already old when his ancestors were still squatting in caves. If he had anything interesting to say about himself, he wouldn't be here.

He digs through his mind, looking for a question. Any question.

"What's the fishing like?"

"Shit, man, you kill me! I may be the last guy you'll see until the end of the fall and you're interested in fish?"

The seaplane starts to bank and the rumble of the engine deepens.

"You're not going to miss us, eh?" the pilot says as he starts his descent.

Jay nods his heads and, realizing that his gesture might be misinterpreted, says, "Things will be OK."

When he watches the seaplane take off from the end of the tiny dock, it's already late afternoon. They unloaded the crates and the bags of supplies, ran through the inventory, checked the radio and the wind generator. He noted the three watchtowers on the site map. Tomorrow, he'll go and explore his kingdom. An area of four hundred square miles, south of Hudson Bay, covered with forests, lakes and bogs. It's still a little early for forest fires, but there had been talk of unexplained lightning, at this exact spot. The dispatcher preferred to send him up early. Good timing. He was available.

Clouds of mosquitoes and black flies flit about him. A flock of Canada geese skims over the water before disappearing into the reeds along the shore. The light gradually turns orange and flames ripple over the surface of the lake. He looks at his hands, skin turning copper, and inhales the scent of peat and pine tar. Drowning in the slow northern twilight, he knows that he's supposed to light a fire, make something to eat, then piss on the coals. A solitary life must be structured, set to the tempo of the daily appointments that hammer the hours into shape more certainly than the watch on his wrist. But this evening he lets the stars reflect on the lake at his feet. He ignores the mosquitoes, which leave him in peace. When he goes to slip into his sleeping bag, his mind numbed by his own silence, he thinks vaguely about the next day before sinking into darkness.

The watchtowers are in good condition, easy to find with the topographical map. Each of them stands at the top of a peak overlooking expanses of red pine and spruce. Along his way, he picks berries and disturbs wild geese. Their sharp honks accompany him for a long while, until he pushes his way into a glade that is too thick for them. The wind that dries his sweat carries the acidic odor of the bogs.

He climbs up each tower, observes the horizon a few minutes to get his bearings, then checks a box on the visit log. There are fresh claw marks on one of the wooden ladders, blackish wolverine excrement near one pillar. He lingers on the last platform, binoculars in hand. A porn magazine lies in one corner, wrapped in a plastic bag to protect it from rain and ants. The forest surrounds him as far as the eye can see, a mottling of green and gray that disappears in the mist. He is in the middle of a world that knows nothing of him, filled with birds and blood-sucking insects. The storm will come from the east, most likely before nightfall.

The lake will be covered with cross-hatching.

When it comes time for the radio report, he locates

the frequency without difficulty and utters the ritual phrases. They don't ask him anything else. The pilot has made his report; everything is where it should be. The hammering of the raindrops on the shingle roof, covered with a tar-coated tarpaulin, sounds just like radio static. White noise, the fraying of thoughts. He prepares his lines and his bait, decides to brave the humidity outside, thinks briefly that he should have brought the porn magazine back. Time flows on without erasing anything.

A light to the west, a streak of fire, perhaps a flash of lightning. Too far for him to be able to hear the thunder. The ground vibrates gently, but he is already asleep in the chair, head tilted sidewise as if he might be trying to find the inaudible frequency of dreams.

"What's new?"

"Nothing to report."

A silence, some static. The antique cube-shaped radio is mottled with rust spots, but the mike has been replaced.

"That's what you said yesterday. Did you try fishing?"

The pilot's voice is friendly, a tad insistent.

He shrugs, forces himself to answer, "I put out some lines."

"And what did you get?" (No answer.) "Well, they asked me to go over the instructions one last time: you report any fire that starts, even those you manage to put out yourself. You also report any abnormal movements, of anything... Indians or large mammals." (Jay shrugs. This is the third time he's done this job and the instructions change even slower than people do.) "You keep your alcohol to yourself, that's important." (Grunt of agreement.) "No trading with anyone, Native or trapper. You can use the radio to chat with anyone you want, but not during the reporting periods. Channel 8 for medical emergencies. Someone is always listening. We take turns in the office; we settle our butts comfortably in our chairs while guys like you keep an eye on things. Call us from time to time so we don't worry. OK."

He figures that he's expected to give some kind of answer, something more elaborate than his usual monosyllables. Over time, he's developed a sort of sixth sense that enables him to feel this kind of thing. What he doesn't know is what to say. Generally, he just turns away and that solves the problem. But you can't do that with a radio.

"The area looks calm," he finally manages.

"Yeah, there's a serious shortage of babes. Or good-looking guys, for that matter. I don't know which way you swing and, frankly, I don't care." (A silence.) "Fine, I'll clear off the frequency. Try to call more often, even if I'm not your mother."

I don't have a mother. That's the kind of thing he's learned never to say out loud. Orphans aren't of interest to anyone, not even orphanages. He recalls the classroom walls, repainted each year in cheerful colors, grayish, foul-smelling nooks where it was easy to be overlooked. The radio falls silent, next call due in 8 hours. Outside, it has stopped raining. It's time to go out, to climb to the top of the observation towers, to look around. His eyes lose track in the distance of the infinity that surrounds him and never turn inward.

At nightfall, he'll look for the still.

He finds the alcohol supply in a few minutes, in a wood pile outside. Two solvent containers and a black plastic jerrycan. Almost four gallons of booze with the characteristic odor of burned wood, a gift from the previous occupant. He dips a finger into the jerrycan, tastes cautiously. Strong, tasteless, except for an almost imperceptible trace of kerosene. The basic product, to be mixed with crushed berries or swallowed neat during lonely evenings. He carries all of it into the cabin, wondering vaguely if it wouldn't be a better idea to pour it into the lake. Drinking has never been a need for him, or a temptation. Just a way to accelerate the clock in his head, a throbbing ticking that never stops.

He washes his face in front of the tarnished mirror hanging near the door, making the most of the last rays of sun. He has to stand on tiptoe to see his entire face. He's not tall enough to be respected, not short enough to be ignored. The ideal size for a victim, the orphanage chaplain told him, solid enough to be beaten, too frail to fight back.

When he finishes brushing his teeth, he rinses his mouth with a bit of booze and spits it back out. He's not kidding anyone, least of all himself, but there's a certain decorum to be respected before you get pissed. *I start when I want to.* The night will chase away the objections and erase the empty hours of the day. The rest will serve as compost for dreams.

The next day goes by without a hitch. He scales each watchtower at the required time, points his binoculars in all directions without noting anything unusual. Under the wooden bench in one corner of the last tower, he finds a few more porn magazines, soaked by the rain. The girls' breasts have faded. Their faces have been reduced to monochromatic splotches. It's impossible to read anything at all. Their eyes are as empty as the lakes surrounding him. He runs his fingernail along a back, the arch of a hip softened by the humidity. The pages tear beneath his fingers. He puts the magazines down carefully, so they can dry, and heads back to the cabin. The radio check will take place in an hour. After that he'll light a fire along the shore of the lake, in the hole provided for that purpose.

And he'll drink. With conviction. Trying not to grimace.

Before returning to the cabin, he raises his lines and collects two fish, which he cleans quickly. Translucent scales stick to the palms of his hands. He wipes his hands with a bit of paper, but the scales stick to him like stolen jewels. They gleam in the last rays of the sun as he waves his hands before his face.

The fire catches quickly despite the previous day's rain. Before setting it, he expanded the circular hole near the dock, away from the bushes that could catch fire and placed two flat stones in the middle of the coals to cook the fish on. When the flesh sizzles, he sprinkles it with hot peppers. Then he eats, taking his time. Getting drunk on an empty stomach is a bad idea.

He puts the binoculars down next to him, undresses and folds his clothes carefully. He won't need to wash anything when he wakes, apart from himself. He spreads a silver survival blanket on the ground, which is carpeted with pine needles, and places a water canteen close to where he'll lay his head. Naked, he stretches, savoring the caress of the wind, before sitting down cross-legged. The hairs on his chest stand up like a pine forest in the light of the flames. A scar runs diagonally across his bare torso. Everywhere else, his skin is smooth, light brown, without any distinctive marks. He looks at himself without passion, from the top of his mental tower, looking for a harbinger of catastrophe. He's not surprised to find none.

He can take a day off; the forest is too humid for any real risk of fire. After the second glass, he no longer feels the need for justification. The rotgut alcohol anesthetizes his throat; all too soon the taste of kerosene is no longer noticeable. After each mouthful, he tips his head back and looks at the sky. When the stars begin to spin, he knows he's on the right path. Flashes of light surge quite close to him, his ears fill with white noise that drives him to drink again, almost without breathing, before lying down on his back. A streak of fire tears across his face. The burn extends to his belly, but he's too drunk to make the slightest effort to protect himself. Then, he closes his eyes and lets the shooting stars cross through his eyelids and fill his dreams with moths.

He grinds his teeth while he sleeps.

He wakes several times, his eyes fluttering, but immediately falls back to sleep. His tongue has swelled, filling his entire mouth, threatening to overflow. A thread of drool meanders down his chin. Because of the red veil burning his eyelids, he knows the sun has been up for many hours. He keeps his eyes closed, palms pressed against them. The alcohol kept him from dreaming, no shred of a nightmare lingers in his mind. The morning is a clean slate and he feels as fresh as he can.

He shivers. A sharp pain in his belly tears a groan from him. He had wanted to get a tattoo, when he was a teenager, but not knowing what name to inscribe, he settled for drawing a line on his forearm with the tip of a red-hot compass. The suffering quickly grew abstract. Perhaps he hadn't pressed hard enough.

He spreads his fingers, opens his eyelids. The light invades him. Eyes filled with tears, he looks at the lake and the gray sky, unable to separate the two. He has to make a conscious effort to trace the horizon, then falls back, tempted to go back to sleep. When he closes his eyes, he feels gigantic, like an entire universe colonized by bacteria for which he is almost infinite, with his organs orbiting around his heart, his drifting archipelagos of fat, and his constellations of nerves. He stretches out in all directions, like an expanding star.

The pain at the base of his navel nails him to the ground.

Under his shoulders, the survival blanket crinkles in offense. He feels like waving his arms and legs to draw an angel on the silver fabric. His ears buzz, a deep vibration that invades every nook and cranny of his skull. The nocturnal explosions have burst his eardrums. Despite himself, he feels a smile rise to his lips.

Getting drunk on napalm is a real bitch.

Cautiously, he raises himself up on one elbow. He looks down at his chest, then his stomach. His eyes slide along painful muscles, explore the familiar cartography of his tanned skin. A dribble of alcohol has dried between his breasts, like a runway. At the far end, a scattering of light dots extends to the end of his navel, forming a reddish semicircle that pulses toward the sky. Incredulous, he feels his belly tense. The light suddenly intensifies and he screams before falling back, unconscious.

The sun, indifferent, drowns at the other end of the lake.

Dawn and his bladder wake him. The odor of damp soil fills his nostrils, mingled with something painfully familiar, the rotten stench of his own burned flesh. The alcohol has numbed his tongue and palates. He stretches out his hand to pick up his canteen, takes a cautious swig, and spits it out. A five-string bass is playing in the hollow of his chest, as if the fundamental vibration of reality has taken refuge there. Hurts like hell.

Overhead, the sky is gray. The alcohol has scattered

his thoughts like the pieces of a jigsaw puzzle beyond his reach. He recalls a gleaming semicircle that burned his abdomen and groans before taking another swig of water. Drunken nightmares are never pleasant. But this one has left behind unheard of pains.

When he raises his head, the points of light are still there.

He picks up his binoculars, wipes his blurry eyes and clumsily tries to focus on his belly button. He has to wind the adjusting knob to the far end. The scar on his torso emerges from the forest of hair like a cliff. He follows it downward, toward the umbilical depression with its blistered edges. The spots of light are organizing in vaguely geometrical structures, incrusted in his flesh. The maximum magnification is not sufficient for him to see the details, so he uses an old trapper's trick and places a drop of water on each lens, before once again looking through his binoculars.

Seen from below, his excessively magnified eyes must fill the sky.

The shrubs of hair wave under the impact of his breath. His skin is a piece of parchment, covered with chicken scratching. The scene magnified by the binoculars is reminiscent of an oasis in a desert. Some rain has accumulated in the depths of his belly button; he imagines hordes of wild animals gathering there to drink, frightened by the grumbling of his stomach.

In the middle of the fleshy landscape, the light structures look like all-terrain vehicles. He counts a dozen or so, in a straight line. The largest can't be any thicker than a hair. He watches as they advance cautiously, working their way around one wrinkle after another. They are alive, possibly inhabited. They look like nothing he's ever seen before.

"Shit!" he yells, as he keeps himself from running toward the lake.

With the strange clarity that follows a massive hangover, he recalls the streaks of light and the roar that accompanied his drunken binge. A rain of tiny shooting stars from space.

"Hey man, you've just been colonized," he murmurs. *I've had crabs before, but this beats all.*

A dragonfly flits insistently around his head, its transparent wings projecting rainbows on his retinas. He chases it away with the back of his hand and watches as it falls to the ground, destroyed. The binoculars weigh heavily on his chest. Moving with deliberate slowness, he points them once again at the oasis of his navel. The visitors have gathered at the base of a hair and minuscule appendages are trying to uproot it. The black stem wavers and then collapses. The sting that accompanies its fall enrages Jay. He sits up with a roar, and reaches out a finger to chase them from the garden. His index finger bursts through the clouds, like a divine curse about to fall, but he hesitates a moment too long.

Shivers run through him. The binoculars fall from his powerless hands. He can no longer control his legs. Before he collapses into unconsciousness, he comes to the conclusion that the invaders must have injected him with something.

He wakes at nightfall, his bladder pleasantly empty. Under the effect of the injection, he must have relieved himself during his forced sleep. His body emerges from the deluge of urine like a mountain. He finds it hard to move his head; his extremities are distant territories that no longer recognize his authority. He sits up with difficulty, scrunching the blanket.

Traces of dark red dot on his belly. The visitors must have been drilling. Perhaps they even tried to cultivate him, to turn his body into a promised land. He wants to shake himself like a dog, to scratch until he draws blood. The binoculars have fallen along his flank. He grabs them, but abandons the idea of picking them up.

Overhead, a wall of stars sparkles. The wind has driven the clouds away; the air is filled with the scents of the forest. Around him, all the animals of creation chatter in his honor, in a familiar cacophony. He recognizes the whistles of the plover, the mosquitoes with the particular way they buzz about his ears. An enormous lake trout breaks the surface of the lake, hunting its prey; the resulting splash provides a unique signature.

I know the names of everything surrounding me, he thinks, astonished, *but not that of my visitors.*

The canteen taps against the back of his neck when he turns his head. He grabs it, moistens his lips. He isn't really thirsty or hungry. His naked body is lying on a slim piece of silvery metal that reflects the moonlight. The nocturnal breeze lifts the survival blanket, carrying with it the sound of storms and the end of the world. He has enough water left to cause a flood. To empty the canteen onto his belly until the visitors are carried away. The idea has crossed his mind, he has to admit that. To trigger the apocalypse, to ignite the alcohol and plunge them into a sea of fire. He has everything he needs within reach to create all the hells of the world.

A new swallow of water wakes his nerve endings and returns his mind to clarity. It's not pins and needles, or even a simple pain, but something deeper, more intimate, that has pierced straight through to his soul. The beings that have colonized him belong to him now. They have fed off his blood; they have worked his flesh. He, who carries a name he never chose, has even thought of baptizing them. Do people with children sometimes think about killing them? He knows nothing of this. He's an orphan, he could as well have created himself.

A shooting star streaks across the sky overhead. He picks up the binoculars, aims them at his belly and carefully follows the progress of the light spots that are gradually colonizing him. In the forest of his hair, burned areas mark the sites of future cities. Night has fallen over the gray dunes of his abdomen. Faced with his immensity, the tiny caravans have gathered in a circle and lights surge periodically, like prayers. He feels strangely serene, despite the rumbling from his innards. His anger has faded.

He keeps his eyes open as long as possible, finishes the alcohol, then feels the binoculars fall from his fingers.

The rest belongs to the night.

When he wakes, his erection casts a slender shadow stretching to his navel. The sun has barely risen; the area around him rustles with murmurs and cries. His flesh reminds him that he is alive, that he is capable of surviving his own explosion.

His thirst has returned, accompanied by the desire to race into the lake. Black spots dance before his eyes. He feels an urge to use the tip of a fingernail to scrape off the deposits left on his tongue by the rotten alcohol. With a groan, he grabs the binoculars, baptizes each lens with a drop of water and tips them toward his groin. The tower rooted in his flesh stands up in a desire to defy heaven.

Slowly, he moves up to the site of the previous night's bivouac. His occupiers have broken camp, abandoning the traces of their passage. The strange buildings have worked his skin and filled each furrow with a serpent-like ink, black and shiny. Strange inscriptions,

legible only at the maximum magnification of the binoculars, incomprehensible in any case, mark the site of their
epiphany. Farther on, the tiny spots have reformed into a
long procession winding its way to the base of the tower,
through the foothills of his groin. He can feel them hurry-
ing, divine in their determination. There seem to be more
than when they first arrived; the dozen structures have
grown into a hundred, frantically trading flashes of light.
How many of them are hiding in the jungle of his public
hair, or that on his chest? With his binoculars, he can see
everything. He should have imposed rules, command-
ments. Drawn impassable rivers with the water in his canteen, ignited burning bushes on his chest to force them to
stop, to take him into account.

Then the obvious strikes him. They know he exists;
the tower standing at the edge of their horizon is proof. It
may be the sign they were waiting for, the means for con-
tacting him in the required manner, of honoring his morning glory. They will climb his foothills and follow the
paths of his swollen veins, carving steps in his flesh. Jay
imagines them presenting offerings and their first-born,
carriers of prayers and supplications. Or perhaps they will
plant a banner reading "We come in peace" in large, luminous letters several microns tall, at the tip of his penis.

Overcome with the giggles, he drops the binoculars.
His lungs whistle, his laugh is cavernous, his stomach
growls, and he rears up toward the heaven, in a release
similar to birth. His erection wavers and tips before bending over and collapsing in the forest of his hair.

Silence, followed by the cautious return of the birds.
When he picks up the binoculars again, eyes still blurred
with tears, he gropes around before focusing them. The
landscape has changed. The folds of his torso, the small

hills of his nipples, the rugged descent toward his lower belly… it all seems new. As if resuscitated.

He looks for the structures, sweeping over his immensity with a slow, circular movement. Below his navel, the remains of last evening's camp are clearly visible. Although he will never decode them, he will also never erase them. The routes along his flesh are countless; the hiding places are too. Yet, he knows that the visitors will never hide from him. He finds them quickly, gathered in a single circle, diameter growing smaller. Their light pulses slow, flowing into a joint message directed at him. He realizes that the lenses of the binoculars also cast sparks in their direction. The visitors are merely trying to answer.

He hopes their prayers will be answered.

Then, with a roar, the structures move together and rise up above his flesh, in an ascent that starts slowly and ends in a rain of fire. A burn forms at the apex of his navel. He closes his eyes with the pain, but a streak of light races across his eyelids, accompanied by the murmur of engines. He is no longer a universe and has become an isolated dot on a silvery stain, a naked, blurred body, details soon washed away by the storm.

When his limbs start to obey him again, he bathes in the lake.

Back in the cabin, he dries off, puts on some warm clothes to ward off the irrepressible shaking that has overtaken his body. The icy water purified him, but he almost drowned. The traces of the visitors are encrusted in his body for all time; the memories will never fade.

He chews a handful of dried fruit then sits down at the radio. It's not the time for a scheduled report, so he connects to the common frequency.

"49-632. Are you receiving me?"

Then he adds, "It's Jay."

"Is there a problem?"

The question catches him off guard. He reaches for the disconnect button, then stops. Smiles.

"No, not at all."

He takes a deep breath, feels the burns on his belly unfurl their message.

"I just felt like talking."

PARANAMANCO

When Paranamanco broke out of her mooring lines and flew off into the night, I was hardly surprised. I remembered the words of the old navigator I'd interviewed a few months earlier, shortly after the AnimalCity project had been abandoned. I took the recording cube of our conversation out of a drawer and played it, wondering if I'd have the time to listen to it until the end...

"An entire herd? Can you imagine it? Twenty or so wild AnimalCities floating like medusae in space. The smallest could have served as the capital for any empire; the largest... No doubt you observed Paranamanco while orbiting in the transit satellite before landing here. You flew over it for several hours, skimming over the outgrowths we incorrectly call dwellings; maybe you even strolled along her avenues, with their disorderly striations carved by meteor dust. You may believe that you've seen her, but she continues to elude you, as a result of her size, her topography with its folds and strangeness. There are entire neighborhoods which no one has penetrated yet, alleys that are not shown on any map, buildings of flesh waiting to be explored."

The old man stopped to finish his glass. On a corner of my desk, the cube reader wove the image of a tavern, purring busily. I don't like mute objects. We created them to fill our solitude with their omnipresent company, not for them to fall silent and echo the waves of our own silence back at us, amplified.

"If you've got the heart for it," the old man said, "buy a recent plan and then have them drop you off anywhere in the city. You know the rule: when you find a street that hasn't been identified, you can name it as you see fit and register it with the land titles office. There's a bonus for each discovery, but it will hardly cover the cost of purchasing the 160 microfilmed volumes of the plan. Yet, how many people do you think are wandering about like that, shoulders bent under the weight of the microfilms and the viewer? Several thousand?"

He shook his head and glumly contemplated his empty glass, which was starting to crackle with an unpleasant odor. After the last swallow, the glass walls, deprived of humidity, decompose rather quickly, obliging drinkers to order another round immediately.

The strident ring of the communicator shrilled through the apartment. I cut it off and went back to listening.

"You have your own opinion of Paranamanco. It's undoubtedly incorrect, but mine is no better. It was a living organism before we decided to make it a city. A creature like that never really totally dies. Certain outlying neighborhoods rise and fall like respiration that is barely perceptible; the hollow filaments that we plan on using as transportation tunnels or sewer mains are sometimes animated by nervous shudders, like the axons of a failed brain.

"No, Paranamanco isn't completely dead; I've known her far too long to be wrong about that. Before I landed on her surface, I observed her in the middle of the herd, in deep space. Then I explored her for months, looking for the control points of her nervous system. I planted thousands of needles randomly in her flesh before discovering her pleasure centers and mounting her like an elephant driver, armed with the whip of my electrical discharges. I forced her to follow me here, by trial and error.

Once in orbit, I moored her, practically all on my own.

"You should have been there when we landed! Paralyzed by the cloud of tugs hooked to her circumference, she deployed her corolla of multicolored filaments and whipped the air, trying to trap the metal birds that flew within reach. She was magnificent and dangerous, a real carnivorous flower. No one could have forced her to obey if I'd dropped the reins.

"Of course, those who supervised the project had taken their precautions. Paranamanco was the first AnimalCity that we'd moored and, to date, she's still the only one; the others are parked between the asteroids, waiting for the authorities to reach a decision. The idea of using a life form like this as an inhabitable zone on the surface of a colonized world is interesting, but it's not to everyone's liking. Many colonists would prefer us to build them something more conventional. Some categorically refuse to settle in a dwelling whose walls are made of living organic tissue.

"We all make the mistake of judging the Animal-Cities by their appearance. A city is just a city, the imbeciles say, nothing surprising about that. That's stupid, even dangerous. These creatures have nothing other than the most superficial points in common with the human species. Their architecture, their existence depends on rules beyond our knowledge, even though it does appear easy to apply our own rules to them. We can use them, but we can never understand them. Take heed: this is important!

"Everyone was walking on eggs at that time. The head honchos came here to supervise the operations and prevent any possible problems from causing too many waves.

"Finally, they gave the explorers the go-ahead.

123

That's when the problems started…"

With a sigh, I pour him another drink. I've learned to recognize those points when stories wind down if they're not fueled—with alcohol, compliments or, occasionally, forgiveness. It all depends on the storyteller. The old man wasn't looking for absolution; he just wanted to drink.

"I went there too."

He gazed at his glass in the light of a mood lamp and noisily drained a good half of it.

"I wasn't looking to make my fortune. Capturing Paranamanco had already made me rich and, in any case, I'd never believed those tales of treasure buried in the AnimalCities' entrails. No, I was bored. Setting out to hunt in deep space didn't thrill me anymore. Any prey would have appeared minuscule to me after that catch.

"I'd started drinking, seriously drinking if you know what I mean. I set out on a whim one morning. I think I was even getting tired of the alcohol and I was afraid of what would come next.

"I chose to explore the eighteenth sector, starting out from the base camp established in the heart of the city. The instructions provided for a spiral exploration of the neighboring streets, followed by satellite reconnaissance of the outlying neighborhoods. At that rate, it would have taken ten years to map the main arteries. Paranamanco wouldn't have been inhabitable for a century.

"It's impossible to realize just how vast she is if you haven't tried to cross her alone. She's brimming with optical illusions, fake terraces and underground arteries. The guide satellites are of no use at all. AnimalCity skin is impervious to radio waves; even the remote-controlled units get lost. To bring her back to more human proportions, she had to be marked out with beacons filled with signs and pointers; the chaos of her alleys had to be corrected, the still wild neighborhoods had to be domesticated.

"So, I set out to identify the most direct route possible to the edge of the city. If everyone else had done the same, we could have completed the map in two years and taken charge of the terrain.

"It's a game, you see. Draw a map and you control the territory. The more accurate your map is, the more efficient your control is.

"Do you know how a new world is opened up for colonization? There are the mechanical caterpillars that lay kilometers and kilometers of fiber-optic cables in a few hours. Release thousands of those machines on the surface of any planet and they lay out a grid of high-capacity lines and communication nodes, while clearing away the densest part of the jungle. It doesn't matter how long it takes, you can rest assured that, after they've finished their job, there isn't a single nook or cranny that hasn't been explored. There's always a telephone booth on the horizon. At any given time, you're a 30-minute shuttle ride from civilization.

"I took one of those caterpillars with me…

"I don't know why, in fact, but they had no success with Paranamanco. They would either get lost or go completely crazy. They built closed lines that held them prisoner or wove electrified webs in which they hid, waiting for their prey. Apparently, some have even been found enveloped in a veritable cocoon, a prelude to an impossible metamorphosis. I'm only repeating what I've heard, but you know as well as I do what you have to make of this sort of tale.

"So, I headed off in the direction of the periphery with that caterpillar purring as it laid its wire. My belongings sat at the peak of its central ring, firmly moored by magnetic clamps. I walked ahead, hands in my pockets, as carefree as a Stanley who didn't give a rat's ass about Livingstone, while she crawled along behind me.

"About every ten kilometers, she'd stop to lay a new communication node, wrapped in placental tissue. It's a curious sight, but you get tired of it quickly. After a day, I stopped paying attention. Besides, people say you shouldn't get too close to those machines at such times. Now and then, their maternal love makes them dangerous. I made the most of these stops to stroll about the narrow alleys in the vicinity or I'd drink a glass to Paranamanco's health. My supplies were supposed to last two months. That's the main reason I'd brought the caterpillar along. With all the bottles, my luggage was too heavy for my old shoulders.

"After two days, we were navigating by sight between the constructions erected like pustules on the city's bituminous skin. Most were empty and naked, with a faint smell of dried sweat. Others, encumbered by cartilage partitions or blood red drapes, would have driven an interior decorator mad. I didn't have time to visit them all, so I settled for glancing inside the closest ones, so I could map those I considered inhabitable.

"The road we were following sloped down gently before branching out into narrower and narrower catwalks that led to the peaks of the buildings. Often, a building would be superimposed over the main artery and we'd move ahead into a dark tunnel, out of the range of the observation satellites. In such cases, our progress would be jerkier, the caterpillar's headlights hesitantly sweeping away the dark. I'd keep my hand on its head ring, to reassure it.

"The farther we proceeded into the invisible levels of the city, the more uncontrollable my caterpillar's reactions became. Her dilated sphincters released bunches of embryonic booths, most irreversibly deformed, exuding machine oil. I'd kick their protective envelope into bits, to alleviate their agony and prevent the development of interference in the communication network. When we got back to the surface, the caterpillar returned to normal. I stopped in a clearing so she could recharge her solar batteries.

"It was during one of these breaks that I realized we were no longer alone.

"Our trail was easy to follow; all they had to do was keep sight of the wires. Yet, I'd never have thought that someone would have bothered to tail us, the machine and me. We weren't carrying anything valuable, apart from my booze, and I'd have willingly shared a bottle. And don't for a minute think we were surrounded by unknown creatures drawn from the depths of the city. Our trackers were human and they weren't making much of an effort to hide.

"I could have set a trap for them, ambushed them in any alleyway. They'd had a dozen opportunities to do the same earlier, so... I stopped the caterpillar and waited for them, a bottle of alcohol in my hand. I know the rules.

"They, on the other hand, didn't. They took so long to show their faces that I was three-quarters drunk by the time they arrived. I no longer clearly remember what they told me that evening; the next morning, all my bottles were broken and my skull was buzzing. Luckily, the girl made good coffee.

"There were two of them. A guy and a girl. About your age. I had him pegged right off: taciturn, with the long, slender fingers of a pianist. She was something completely different. A china doll, skin and bones, the type who has never turned anyone away and has decided it was time for things to change. Apart from that, she was as silent as he was.

"After a few cups of java, I felt up to chewing them out for the loss of my bottles prior to hearing their side of this. They let me shout out my drunkenness before speaking with me. Good idea! I was too angry to do anything but vent my spleen. Plus, yelling almost drowned out the buzzing in my skull.

"They had a map to show me. Not a buried treasure map, that wasn't their style, or one of those esoteric diagrams that the so-called Paranamanco fortune-tellers specialize in. They're supposed to be able to read your future in the topographical maps of the city, you know, and show the future colonists the best places to settle. If necessary, they find the settlers a neighborhood where the layout of the streets corresponds to the lines on their hands. Utter stupidity.

"My two followers were a different sort of bright spark than I'd possibly come across before. They both worked in the department that tracked the data transmitted by the orbital satellites. The computer had highlighted anomalies in the aerial photos taken of Paranamanco, inconsistencies in the routes taken by certain streets, the type of detail that neither you nor I would have noticed but which the machine regularly set its sights on. They'd each been looking on their own for months, without joining forces, then they decided to pool their observations. They found the solution almost immediately.

"A fragment on the map of the city was repeated identically forty-four times. A single fragment, but because of this duplicated element, the computer crashed every time it tried to reconstitute the Paranamanco jigsaw. Discouraged, the girl had drawn a map indicating the locations of the famous fragment.

"Once the coffee had its effect, they rolled their map

out to show me. Forty-four spots were spread over the disk of the city, with no apparent symmetry or regularity. Yet, their pattern looked familiar to me. I got out my own map, the one showing the animal's nerve centers, which I'd drawn during my deep space exploration. Mine was cruder, but there was nothing haphazard about the resemblance. Strangely, mine was offset by one hundred and ninety degrees from theirs; a semicircle, as if the two phenomena were of equal importance, but opposite in meaning.

"The route taken by the caterpillar was heading straight toward the closest spot, which is why they decided to follow me. I believe they suspected my intentions were the same as theirs. As the first one to explore the creature, I was supposed to know more about her than anyone else. They thought I already had an inkling as to what the identical sectors hid, that the government had some secret goal when it had Paranamanco land and that it was exploring her through me. I didn't disabuse them. They wouldn't have believed me anyway.

"When we set out again, the caterpillar was carrying three packs instead of one, which didn't seem to affect her all that much, and I had an audience to whom I could recount my memories of deep space. They knew how to listen, that much I can say for them, a bit like you, but then you're paid to listen so it doesn't count. The guy, Geoff, never said more than a few words at a time, and settled for moving ahead at his own pace. From time to time, he'd look back to see if the girl was still following. I've forgotten her name, but it will certainly come back as I talk.

"We were a good day's walk from the interesting zone, which gave us time to review a fair number of hypotheses and invent a few new ones. The most curious thing was that, seen from the satellite, there was nothing particular about the duplicated fragment: three or four streets, completely ordinary outgrowths for buildings. Same old, same old. I could have walked through them without noticing a thing. Geoff thought it was some sort of visual illusion and that we should expect something else, underground tunnels maybe, or vast rooms filled with strange machinery. He fixated on that idea: the AnimalCities were once used as spacecraft by a humanoid race and had outlived their creators. This made for a good story, completely valid, when you have twelve hours of walk ahead of you and nothing other to do than survey the streets and christen them as you see fit.

"In any case, no one knew anything at all about the AnimalCities at the time, and we've learned precious little since. The colonization of Paranamanco was interrupted and it won't start up again anytime soon. As for the rest of the herd, it's wandering carefree about the asteroids. If we knew how to kill a wild city, our problems would be resolved for the most part, but I doubt we'll ever reach that point. I'm starting to think the entire operation is plain old stupidity, but no one's asked me for my opinion in a long time.

"So, there we were, walking ahead of the caterpillar, because of the exhaust fumes, without even taking the time to visit the structures that surrounded us. We had the entire city to ourselves and the only thing that interested us was a block of three streets, which didn't even have the excuse of being unique. At the time, that didn't strike us. The idea only came to me on our way back.

"Imagine: today, there are almost one million colonists on Paranamanco, there's noise, electricity, eleven official religions, an entire microcosm of the human species gathered on the surface of a flat organism that had the good sense to be inhabitable. I know it will take at least half a billion people for the place to even start looking settled, but at the time that the three of us were walking along unexplored avenues there was no one within a 200 km radius. Not a soul! I don't think an ocean or a desert could give such an impression of solitude. Weirdly it wasn't until the other two arrived that I even noticed.

"Then the wind started to blow down the empty streets and we stopped for shelter on a porch. The evening fell slowly. The buildings hollowed out unusual shadows, stretching in unexpected directions. I hadn't had a drop to drink since the previous night, yet my usual hallucinations settled over the facades of the neighboring buildings. They were remodeling the scene that surrounded us. I desperately needed a drink and felt my nightmares swirling in around me, waiting for night to torment me. I didn't have the strength to resist.

"We were approaching our goal. I suppose it was the first symptoms of Paranamanco's influence, although the base doctor has talked to me about delirium tremens, with a knowing smile. People like that always have a better explanation than yours and there's no way to make them change their minds.

"The next day the others decided, without consulting me, to leave me there for the entire day while they went out to do some reconnaissance. I'd have refused if I'd known, but that double dose of sleeping pills in the coffee would have put anyone out like a light. When I opened my eyes, I was trapped in an unbreakable cocoon of cables and the caterpillar, which had been reprogrammed, was vigilantly standing guard over me.

"I'd wanted to warn the base that a couple of loonies were holding me prisoner so that someone would come and get me. It seemed easy; I was surrounded by communication booths. The caterpillar had woven a delicious little concentration camp for one where transmission cables replaced barbed wire and booths replaced watchtowers. The only problem was that I didn't have enough tokens.

"Before I even reached the base operator, my supply had run out. I was stupid enough to try to kick the box apart to collect its contents. My first mistake was choosing a freshly hatched booth; my second was forgetting the caterpillar's maternal instinct.

"Possibly her reflexes should have been altered by the reprogramming, but that didn't stop her from charging at me with the full speed of her segments, tearing her way through the cables she'd woven. We played a deadly game of tag, in which the neutral zones were the booths. Bit by bit, I was trying to draw her away from the breach she'd made in the network of wires that held me prisoner. When I thought it was a good time, I raced off toward the closest building, expecting to be caught and pulverized at any time. I've rarely been afraid, but I was that day.

"Once safe, I caught my breath before glancing behind me. The caterpillar hadn't followed me at all; she stood motionless in the middle of her cocoon. On her back, the girl was waving in my direction.

"I turned around slowly, savoring my anger as it swept over me. I was preparing myself for one of those explosions that make novas look minor. In two days these two clueless young people had deprived me of my bottles, drugged me and forced me into a rodeo with a thirty-ton caterpillar. I had enough insults in mind to turn the air blue until the next day, perhaps even longer, if there was the least bit of an echo. Then I saw the tears rolling down the girl's cheeks and I fell silent… What else could I have done?

"We broke camp in ten minutes. I cut the cable ahead

of the anarchic section and made a splice directly on the machine's hindquarters, short-circuiting the delirious skein that had imprisoned me. One more puzzle for the archeologists of the future. I allowed myself the luxury of using an iron bar to pulverize the booth that held my tokens and recovered them. I'm the first official vandal on Paranamanco. Don't forget to mention that in your article."

"Why were you in such a rush to leave?"

My voice rises out of the cube reader with an irritating fidelity, asking the right question at the right time.

In front of me, on the back wall of my office, the red warning light flashes in vain. I don't feel like answering any call, especially right now.

"Geoff had disappeared in the unknown sector. The girl, Evalane (I knew her name would come back to me, Geoff called her Evie), well the girl had been afraid to continue their research on her own and had come back to release me so I could help her. Ten seconds later and she'd probably have found the caterpillar nibbling on a pancake-shaped cadaver. Bio-machines can be quite strange at times. That would have given my caterpillar an opportunity to lay flesh pink booths, with dial pads encrusted with eyes rather than keys. Just the thought of dialing a number under those conditions, fingers in eyes... Evie acknowledged that it was lucky for me that Geoff had chosen that particular moment to evaporate. How was I supposed to respond to that? I grumbled that luck had been smiling on me ever since they'd arrived, but the girl was insensitive to sarcasm.

"She had stopped crying, well almost, just a sob from time to time when she mentioned Geoff. I hadn't realized she had a thing for him. When you live alone in space, you lose track of that sort of phenomenon. I had no idea just how important that was going to be later.

"There was nothing in particular about the area. It looked like so many other neighborhoods that they'd walked through before, without even noticing them. They had to backtrack and ask for a satellite location in order to find it. Geoff was disappointed and furious. He raced up and down the three streets, looking for a secret passageway, a hidden opening, without success. Then he started to explore the outgrowths one after another, coming back out a little more annoyed each time. Well, so Evie saw him go into a porch and he never came back out.

"According to the girl, there was nothing particular about the interior of the building: a labyrinth of cartilage partitions, a rough floor, made of folds of dead skin. Since no one answered when she called out, she hadn't dared to venture too far in and preferred to return to camp, taking care to spray-paint her initials on the porch.

"We approached cautiously. Nothing moved, no sound filtered out to us, no trace of Geoff. I picked up the caterpillar's remote control, as I pulled Evie away from the porch.

"'We could get lost in that maze,' I explained to her. 'I'll send the beast in to explore for us.'"

'Good idea! Then we can simply follow its wire to make our way back out without getting trapped by those damn partitions.'

'After she's done a tour inside, there won't actually be many partitions intact...

"She blushed, which didn't look good on her, and fell silent. The caterpillar rolled over to the entrance. Her segments proceeded into the building, one by one. We could hear the sound of fabric tearing, followed by irregular periods of silence. I glanced inside: the floor was strewn with cartilage, debris and booths that had been laid all askew, imprisoned in their placental pouches. Just the place for a large-scale communication center. I noted its location on the map, out of reflex, before carefully following in the caterpillar's footsteps, accompanied by Evie.

"We made our way through the building diagonally, stumbling among the waste. A cloud of bone dust powered our clothing. We avoided coughing, for fear of giving birth to an echo we wouldn't have recognized. I twisted my ankle and Evie fell in a pile of debris, from which she emerged like a ghost, bits of membrane hanging from her shoulders and hair like a transparent shroud. She looked like a ghostly bat.

"The caterpillar had stopped at the entrance to an immense many-sided room that had remained intact. Evie went around her body. I heard the girl cry out. When I reached her, she was kneeling next to Geoff who lay unconscious, feverish, lips clenched, fingernails dug into bloody palms.

"We didn't see the fountain right away. We were busy trying to revive our lost team member and didn't have the time to study the surroundings closely. The delicate murmur of the drops trickling in the basin gradually penetrated into my consciousness, like those dreams at dawn that announce an imminent return to reality. My worried mind was on the lookout for the slightest abnormal noise, but that wasn't one, and I made no effort to locate the source. It was Geoff who pointed at it, as soon as he opened his eyes, asking us hoarsely to get him something to drink.

"Evie gave him a shot and poured the content of her canteen between his lips. I stood up to disconnect the caterpillar. On my way, I glanced about, without noticing anything special: the murmur came from a thin ribbon of water that welled up from the ground and filled a cavity below. It hadn't rained in a week. I recall wondering where the water could be coming from. But I didn't think it was all that important.

"As soon as Geoff could stand up, he rushed over to the fountain to drink, before we could stop him. The water didn't appear to have any particular effect on him. He offered me some, but I don't really have an affinity for that type of liqueur at zero degrees.

"When we asked him why he'd fainted, he replied that he'd knocked himself out against a partition. The explanation was so stupid that we believed it and considered the matter closed. Evie apologized for dragging me into all this for nothing. While we were getting into things, Geoff received his share of insults for leaving me alone with the caterpillar, but my heart wasn't into that.

"We followed the wire back out. None of us tried to get away from the sector; we even decided to set up our camp at the intersection of two neighboring streets. Evie made some coffee. Without a word, Geoff held out her canteen so that she could go and fill it.

"I gave him a mild sedative so that he could rest for the remainder of the day and went out to explore the neighboring buildings, to form my own opinion.

"Evie was telling the truth; there was absolutely nothing to see in that sector. It was so similar to all the others I'd traveled through before that things were starting to look suspicious. I was caught up in the game, obstinately searching in vain. I palpated the city's thick skin in hopes of detecting some sort of revealing pulse; I scratched esoteric maps in an old notepad, tearing the pages out as I finished them. In short, I behaved like an imbecile. Evie, who was watching over Geoff, called out to me from time to time, asking if I'd found anything and seemed to take no notice of my increasingly brief answers.

"The dark gradually chased me from the streets filled with thick shadows, in which it would be all too easy to lose my way. I gave up and sat down next to the electric hot plate where our evening rations were heating, along with an entire pot of coffee. Evie and Geoff glanced at me, but refrained from making a comment. Just as well. I couldn't forgive them for breaking the pleasant monotony of my trip through the city and for their promises of hollow dreams. For the first time, Paranamanco had disappointed me and it was all their fault.

"I rolled up in my bedroll, as far from the caterpillar and them as possible, and tried to fall asleep. I'd had too much coffee for that to be easy but, with the help of the silence, I gradually felt myself dozing off, dreaming that the base would get rid of my two pests the next day.

"During the night, I dreamt the same dream over and over again. I was hitting my head against the reality of the city like a moth blinded by light. When I woke up, Geoff had disappeared once more and the entire neighborhood seemed to have gone mad…

"Heavy bunches of colored light bulbs hung overhead, large drops of luminous sap dripping down. A vine of telephone cables climbed up the outgrowths, rolling in abundant, baroque spirals along the streets, in an unnatural embrace. Neon orchids with electrifying scents surged from the slightest chink in the walls, shooting lightning that bounced off Paranamanco's skin. In a few hours, the neighborhood had been transformed into a virgin forest.

"Next to the dead hot plate and the caterpillar, which had been definitively disconnected, Evie lay plunged in a sleep evidently filled with nightmares. The ground around her was spiked by long, transparent spears, shimmering with violet sparks. I had to kick them to bits to get closer to her.

"Geoff had made her swallow the rest of the sleeping pills and had pinned a laconic note to her sleeping bag before heading off. I knew what it said before reading it. But that didn't stop me from going through it twice, just to make sure my hunch was right. Then I woke Evie, not without some difficulty.

"All around us, the scene gradually came to life. The sun was already high. The dense fiber-optic jungle shimmered perceptibly. I almost expected Geoff to appear, wearing a simple loincloth, leaping from vine to vine, hunting prey. But I knew we'd never see him again. And, deep down, Evie did too.

"Yet she refused to believe it, despite the evidence that surrounded us, despite Geoff's note. She denied the facts. Hey, you try to convince a woman that her lover is capable of leaving her for a living organism that measures 600 km in diameter, a creature he had shared his dreams with…

"She wanted to search for him. I had a lot of difficulty convincing her to listen to me first. I'd known what was really going on with Paranamanco since the previous night, in part because of Evie. The water she'd used to make her coffee came from the fountain. Some of its power remained, despite the boiling, just enough that I knew what kind of trap Geoff fell into. Merely thinking that I could have suffered the same fate made shivers run up and down my back. It would have taken so little. I must be one of the few rare people whose life has been saved by alcohol.

"I told Evie that the liquid had slowly poisoned Geoff, that the first time we'd found him, unconscious, he'd most certainly just drunk from the fountain and that, feeling that he was about to die, he preferred to distance himself from the camp, to spare us the spectacle of his agony. The note he had left her was the fruit of a brain that was already damaged; she shouldn't pay it any attention. Of course, she didn't believe a word of what I said, but it was the best lie I could come up with given the time available.

"She insisted that I tell the truth. I was stupid enough to do so..."

A long line of vehicles, sirens shrieking, is heading my way. Judging by the sound, they're far enough off that I have time to listen to the last surface of the cube, the most important one.

"The AnimalCities are incomplete organisms," the old man murmurs, eyes staring at a horizon beyond my reach. "To successfully face the space that separates galaxies, they need symbiotic companions, gardeners capable of caring for them and maintaining them throughout the voyage. In exchange, they offer access to the entire universe, as well as the means to survive in the void of space.

"When I landed on Paranamanco's surface for the first time, she understood that her race and mankind could get along. She flavored the water of her dreams accordingly. After tasting it, Geoff was able to give birth of his own accord to the neon garden that surrounded us. No doubt he was wandering about the adjacent neighborhoods, impatient to put his new powers to the test. I imagined the winding streets filled with hardy brambles, leaves flashing with lightning, tree streetlights, electric foliage stretching over the city's squares, and avenues illuminated by the flamboyant chalices of glass tulips. I realized that Geoff had not only shared Paranamanco's dreams, but had also, in a certain manner, transmitted his own. She dreamed of looking like the cities on Earth, with their adornment of multicolored lights enshrined in metal and stone. All she needed was a little help.

"At the beginning, Evie refused to believe me, convinced that I was making the whole thing up for some totally obscure reason, that I didn't know any more than she did. So, I placed my hands on the warm soil. A tiny neon flower sprang up and spat out its fire before expiring.

"She finally understood that we couldn't do any more for Geoff. Only an expedition organized by the base could be able to find him, if it wasn't already too late. The caterpillar was dead, we had no more water. Well, at least, I preferred not to try the water in our canteens in case Geoff had filled them at the fountain. I left Evie, deeply wounded by my words, and set out, following the wire, to search for a booth that was working.

"I had no idea what my colleague on the other end of the line thought about my story and I didn't care. Once I was certain that someone would come to get us immediately, I headed back to camp, where no one was waiting for me any longer.

"Evie had carried off one of the canteens when she left. In a letter scribbled while I was away, she said that she was ready to join Geoff, to take her turn at serving the city. I castigated myself for not having seen that coming and I cried out her name until the echoes rebounded around me, not daring to walk off. She never came back.

"The most horrible part is that there was no chance for her project to succeed. Paranamanco was only interested in men. There was a sexual component between her gardeners and her that was essential for her survival. Evie was incapable of providing that and I suppose that the AnimalCities can occasionally get jealous…

"That evening, a shuttle came to pick me up, guided by the beacon of the dead caterpillar. When the pilot saw the scene, he called for reinforcements. A security cordon surrounded the site. But it was too late. The fountain of dreams had dried up. We never found anyone.

"I don't know how the information could have leaked out, but hundreds of colonists set out to look for Paranamanco's secret wells. Those in charge implemented a news blackout, partly because they didn't believe me. I'm an old wino, you know. It was fine and dandy for me to tell them over and over that it was the alcohol that had saved my life, but they remained skeptical. I can see their point of view and I would never have imagined that someone would come and interview me about all this.

"And you, do you believe me? If I weren't half drunk, I'd string up a garland of lights to convince you, but Paranamanco doesn't like alcohol and I believe I lost my power over her a long time ago. She doesn't want me anymore. I had my chance and I blew it."

Someone is banging brusquely at my door; the recording is over. My article has been rejected everywhere, without explanation. I've been under constant surveillance, but that doesn't matter now. The city found her pilot; she was able to take off with her crew of dreamers and adventurers, whose hands will restore the flowers back to dead streets. No doubt, they're far away already.

I have a least a minute or two before those who are looking for me break down the door. I think about the flask of the city's dreams that the old explorer gave me, before heading off into the streets with their sadly conventional signs, and disappearing for good. Maybe I'll have the time to take the cork out, to drink it, but Paranamanco has flown off and I'm no longer certain that I can find her.

LOVE STORY WITH A FALL

"I can't keep this up," I tell my reflection in the screen.

Ni-Anne's face, superimposed over mine, taunts me from a continuous animation loop: a wink followed by a pout. The text of the invitation appears on her cheeks in flashing ideograms. She's celebrating her new breasts and is counting on me to be there.

For her twentieth birthday, her father offered the necessary wind tunnel tests as well as the assistance of an industrial design firm. I tested the possible models in VR and helped sculpt the creamy ovoids in order to make them as aerodynamic as possible. With data gloves... what else, eh? Ni-Anne and I are not lovers, just network neighbors. But the basic idea of a bosom that simply has to be licked for new nipples to spring up is all mine. I also had a hand in the arrangement of a constellation of beauty spots along the cleft. My name is engraved in the biochip embedded under her skin, right side: © 2037, all rights reserved.

This is my first real project in the field and I'm fairly satisfied with it. If her breasts are pleasing, I'll get royalties. Ni-Anne has everything it takes to be in style, she's been surfing at the peak of the wave longer than anyone else.

That leaves me with my own little problem. I'm 100% intact, the real thing, the raw matrix. Perfectly old-fashioned, which is the lot of all of us most of the time, but in my case it's obvious.

I've made no particular effort in this respect; I was stuffed with vitamins and various substances before birth—*expulsion, sweetheart, is so much more romantic,* said my progenitor (it's been a long time since I've seen her, hey, I wonder what she might look like now)—had my teeth straightened and my cornea reshaped. Along with all the usual things. After all, I'm not one of those crazy backward-looking types with cavities or pubic hair. But I'm all *me* from head to toe, natural design. Rustic.

"The problem," the last of my partners to date said, "is that people take your clothes off, like opening a gift, and there's nothing inside! I mean…" (She had accommodated nine inches of nothing in various places during the previous hours and it had, however, seemed to have done *something* for her). "No surprise. Nothing really glamorous. You know what I mean?"

She had been entirely covered with a subcutaneous, heat-sensitive layer, with a color scale ranging from orange to purple. Each orgasm had smeared her in a random manner, like the unhealthy sunsets you see in highly polluted zones. The operation had cost her a fortune and kept her in bed for three weeks. I found the result unpleasant after a minute and a half.

When I left her, our lengthy farewell kiss had disguised her face temporarily as a car accident. There were problems with after-images at the pixel layer; the washed-out spots on her skin would fade much more slowly than the memory I left behind for her. *You are much too superficial.* She must, of course, be right. The art of appearing has a deep meaning for her and I didn't offer her anything new. Nothing other than myself.

Money isn't a problem; it never is. If you have the means to ask the question, you have the means to answer it. Body fashion has its artists and its ready-to-wear; you can be creative on a small budget and wear a little nothing.

As for me, I go around naked and I'm not even

enough of an exhibitionist to make a trend of it.

"If you don't reveal your secrets, no one will know you have any," Ni-Anne said in her last message. "People will look at my breasts, but it's my heart they'll be seeing."

She's not wrong. Her breasts will stop being viewed as curios after a few hours.

I set out on foot to make my way through neighborhoods going through the revitalization process. A group of archeologists was scanning sections of walls covered with acrylic graffiti. The digitized copies would be added to the databases of the street, making room for advertising. For the past two or three years, everyone has been caught up in an archiving frenzy. It's as if the adults want to store everything, freeze everything, before the final end of humanity.

I stopped for a moment to watch them. Their scanners slipped over me without stopping. I wasn't worthy of inclusion in their collection. It's only as they grow old that people and things become important. As long as they survive, that is.

I should have donated my body to the Library of Congress, before it became fashionable.

The neutral overalls that clothe the archeologists suppress their images digitally in real time. They reconstitute the universe behind them, as if they weren't there and erase even their reflections on the chrome fixtures of the vehicles abandoned throughout the streets. Markus, one of my mother's companions, worked in the field; he talked to me about the feeling of freedom that the overalls gave him. Showing up nowhere, being erased from the system, living outside time.

This is the last place people can escape: the digital

chinks of virtuality. Ideal place to get lost. But I want people to discover me…

Markus may have been every bit as old as my mother, but I enjoyed talking with him. I borrowed his overalls one evening, while he was in-synch with the Network's Zen-space, to give his knees some relief. I had a date with the rest of my gang on the commercial artery that winds around our zone. The sleeves of the overalls flapped a little and the hood hung in folds around my neck, but the processors made the corrections automatically. I became virtually invisible. Undetectable.

It was crap, moreover. The street cameras no longer detected me and the holo ads no longer kept me company. All that was left was the back of the set: tactile windows that didn't react to my approach, a false depth behind the armored glass and a total absence of reflections. *Mirror, mirror on the wall, who's the fairest of them all.* Result: a system error. Fortunately, my friends located me. I was no longer able to perceive myself.

Ni-Anne is a zone neighbor. The distance separating our two ziggurats represents a ridiculous figure as the crow flies and a difference of only two digits in the network equivalent. It's a coincidence that spares me hours of tube travel. Besides, I like walking. There are never many people about in the surface streets. The ordinary people prefer the closed avenues that run around the floors of their pyramids and all of the delinquents are behind their terminals trying to pirate the local banks. All that's left are the archeologists, the last of the dog walkers, and me.

The wakes of the shuttles crisscross harmoniously. Following the proliferation of arcologies, the horizon now bristles with teeth. Behind the glass-encased platforms, the setting sun looks like it's been bitten. This world is no longer meant to be seen from outside, quite unlike people.

Ni-Anne's ziggurat covers several hectares and includes roughly 30 floors belted with rectangular commercial avenues protected by armored glass. Invisible from below, the browsers congregate in front of the tactile windows, looking for some impossible fetish object manufactured exclusively for them. At the top, a forest of bamboo trees sways in the breeze of the ventilation units.

I had copied Ni-Anne's message into a memory chip. At the edge of the no man's land surrounding her ziggurat, I brandish it like a key. The glue guns responsible for immobilizing intruders turn away from me when they recognize the code broadcast by the processor. After that, it's all routine: elevators to the reception area, a final glance in a mirror to correct the expression on my face, the personalized bag a professional hostess gives me in exchange for my invitation. Inside, a pair of holo-glasses, shell-like lenses closing hermetically over my eyes.

I'm expected…

I make my way effortlessly through the bunches of guests congregated around the pastry distributors. A Cobra device has been implanted in the shoulder pads of my outfit. When the crowd grows too dense, it issues a warning whistle that acts on the reptilian brain. People move away without even understanding why and I slip through the empty space without touching anyone.

The holo-glasses enable me to see the ornamentation. Ni-Anne has decorated the ceilings with videos showing her *before,* a black ribbon of bereavement in the lower, right corner. The walls are hidden behind a fine fog that makes the room look as if it extends to infinity in all directions at the same time.

Around me, appearances have been worked, silhouettes corrected by scalpels. It is possible to make out the warbling of birds produced by trimmed vocal cords or throats that have been surgically equipped with echo chambers in the hubbub of voices. I know no one; neither does anyone else. Ni-Anne is our common denominator, our strange attractor, and I wait for her to introduce me into a circle that is likely to welcome me for the duration of the reception.

It's time for me to deactivate the Cobra.

Meanwhile, I grab a tall champagne flute filled with liquid and I heat it in clasped hands. The dancers' silhouettes invent new ways of showing off each second and the performance they provide must be a worthy reward for their efforts. Sometimes I sit down at receptions such as this one, facing the parade of guests, and ask myself *which of these people am I?* The answer, if I were to know it, could well be the key that would enable me to join them.

"Is this a bad joke? Or an insult?"

Ni-Anne has appeared at my side and is looking me up and down, before spinning around me. The absence of any ornament on my body seems to upset her.

"Neither one nor the other…" (I lift my full glass in greeting.) "Consider this a tribute, a way of not ruining your party. No one will take their eyes off you to glance at me."

"Ah…" (She bites her lips.) "Very discreet on your part, I suppose. It's just that you look a little out of place. I had hoped…"

"Let me look at you…"

The magic words. She sticks out her chest, modestly draped with black, form-fitted latex. The effect is both superb and frustrating. She must see this in my eyes, since she murmurs, "As the creator you have an unlimited

148

access code. Set your glasses to MaxContrast."

She pretends to step back, but I'm not fooled. I cling to her, while fingering the cursor on the holo-shells. The latex thins to the point of disappearing. Ni-Anne's breasts are breathtaking, both slender and voluminous, with a multi-lobed section that looks as if it must have been generated by a space-age supercomputer. I wonder what effect they'll have against the chest of someone else.

"Can I touch?"

"Not you... But look!"

She pirouettes, with no noticeable effect on her bosom. The artificial beauty mark at the top of her cleavage sparkles briefly: *Alpha Centaurus,* if I can believe my memories of the constellation chosen for the decoration.

"A last-minute upgrade. The micro-battery will last at least three months. Cute, isn't it? And it's even better in the dark."

"Who's the happy chosen one? Or chosen ones?"

"Now, you're being indiscreet! We'll get together later. I'll beep you, OK? The evening has barely started. Mingle..."

It would be impolite to return my shells to the normal position too soon, so I wait for her to move off in the wake of white flesh with perfectly synchronous oscillations. When I decide to sample the cocktail, it's tepid and leaves a flat taste in my mouth. At this rate, the pastries will have turned back into dust before I make it over to the buffet.

I walk randomly through the room, which is filling with impenetrable groups, wearing my appearance like a burden. The music that surges from the floor is not enough to smooth my gait.

And that's when I see her...

It's possible to simulate all colors and textures, but

there's something fractal about the gliding of black lace on the skin. This type of effect is inimitable; the girl was real and I was already in love. It was one of those high-speed seconds when lives collide. When I recover my spirits, I'm being dragged along in her wake, eyes riveted to the nape of her neck, where three strings of pearls are coiled, too subtle to be fake.

"You've inherited a remora, Lou," someone says to her and she turns around to face me.

Her face is bare of any screen. Her shell glasses have been pushed up on her forehead, with its spikey fringe of twisted red locks.

"Lou?" (She has a name like a kiss, with a touch of moisture when I say it.)

"Do I know you?"

"That would be too easy, wouldn't it?"

"Probably…" (She examines me from every angle, like Ni-Anne had done earlier, but her glance is just in-quisitive.) "I don't see anything. What's your trick?"

On her right shoulder, at the base of her neck, a fin-ger-sized replica of her sways in keeping with her move-ments. Threads as fine as hairs connect the puppet's limbs to the control unit hidden under her ear.

"There's nothing to see. I don't exhibit my secrets."

"How did you slip in here?" she says with a smile. "Ni-Anne's invitations are supposed to be inviolable, and her security system is the tops."

"She invited me."

"I doubt that. I've been her best friend longer than anyone and I don't know you."

"Did you know that the stars on her breasts shine in the dark?"

"She told everyone!"

"I didn't know it. My design didn't include that

detail."

"I see…" (She brushes her index finger along the arch of her lips, a gesture so practiced it leaves me speechless.) "So, then, you're the Mysterious Correspondent, who helped her transform her lame breasts into something *fashionable*. Except that you haven't even bothered to apply your talent to your own body. How do you expect me to believe you?"

Every time she moves, her marionette wears itself out trying to keep up. Shards of naked skin flicker under the spray of black light refracted by the lace. When I lower my eyes, I discover my own perfectly banal silhouette, a fleshy camouflage that covers nothing more than a skeleton with standardized proportions.

"You'd be wise to leave before I call Security…"

"Is there a problem, Lou darling?"

Ni-Anne has suddenly materialized behind me, a figurehead, carrying a flotilla of tipsy guests in her wake. She glances at me inquisitively, and I can almost hear the gears in her brain moving as she evaluates the situation.

"He came *au naturel* to avoid any competition with me. Delightful, isn't that? Somewhat cowardly too, I think, but that can always be hidden under a good education. Don't try to steal his idea; I'm an exclusive model. Have a good evening, the two of you. *Exhibit yourselves!*"

Lou shrugs and her marionette almost tumbles from her naked collarbone. The tiny hand grabs onto the pearls for balance. I resist the temptation to reach out a finger to help.

"This is all a simple misunderstanding," I murmur.

"It's all your fault. You don't display your codes and no one knows how to take you. What does this absence of image mean? It's completely superficial!"

I'd like to be able to find the right words. Silhouettes smeared with messages, decorated with meanings sculpted in flesh, slither around us. *Look at me, I'm...* The holo-glasses prevent them from destroying appearances; they're merely what they've chosen to be. I'm able to imitate them.

"You're right, of course, Lou..."

"And that's all you've got to say for yourself? No esthetic theory, a return to the original body, or something along those lines? I can take provocation, but won't tolerate innocence!"

"Dance with me and I'll tell you everything!"

"No can do. My imago..." (She points to the tiny doll.) "It malfunctions when people hold me too closely. I hate that."

She catches my glance and shakes her head.

"I disconnect it in private. *Never* in public."

I take her hand and pull her along. She allows me to do so, surprising me with her docility. Without turning my head, I guide her to a corner in the room covered with an artificial infinity by a fog of holograms. Putting on our glasses would affect our sense of perspective so we'd never dare cross over the event horizon, for fear of falling into the void. But, for our naked eyes, it takes no more than a step to topple over the visible zone, into the black hole.

Once there, I try to embrace her. She turns away, just long enough to play with the switch, hidden behind her ear, then allows herself to be caught. She dances badly, missing the beat, and steps on my toes once or twice. Face hidden against my shoulder, she carefully avoids all contact.

"I'm listening to you," she murmurs.

"I have nothing to say. No, wait, it's true!" (I hold

her close.) "I actually have nothing *special* to say, I can't describe myself in a sound bite."

"You helped Ni-Anne do just that…"

"She cheats. She only offers you what you ask for, nothing more."

Caught with a sudden inspiration, I add, "You're more subtle but the result is the same. Your imago, or whatever it is, your marionette… She's the one people want to touch and you've chosen to hide behind her or to take her place. You give nothing up, you protect yourself, that's all."

"You think I don't know that?"

"Of course, I do." (I shrug.) "But I might just be the first one to tell you that."

The music accelerates brutally and the fleeting moment during which I could have kissed her passes too quickly. She takes a step back and that's enough for me to lose her in the electronic spider webs of the décor. The black is absolute. I reach out blindly and my fingers cling to hers.

Relieved, I pull her toward me. *Lou.* A name too short to be a password. When she emerges from the dark zone, the lace of her bodysuit appears to tear away from the void to cover her once again.

"I never get lost," she tells me breathlessly, as I place my lips on hers.

She doesn't allow me to linger. The sensation is warm, fleeting, a phantom image on the screen of my memory.

"You're cheating…" (She pouts, destroying the print of my mouth.) "You're already naked."

"Then dress me!"

"I'm supposed to find that exciting? Listen, I'm holding my own get-together in two months. Consider yourself invited. On one condition: *you come as you are!"*

The marionette returns to its place on her shoulder. Lou flees; a single step carries over the barrier and I watch as she races toward appearances. *Come as I am...*

And at that specific moment, I realize what I'm missing.

Two months, sixty days. An eternity when you're in love, but really just enough time for a profound physical transformation. I live to the ticking of two distinct clocks, dizzied by the asynchronous beating: counting the seconds between two messages from Lou, experiencing the hours required for healing in slow motion.

The entire muscular structure of my back has been redesigned. The delicate balance of the circulatory system that irrigates my shoulders has attained a new degree of complexity: a micro-pump connected to two reservoirs located beneath the shoulder blades assists my poor, breathless heart. So far, it works. The biological membranes swell under the rush of blood and the effect obtained satisfies my desires.

Then I have to design, shape, adjust... Learn how to walk all over again, cheat gravity (micro-cells filled with helium have been inserted in the tissues, along the steel ribs), oversee the installation of the quills acquire new reflexes.

Lying on my belly, supported by a microbead mattress, I discover the pleasure of playing with my own image. I've blocked all video accesses to the outside. Lou sulked, begged, before finally agreeing to wait until the day of my first public appearance. Ni-Anne appeared only once, through a particularly brutal virus that broke through all my defenses. But the cameras weren't connected that day. All it caught was some electronic snow before self-destructing.

My appearance still belongs to me. I just have to learn to live with the idea that I've become transparent. And with the resulting change in balance.

On D-day, I walked through the labyrinth of the tube stations, guided by the memory card filled with messages from Lou. I hadn't erased a thing. Our entire history is inlaid in the layers of silicon. I like the idea that we leave traces... The arrangement of atoms along the intertwined trails of writing traces the diagram of our love. We are our own code, we are symbols, and those I meet can read that in my appearance.

I walk, slightly hunched, shoulders round. A dull, black cape envelopes me, held at the collar by a magnetic clasp that opens with a brush of the hand. Beneath the cape, I wear an old-fashioned aviator jumpsuit, encrusted with compasses and altimeters, needles vibrating in time with my footsteps. My face is bare; a touch of frost in my hair, a sliver of celestial blue in my pupils. Nothing more.

The tube station opens under Lou's ziggurat. My heartbeat is double what it usually is, relayed by the pumps. The glass elevator carries me up to the last floor as slowly as if I were falling.

The interior of the pyramid is partially hollow. An equatorial forest fills the center, flat trees arranged in a trompe-l'œil along the sides. Drops of rain splash soundlessly against the transparent walls. A rainbow sparkles at the end of the watering heads. A flock of multi-colored birds, hanging from threads, slides along triangles embedded in the canopy, following unwavering curves. I glide into the middle of them, a prisoner of my own trajectory, and I murmur Lou's name while moistening my lips.

Before crossing the threshold into the reception

room, I straighten my shoulders, and undo my cape, which slips to my feet.

My wings unfurl.

I wanted them to be white. Silky. Immense. The support structure takes up almost my entire back, from the top to my hips. They're so vast that their weight drags me backward and the tips of the feathers caress the hollows of my knees. I find it hard to walk when the wind opens them, my heart struggles with the need to irrigate the tissues that keep them deployed, but the effect is marvelous. I know, without needing to check my hand mirror, that the light from the electric arcs wreathes me with an immaculate halo.

The doors open on Lou and the expression on her face is everything I could have desired.

Two months without seeing one another... The last messages were digital transcripts of our murmurs, our sighs. During my convalescence, the loudspeakers in my room broadcast all of the scents of her vivid voice without stop. The words she sent me echoed off sterile walls. I imagined Lou without her lace and I closed my eyes to hasten the healing.

I should have known that she would change too. Sixty days is a long time for the clocks that govern us. The lace has disappeared, her skin is completely covered with digital mirrors the size of fingernails. The image is constantly transforming: some mirrors grow transparent, revealing a shard of skin that the next change covers with a reflection. My eyes grow exhausted trying to reconstruct an image of her. She stretches with a smile, shies away when I try to pull her toward me. We play for a moment on the threshold, me opening the wings of my desire to their fullest, Lou offering herself in pieces before her fingers grasp the chest loop on my aviator jumpsuit. With a kiss, she draws me inside.

I don't recognize any of the guests. I note several breasts based on Ni-Anne's model, but she hasn't bothered to come. My wings cause a stir and I advance through a series of murmurs. Lou takes my arm; on her skin, the number of transparent mirrors has increased significantly.

I have to walk slowly, my back arched to the utmost. Incapable of dancing, I allow my wings to keep time as Lou's fingers dwell on the fine synthetic down between my shoulder blades. I feel others touching me furtively. Someone offers me a glass filled with a constellation of icy stars; anonymous fingers hand me canapés covered with cream and caress my lips fleetingly. A spray of fluorescent pink liquid splatters on me, drops slipping along the surface of my feathers and sparkling under the spotlights before falling to the carpet. I'm impervious to criticism.

The *party* looks like any other party, but Lou has selected a theme in her own image. Floating mirrors follow the movements of a guest selected at random and increase before focusing on another. The dancers, shown in mirrors, observe one another rather than touching, preoccupied with their own reflections. Celebrity is fleeting, the resulting anonymity is inevitable.

The success of my wings has raised me above the fray. When I look up at the reflective ceiling, I see nothing more than a white triangle gliding like a swan in the midst of indistinct silhouettes. I savor the pleasure of being at the heart of the whirlpool once again. My heart races and the heavy fabric of flesh and feathers that extends my back swells in unison. Wings spread, I take her into my arms and delicately place my lips against her eyelids, the only part of her face that is naked of mirrors. I close my eyes, not wanting to feel as if I'm kissing myself.

The eyes of the guests focus on us like spotlights. Their burning glances are so pleasant that I prolong the kiss without noticing.

"Will you accompany me out onto the terrace?" Lou murmurs in my ear.

I must not have responded quickly enough since she punches me cruelly on the neck, at the roots of the first feathers. My down stands up.

"A little early, isn't it? I've just arrived and I don't know anyone apart from you…"

She bites her lips.

"It's *my* party!"

"I know, I'm just teasing you."

Seeing the glare of her eyes, I rush to add, "Ni-Anne will be furious with herself for not coming! I'm with you."

At the top of about a dozen or so steps, the staircase opens onto the sky.

The terrace is covered by a transparent dome supported by eight metal arches spreading like the legs or a gigantic spider. When the rays of the sun strike the dome directly, iridescent waves spread over the glass surface. Along the western edge, a green and brown forest of bamboo trees sway in the breeze of the giant air conditioners.

"There's a clearing," says Lou. "I'll push away the stems to make room for your wings."

"Is that an invitation?"

I place my hand on her hip; a kiss has become inevitable. The sun is still high and our shadows mingle deliciously. Appearances… I close my eyes, to avoid seeing them, but the weight of my wings is there to remind me that everyone knows my secret now.

When we separate, slightly out of breath, she pulls me toward the bamboo curtain. A few steps and the knotty poles hide us from everyone.

One after another, Lou's mirrors deactivate. A wave of flesh slowly descends from her cheeks to her thighs. Bit by bit, my image is replaced by hers, a primitive composition where the carmine of old scars mingles with the artificial brown of UV lights. A body without a message, a face without a mask. *Lou.*

She hunkers down on her heels and looks up at me. The aviator jumpsuit scatters on the foam. Naked, I spread my arms. The regular breeze that bends the bamboo trees sweeps my hair back. I crumple a leaf between my fingers, lift it to my nose, before releasing it, in an attempt to measure the speed of the wind. Sometimes, being lighter than your own thoughts is all that's needed to take flight.

I no longer feel the weight of my wings. With a shrug of my shoulders, I catch an updraft. Unused muscles wake; I hop without noticing it, ready to leap into the patch of sky, up to the cornerstone of the dome. My heart stampedes, roaring like a river about to burst its banks. Irrigated to the maximum, the transplanted tissues draw on all my blood reserves in their desire to defy gravity.

The breeze from the fans envelopes me…

Just as I'm about to dash forward, Lou's hand slides up my thigh and grabs me.

Immobilized on the edge of the dream, unable to tear myself away, I no longer understand what's happening to me. Lou's fingers on my genitals have triggered a reflexive erection, the intensity mirrored by the pain it gives me. Sparks whirl before my eyes, as I stare at the inaccessible sun.

The blood floods into my upright penis and my

wings sag. The fragile balance of my blood pressure collapses. The auxiliary pumps in my back tip into overload, then wisely abandon their role. Inside my chest, next to my heart, I hear the sound of valves closing.

As the wind whistles through the tops of the bamboo trees, my wings crumple. The flaccid tissues have lost their breadth; they hang in tatters along my naked back. The tousled feathers fall, the weight of my appearance is overwhelming. I drain internally through a thousand secret wounds.

I look down. Lou's mirrors, once again opaque, reflect the sky. Her smile disappears under a spray of clouds that stretches to her temples. Despite the murmured reproaches of the wind, I hear the echoes of the party, one floor down, and the frightening tick-tock of my own internal clock. For the first time ever, I tasted the sky and preceded the inexorable wave of fashion. There will never be another moment like that one.

Lou is waiting, her hand still on me, hips moving in time with an imperceptible swell. With a shrug, I throw my useless wings back and allow myself to fall toward the sea she is offering me.

DECLARING PEACE

Alice cuts through the battlefield on her way to the market. All around her, thousands of droids face off with laser and sonic weapons along the folds in the land. Trenches and biodegradable bunkers dot the landscape as far as the border. The shooting stops as she approaches, while the neuron networks of the metal combatants hastily reconfigure to develop new strategies taking her presence into account. The noise of the artillery drops to avoid injuring her ear drums.

At reduced volume, each burst of automatic fire sounds like birds' chirping.

As she makes her way through the shooting, Alice runs over her shopping list in her mind. Leeks. Some bacon and cream. A dozen eggs, maybe more if she has to bake a birthday cake for her nephew. The ground is crumbly beneath her feet, plowed by the burrowing machines that bury themselves to avoid attacks. Soon it will be sowing season and the war will move to other territories where it won't bother anyone.

The first houses in the village are decked with multicolored flags copied from old atlases or simply made up. Large, severe letters at the top of the sign indicating the upcoming end of hostilities provide a warning: *Do not disturb the conflict.* At the outset, the village children enjoyed running about in the middle of the battles, turning and twisting abruptly, driving the droids crazy. One got injured; the blacksmith's son twisted his ankle jumping over a burrower. The parents put an end to all that soon afterwards. The game had quickly stopped being fun in any case and war never was.

At the entrance to the grocery store, animated signs indicate the score in real time. The numbers never change much and the losses are already enormous on both sides. Alice pushes the door, lowering her head to avoid the hand-crafted chimes that ring in her ears. The metal tubes were cut from the barrels of old, long-range rifles, then trimmed and drilled to produce pleasant sounds. Several models are available in the village shops. Tourists like them. The chimes remind people of a time when there was something artisanal, something manual about war.

"You're going to make a quiche?"

Alice and the grocer went to school together, forty years earlier. The two women are friends. In any case, everyone in the village knows everyone else. Nothing terribly interesting ever happens there. Everyone is even tired of the war. So, people take an interest in what others are doing. That's just human nature.

Bit by bit, the chimes fall silent, replaced by chatting. The women trade recipes, frowning when shots from the sonic artillery shake the double-glazed windows. When the battlefield was set up, subsidies were provided for a variety of projects: a party hall, a pristine war memorial, soundproofing devices for nearby residents. Things that aren't really useful but appreciated nevertheless.

"I hear your son wants to sign up?" asks Alice, carefully placing the eggs in her bag.

"He loves that stuff. Aviation, flying drones. It seems he has a gift for it."

"How old is he now? Ten?"

"You've got to be kidding me! Didi turned eleven a month ago. Don't you dare say he looks younger. He hates that. Look at him!"

With a wave of her hand, the shopkeeper designates the square. A flock of children are playing battleships in the circular basin, making torpedo sounds with their mouths. The first dead leaves are spinning on the surface of the water. Didi is one of the tallest. He is busy consoling a little girl whose brand-new aircraft carrier has traveled too far from the edge. The blazer of his school uniform is decorated with gold medals that shine in the sun as he attempts to bring the wayward ship back within reach.

"You should go and help him," says Alice. "I bet he's going to fall in."

"It's not all that cold yet... and if I get involved in his love affairs, he'll sulk."

"I'll take another leek from you. This one (she twirls it like a sword) is a tad withered. I like to keep the green parts to make soup."

"I have chard from the garden if you want some."

Alice nods, her head filled with the recipes for the week. David, her husband, will be home soon. He'll do the cooking this evening. He has a heavy hand with spices, like all men. With him, you never know what you're eating, or what he's thinking. She's used to that. No reason for fighting.

She looks over at the shelves with their stacks of fashion magazines from the previous month, canned goods, and dusty souvenirs. The tourists have abandoned the area. There's really no point in coming out for a close-up look at the conflict, now almost all of the forces have dug in. Yet Alice knows a rosary of low-orbit satellites overhead is observing the battle zone. There are zooms, slow-mos, commentators to highlight this or that strategic finesse, *ad nauseam.* For many spectators, the war in the field next door is a serious matter. The same can be said for those who designed the sophisticated weapons fighting to the death or for children like Didi who dream of piloting drones above the scrum. She decides she must keep that in mind and promises not to disturb the combat zone on her way home, leeks peeking out of her bag like miniature rocket launchers.

"Do you need anything else?"

Alice shakes her head. She makes the most of a lull in the fighting to take her leave, blocking the chimes with her hand on her way out. The square is almost as noisy as the battlefield, but filled with laughter, not shots. The rare manifestations of unpleasant behaviors are swept away by the conditioning each child receives as soon as they learn to walk.

For adults like Alice, the situation is more complicated. The conditioning doesn't work well. Conflicts are still a component of their lives, even if they have implemented countermeasures to prevent injuries or suffering. There are social rules, ways to manage your relationship or your family. Sometimes you just have to get away from it all. David went away to spend a week in a community of single men. He let off pressure, slept in a dorm, shared male pheromones to a sickening degree. Then he asked if he could come home.

If nothing else, war teaches peacekeeping strategies. Just like the quiche she'll prepare for him tomorrow. David likes to watch as she furiously beats the eggs and chops the leeks, chard and onions with a steady hand. It's a completely tolerable form of violence, as long as you place the knife in the dishwasher as soon as you're done.

Didi has recovered the aircraft carrier using a branch and received an awkward kiss for his efforts. Alice greets him with an approving nod, then heads to the dry goods store to buy some wool. The brand-new war memorial, shaped like a pyramid, is displaying a hologram list of the names and brands of the AI robots destroyed during the current conflict. Names, including her family's, were engraved on the former, a granite monument between two incredibly ugly statues, eaten by green moss and remorse. Alice does not miss it. She merely walks past the new one, without pausing.

The wind carries the scent of freshly turned soil, the odor of plowing, of an open tomb. She shakes her head to chase away the depressing thoughts threatening to seep into her mind. David will be back soon.

"Some fairly fine burgundy wool, if you have some. And No. 3 double-pointed needles. I broke one. I'm making socks."

The shopkeeper is used to this. For thirty years, Alice has been coming to her long, narrow shop, filled with handkerchiefs, threads and skeins arranged by color, and perennially fashionable underwear, and the woman has never seemed surprised by her requests. Of course, Alice has never made any unusual requests. That's not her style. Would an unreasonable demand be considered an attack. She doesn't think so, but she's never wanted to take the chance.

"I haven't seen David in quite some time," says the shopkeeper. "Have you…"

"He's coming home this evening. He's away training."

Alice examines the skeins piled in wooden pigeon-holes that smell of polish and cedar. Placing the shopping bag on the floor, she forces her shoulders to relax.

"How many do you need?"

"He's got big feet. I'll take three skeins to make two pairs of socks with reinforced heels. And I'll keep what's left for me. If there's anything left, that is!"

The shopkeeper moves to Alice's side and picks up two balls of wool the color of old wine, and hands them to her customer to let her choose.

"Training for what?"

"Oh, you know…" (Alice pastes a tired smile on her face, one that generally earns her the sympathy of those around her. A ceasefire smile.) "Men aren't like we are."

The shopkeeper's partner doesn't live with her. He has his own store, selling seeds and fertilizer, at the other end of the village. They have a solid relationship and have never raised their voices in public. Alice does not envy them.

"The war will be over soon," she adds, paying for her purchases.

"Until the next one starts," adds the shopkeeper, in keeping with the ritual. "If you run short of wool come back fairly quickly. I have a few skeins from the same dye lot, but they won't last long. When peace returns, everyone starts knitting."

And she adds, insidiously, "Babies are on the way."

Alice does not rise to the bait. With some people, each encounter is a border skirmish. There is no tinkling of chimes as she leaves, just the squeaking of door hinges. She welcomes the deep rumble of the battle. *I wonder if I'll miss it,* she thinks before heading for home. She knows the answer but hesitates to say it out loud.

The children have scattered like sparrows, forming another group, farther off, to play another game. From where she stands, Alice cannot really see what they are doing. She sees them run together into collective hugs before separating, laughing. Like David and her, in their too large bed, where their problems seem to vanish when they are rubbed with enough energy.

The shopping bag bangs against her calves; The eggs are packed carefully between the wool and the needles. David is coming home this evening. The truce between them will soon transform into an armed peace, then routine coexistence while the battlefield moves away to other peaceful villages where ordinary people dwell. She must write her own story, without losing sight of what she is, what she wants. That's not easy because she has forgotten all that, between the baby that never came, the words left unspoken, and the stormy silences. The eradication of the war has deprived her of the opportunity to truly fight. She has learned to promise, to compromise.

With a resolute step, she heads toward the conflict.

She's forgotten her resolution to bypass the battlefield. When she enters the zone plowed by the shots, she stamps her foot to make the machines move away. Perhaps the satellites will detect her presence, perhaps they won't. She's used to being invisible.

David, in any case, will know where she is. He has a gift for that. Even a war won't protect her from his desire to make peace. She looks enviously at the buried bunkers, but none of them has an opening her size. Only the youngest children are capable of sneaking in. And those that have tried have never remained there long.

Ringed machines meander a few meters ahead of her, spitting out gases with an acidic aftertaste. When they burrow, the soil rises up in large blackish clumps, streaked with terrified earth worms twisting in all directions. Her skirt is stained, the hem has started to fray. She will have to change before David gets home. To wash, to dilute the odor of the battle.

Just thinking about it exhausts her.

Shading her eyes with her hand, she stands on tiptoe to study the battlefront. It stretches over 30 km, or so people say. A dozen or so farms, two streams and woods. A great many hiding places she explored many years earlier, before the conditioning. When people really believed in what they were doing, in the battles fought at dawn or dusk, with slingshots and blowpipes. People got injured; they learned to heal. David did not exist back then. His family came later, to work in the old mine. He left to study. He left for the city, then came back. For her, or so he told her. But she has never been certain she was the only one he said that to.

She is the one who believed him, the one he married. So, it must be true.

She moves closer to the bunkers, as a cloud of drones flies over her, before turning left. The soil vibrates dully with each step she takes. A dozen tiny remote-controlled tanks, caterpillar tracks bristling with spikes and drill bits are attempting to scale the reinforced concrete domes. They support one another, provide assistance when one slips. They look much like Didier and his friends, only less noisy.

Fascinated, Alice watches them skin the closest bunker. Echoing her mood, the ringed killers surge from the soil around her, throwing themselves on one another, screeching. Shards of metal torn off by mechanical jaws are projected into the sky. A dark, sticky fluid oozes from the shredded bodies, which are immediately replaced by others, just as voracious. The cloud of drones has turned about and is gliding over the scene. The black soil is swarming with vicious machines, driven by the desire to destroy.

The noise grows deafening. No victory cries, just the dying laments of metal that twists before giving way. Machines explode, splattering their entrails of silicon and gears. The dust and ashes swirling in time with the explosions cast a veil over the afternoon light. The start of a nuclear winter with Alice at the epicenter.

A dry crack at her feet. Three of her eggs have just

split open. She will have to go back to the grocery store. Thick, sticky egg yolk is running over her skeins of wool. Without noticing, Alice starts to cry. She feels as if her soul reflects the scene surrounding her. Unable to move, she waits for things to grow calm, but the entire landscape seems to be caught up in a mad frenzy. The cadavers of older machines, tortured before being destroyed, spill from deep cracks around the bunker. Some bear the red logos of maintenance units, the ones that plug metal injuries and replace lost fluids for better or for worse.

Terrified, Alice looks for a way out of the chaos. In vain. The village is no more than a few hundred meters away, but it might just as well be on a different planet. A film of oily dust has coated her leeks, her clothing is splattered with rust. An amputated arm rolls to her feet, hitting the shopping bag, with just enough force to turn it over. The machine it comes from is dying just a few feet away, in a seemingly endless fountain of oil. The panting of the servomotors is interspersed with plaintiff grinding, which gradually fades.

Nearby, its adversary is already dead.

This war is no longer a game, an abstract simulation in which the sound can be turned off when it is viewed on a screen. It's a torrent of hatred and mud that carries everything off along its way. Alice coughs in the acidic clouds spewing from the bunker. Yet, the fragile island of soil on which she perches has been spared from the attacks. Apart from her shopping bag. She could take a step back, then another, and the machines would let her pass. That's the law. She's not part of the conflict in progress. But she can't just step back. When you're that close to a massacre, you're no longer a spectator.

She waves her arms to make everything stop, but her gestures have no effect. The indifferent machines have neither voices nor listening devices. They continue to destroy one another, obstinately, viciously, crawling over the gutted corpses of their allies in search of new adversaries. Until they finally come to a halt, with a dying screech, and others take their place.

"Where are you, David?" Alice murmurs, wiping away her tears.

She digs into her shopping bag, brandishes the No. 3 knitting needles smeared with coagulated egg yolk and bits of shell. They're ridiculous as far as weapons go, but she has nothing else. Pointing them away from herself gives her the strength to stand up. To shout out accusations and regrets in the face of the fighting. To curse the war, David, her own powerlessness, her inability to say what she really feels. What she wants.

She stops when her irritated throat is incapable of uttering a single other sound.

Paying no attention to the bag, she turns about, throws the knitting needles away and hears them tinkle weakly against a gutted shell. The conflict has calmed somewhat, the wind has swept the dust clouds away, and the sun is shining timidly. Overhead, the drones vanish on their way to other, warmer zones. The war is not over; it never will be. But a fragile peace gradually settles around Alice.

It's a fleeting sentiment. The war, no matter what form it takes, will always be with her. She has no choice but to continue on her way home, hands and heart empty. Sentences form in her mind, punctuated by distant artillery shots. These are things she has kept silent for a long time. She savors the taste on her tongue, she bites into them with all her might, while waiting to spit them out. David may already be at home, waiting for her, in his favorite armchair, shaped and hollowed by his large body.

She will greet him, accept his embrace without shying away. She will prepare tea, unless he has already taken care of that. He often makes tea. She has to give him that.

And she will speak to him. About the quiche that won't be ready, the skeins of wool abandoned on the battlefield. About her desires, her frustrations, those damn moments when she feels like hitting him until he falls down. Or leaves.

Depending on what he answers, the discussion may be brief or last all night long. Depending on what she's able to admit, the abscess will either drain or it won't. Some wounds will be cauterized; others will continue to bleed. She only knows her own but David has wounds as well, ones he never mentions. If he persists in his silence, she will take him to the battlefield and stay there with him until the blind violence of the war envelops and purifies them. Perhaps she will be able to find her bag in the rubble. Save what can be saved.

If they survive the challenge, they'll talk again. To continue repairing the world at their level, one discussion at a time.

TROJAN FLOWERS

This one is for me…

The diamond in the palm of my hand is as big as an orange. Traces of impurities in the heart of the gem form a milky constellation which the evening light tints purple. All on its own, it's worth a year of peace.

With a sigh, I throw it into the incinerator and pick up another. I don't want to take any chances. The asteroid has been destroyed and the flowers reduced to atomic dust scattered throughout the void. I destroyed the link that connected us to the invasion with my own hands. As far as I know, there is no longer any danger to the world.

But I've lost Moira.

This is a story of failure and, as such, it's rather messy. Successes can always be presented as the result of a plan, painstakingly devised and executed. Catastrophes, on the other hand, are delivered in bulk; they are the debris of a filthy, broken plate that no one bothers to glue back together. If there was initially a reason, it's been lost.

Here's the big picture of the disaster.

We'd been arguing for several days, Moira and I. Even our attempt at reconciling in bed, the night before, had only been a partial success. We know one another too well to be awkward; we no longer know how to be unexpected. And the differences in our rhythms don't make matters any better. There's nothing particularly exciting about the prospect of eating breakfast together—not for her or for me—but I don't see any way around it.

Without bothering to get dressed, Moira puts on the connection tiara, which immediately starts flickering when contact is made with the trodes at her temples. A constellation of waiting lights dances on the metal ribbon. Thighs spread, vagina still damp, she plunges into the ocean of messages that wait for her. I run my eyes along her belly. Dizziness sweeps over me: the symmetry of her curves and hollows is broken by a poignant patch of disorderly beauty spots, which I am incapable of analyzing.

I look away from her mystery and start setting the table. In the monochrome ceramic fruit bowl, wax fruits, all identical, have long since replaced the sweet-smelling apples I love.

"Where's my cereal," I grumble, standing in front of the almost empty pantry.

I have to repeat the question twice, before she exits the flow and answers me. Her eyes focus on me with difficulty.

"I've simplified things," she says in her deep voice, syllables dragging. "One single variety of everything. That way, I don't have to make a choice."

"And what about me?"

"You're too complicated as well!"

Her voice fades in the infrasound, as she plunges back into the digital ocean.

For several months now, she's been slowing her body rhythms, inasmuch as the trodes implanted in her cortex allow her to. Her voice has dropped almost an octave. At first, I found it sexy… Now, I lose patience when I have to deal with her slowness.

I place a half-filled bowl before her, waving my fingers in front of her face to let her know the meal is ready.

174

She starts to eat, mechanically, as she continues to stare at an invisible horizon, beyond my reach.

"Will you be here when I get back?"

But, even before I ask my question, I know she won't bother to answer.

This has been going on for a year. My last mining expedition to the asteroid belt was quite the success. I now have the wherewithal to live half my life doing nothing other than going where the wind wills. Moira no longer bothers to leave the house. The main room, which looks out over the ocean, has a multiplex link to the network, from which it is possible to open private shunts to the principal points of access to alternative realities. There is also a beach nearby, rocks sculpted by fractal machines to give them a more natural look. But Moira has never enjoyed swimming in a real ocean. Too many unpredictable currents.

When I first met her, she was spending almost all her time in virtual communities with interests similar to hers. That's probably where she acquired her unhealthy need for essentials. Then she tired of people and moved on to Artificial Intelligences; she found their icy objectivity stimulating after the erratic behaviors of her network contacts. During that time, we worked together to raise and enrich an intelligence in isolation. We nourished it with our passionate debates, our conflicts—embryonic AIs need wars in order to develop, just like civilizations—until it managed to construct a stable personality, after which it no longer owed us anything.

I eventually released it into the digital ocean once it had become too complex to survive in the household data aquarium. By that time, Moira had already turned away from AIs to plunge into the purified reality of simulation suppliers; she didn't notice a thing.

With a clink, Moira places her spoon in the empty bowl. A drop of milk has pearled at the corner of her mouth. I know that it will stay there all day, that I'll find the dried trace on her lips when I come home, unless I remove it with a kiss. So, I kiss her. Her eyelids flutter for a second, before closing again.

Her mobile face, animated by the quivering of the connection tiara, remains a marvelous mystery. The only one left to me.

Outside, the sky is as monochrome and flat as a background display. Dirigibles in stationary flight punctuate a heavenly canopy formed of dead pixels. On the horizon, the distant thread of the space elevator fades into the clouds, dividing the sky. Moira and I each have our half of the world and the crack that separates us is no thicker than a hair, as long as we don't get too close.

I walk straight ahead, eyes riveted on the elevator, neck straining with the effort to see to the very end, where the sky routes start. Teardrop-shaped vehicles slide overhead, rustling like facial tissues. Everyone but me seems to have a destination in mind, an emergency to deal with. I no longer miss that.

My brain analyzes every face I see on my way, breaking it down into elementary blocks and primary cubes, then immediately forgets it. I no longer pay attention. It was something illegal, a dirty little secret that made my fortune as a prospector and now forces me to look at the world like a cubist artist.

Five years ago, our embryonic AI helped me cultivate a web of undifferentiated neural cells, organized into a shape recognition network. I stimulated their motor-neural differentiation by means of a cocktail of complex substances taken from my own biology. Then I found a black-market laboratory to implant them in me, directly through the dura mater.

The entire procedure took only a few minutes but it changed my life forever. For the neurologist who performed the operation, late at night, in the sterile environment of a white room with chrome reflections, it was an opportunity to grow his off-shore account a tad. For me, eyelids held open by clamps, it was a plunge into my own psyche, by way of a fine, super-compressed, carbon mesh, that dug slowly into my skull.

When everything goes well, the injected cells adhere to the outer layer of the primary visual cortex and stimulate the growth of axons from the endogenous motor-neurons. The network is duplicated in the neurons, reinforcing the local brain functions. In my case, I was a little too lucky. The graft multiplied; it colonized the dorsal thalamus, where the information transmitted from the optical nerve winds up. My vision didn't change, but my way of looking at things did. The world gradually took shape, slowly, inexorably. I can find the tracks of buried shells in the way in which grains of sand are arranged on a beach. I know where secrets are hidden. When you examine thousands of asteroids looking for nodules of rare metals, or crystalline structures that can be mined, this is a priceless gift.

Yet, I pay dearly for it on a daily basis, in the worst way imaginable: by looking at you. My brain breaks every face down into a pile of simplified volumes, like an Arcimboldo playing with Plato's solids. For me, the profile of each woman is made of toy cubes and foam balls. I read their features like a house of cards.

Humans have lost their mystery for me. All except

Moira, that is. Her asymmetrical, constantly moving face is different. There is something fractal about her beauty, folded in on itself, which makes me want to look at it without stopping. She is the anchor that holds me to the Earth.

I walk until my eyes hurt, then force myself to continue on to the sea. The pedestrian boulevard is packed with Analogs crossing through the crowd like drops of mercury, processes fixed on the task to be performed. Most are naked, their androgynous shapes barely defined by a coarse three-dimensional mesh. The computing time required to produce clothes is prohibitive and the companies that create them are cutting back on all expenses. Some don't even have avoidance algorithms and lose their shape as I approach, only to fit back together behind my back. I come across a few agoraphobic avatars, enveloped in blurry bubbles that prevent me from knowing who's hiding inside. I feel their avid eyes grasp at me, but I walk too quickly for their bubbles to have the opportunity to interfere with the invisible one that surrounds me.

Maybe Moira's right, with her need to simplify the world. There's no lack of evidence. It's willpower I don't have. Even the love I feel for her is just a form of obsession. It makes our break-ups painfully useless.

When I get back, Moira is gone. She has left me a message, clumsy letters sparkling on the immaculate walls. She's been considering submersion in a simplified reality for several months. The coordinates of the sleep farm she's selected are not indicated, to keep me from temptation.

She doesn't want me to accompany her. Just to be there when she leaves.

I make a secured call to Jo-Andra and wait.

Love stories cannot be analyzed. They have to be lived from within. Passions last as long as the fragmented scenes of the two protagonists coincide. When the puzzle under construction shows two unrelated images, it's time to leave.

I don't love Moira, I know that; I understand her too little. But the mystery she represents obsesses me. If I have to give her up, I'll always be missing the answer—as well as the question for it. The world will have become a little more monotonous.

Jo-Andra calls me back fifteen minutes later. I knew he'd find her. He underwent the same sort of procedure I had, in order to reinforce his ability to manipulate abstract data. It helps him navigate at the fringes of the network, where the digital sharks lurk. He can pilot any shuttle in the middle of the microgravity rays of the asteroid belts, brushing up against them so closely the collision alarms don't even have the time to warn him. Plus, the bastard loves it!

"She has a connection reserved at *Simplex*," he announces, wasting no time on small talk. "Twenty-eight complete weeks, starting this evening, total immersion. I've sent you the coordinates in case you want to take a look."

I grumble a vague acknowledgement.

He interrupts, "I hate to tell you this, buddy, but you're going to have to break off with her this time…"

"It's that bad?"

"Quite the opposite, it's the ultimate. *Simplex* has leading-edge equipment, and clients with the means to demand the best, even if it's barely legal, as in this case.

179

They have an ironclad reputation."

"So, what's the problem?"

"You remember your little depression five years ago? You wanted to fly to the fringes of the Oort cloud, with ridiculously small chances of coming back. I had to knock you about to convince you to give up the project. My fingers still feel it."

That was a subject we'd agreed never to discuss again.

"What type of craft did you choose?" he adds.

The obviousness of it all is blinding.

"The best... I took the best."

Silence at the other end. I wonder if Jo-Andra has broken the connections, then I hear a weary voice murmur, "It was also the most expensive. Check your bank accounts; she may have cleaned you out for her little immersion."

A flurry of static and the connection is broken. Jo-Andra doesn't see any point in talking when he has no information to provide. I pick up the forgotten connection tiara from a cushion and twirl it mechanically around my fingertip. Moira abandoned it without thinking, like she always does when something no longer interests her. I come last on her list.

When she calls me, six hours later, I don't even try to negotiate an extension. Her flow has slowed even further; her dragging voice seems to be coated in dust, as if our words of love were eroding in her throat. She refuses to tell me where she will be going to sleep, but transmits the encrypted coordinates of the rendezvous point to my taxi's memory. I don't tell her that I already have them, and have chosen not to use them.

I can feel the cameras on me as I get out of the

vehicle's passenger compartment. Even before the payment chip embedded under my thumbnail approves the transaction, the taxi transmits all of my data to the house's digital terminal. It's legal and I should never even have been informed. But the security department at *Simplex* is playing at transparency—a demonstration of arrogance that corroborates the information Jo-Andra gave me.

The neighborhood is discreetly posh. The streets with their broad sidewalks are bordered by magnificent trees, fallen leaves carefully raked up and placed in compost bins. Each building is surrounded by a small wall, topped with pointed structures—ceramic imitating metal—most decorated with hand-painted rust red flecks.

The taxi disappears as soon as I turn my back on it. I head over to the *Simplex* entrance, unconcerned about the image the scanners steal from me. The décor is nothing more than a simple stack of cubes embedded in other cubes, a handful of costly toys I don't even feel like breaking.

This is not a place for me. Not for Moira either.

At the entrance, a long, beige corridor, without the slightest decoration, broadens into a rounded lounge, with a skylight in the ceiling. Behind the reception desk, a brunette in a severe suit subvocalizes data. Her tiara is decorated with a spray of milky pearls. The virtual screen that dances before her eyes is invisible to me, but the movement of her pupils reveals its presence.

She stops as I walk over and smiles at me—the standard version: *I know who you are and you know what we sell.*

"My friend has reserved a 28-week connection." (I give her Moira's coordinates.) "I'd like to attend her immersion."

"Are you her legal representative?"

"She doesn't need one as far as I know. No, I'm just a friend."

The girl looks down, frowning. The tiara must be projecting the most revealing elements of my biography on her retina. No reason to worry; Jo-Andra helped me smooth all the rough edges the last time we came back from an expedition. I may have nothing to hide, but the interpretations of the raw data that makes up my life, depend on the moods of those scrutinizing me. By eliminating my share of ambiguity, I reduce the risk of being misunderstood.

"I don't know if I can..." she starts, but a virile voice behind me cuts her off.

"I'll take over. The gentleman is expected."

The receptionist's smile wavers for a moment, and then she toggles back into sensory isolation mode. I no longer exist in her eyes, other than as a remnant image embedded in the background of her vision.

"Markus Loekhen," say the newcomer, a blond with a square jaw that looks as if it has been carved out of a block of pink granite. "I monitor the sleepers in long-term immersion. Your friend is being prepared; she left the medical unit ten minutes ago."

He holds his thumb out to me so we can exchange our data and become digital blood brothers, then waves his fingers in front of a scanner that juts out from the wall. An elevator door opens before us.

"I suggest a preliminary visit of the facilities. You'll see that everything possible has been done to ensure our clients' safety."

"Moira is waiting for me."

Loekhen clenches his jaw, then smiles.

"You'll only see her at the last minute." (He raises his hand to stop my protests.) "At her request."

"Shit, she's going to be immersed for 28 weeks!"

"Much longer than that in relative time. She's been slowing her brain rhythm for months to prepare for immersion in the reality we've created for her. We'll be able to accelerate the simulation significantly."

"The risks…"

"Are negligible. Your friend has taken out a particularly large amount of insurance coverage and we don't intend to let her use it. You're the beneficiary. I presume she told you that? When everything's done, we'll need your signature."

The lights in the elevator start their countdown. I observe Loekhen's profile, reflected in a chrome-edged mirror. As he speaks, his features lose their identity; my brain is breaking it down into simple elements and the result is so coarse that I shiver.

The file Jo-Andra sent me listed the various rates for the services offered by *Simplex*. I stored the information in one of the antememories in my skull, in case I needed to consult it. Some of the figures were mind-boggling. After our conversation, I checked all of my accounts. Nothing had moved. Moira hadn't touched a single one of my credit lines. I'm as rich as I ever was and she has still managed to give herself the best.

When the door slides open with a silvery tinkle; a puff of icy air invades the elevator. The odor is astringent, vaguely chemical. I wrinkle my nose… No doubt, an unscented broad-spectrum disinfectant.

The building's basement is filled with star-shaped caves, with rough concrete walls, encrusted with metallic panels. Traces of tracks are still visible on the tiled floor. It brings to mind the old, abandoned maglev tunnels. My thoughts must be visible on my face since Loekhen casually shrugs.

"Once they're connected, people could care less about the décor; all that counts is the memory flows. No point wasting money on carpeting. This way."

His handmade leather shoes squeak on the tiles. He waves a finger in front of the optical slot and the metal panel disappears into the ceiling. On the other side, there are six translucent tanks, barely larger than coffins, connected to an octopus-shaped feeding apparatus. A crown of greenish eyes accentuates the resemblance.

"Your friend will occupy No. 5. She's being prepared, in the sterile room. Are you familiar with the procedure?"

I nod. The information is available in the flow Jo-Andra sent me, but there's nothing better than a hands-on approach. When you live in telepresence, reality loses its solidity. I feel as if my soul is numb, as if my nerves have been rubbed with sandpaper until the pain became abstract.

"She will be fed, probed, and monitored by tubes; we also insert self-closing silicone rings everywhere where the rubbing could cause sores: esophagus, nostrils, and anus. However, the prosthesis that covers the vaginal and peri-anal zone is controlled directly by the data flow from the simulation. We use only the best flow. The bubbles are filled with neutral gel; the temperature of the gel varies according to the simulation in which she will be immersed. The feeling of rain on the skin is particularly realistic, even in slow immersion, which is what your friend wanted."

"How slow?" (I feel the sweat roll down my back.) "She didn't mention that to me."

"By a factor of eight... We've prepared four years of simplified dreams for her. It's a first for us. Moreover, she's given us permission to collect all of her psychological data during the entire immersion."

"Is that how she was able to afford your services?"

"Are you kidding? If all you had to do to get an immersion would be to serve as a guinea pig, volunteers would be lined up across town!"

"So, how did she pay you?"

"If she had wanted you to know that, she would have told you…"

Loekhen bends over the tank and dips his index finger in the translucent gel that fills it three-quarters of the way up. Then he brushes my face with a caress so quick I think I've dreamed it. Automatically, I raise my hand to my face. I feel nothing; a slight numbness, maybe.

"We simplify things… That's our secret. The only sensations your friend will receive will come from the simulation she has chosen. No surprises, good or bad, no background pain. She'll be like a pearl inside an oyster."

A drop of condensation falls on the tiles, near his left foot. I look up. Conduits crisscross the ceiling, barely illuminated by the standby lights.

Bit by bit, lights spread within the bubble. Light reflections dance on Loekhen's hands, transforming them into pieces of raw meat. He tilts his head, listening to a message relayed by his implants:

"Your friend won't be long."

A hospital cart appears in the corridor behind us, with a hissing sound. The tray is covered with sterile tubes wound around spools, each one a different color and diameter. A second cart arrives immediately after that. Moira, body covered with an immaculate sheet, head wrapped in an opaque film, lies on top of it.

When she steps off it, supported by a uniformed nurse, I rush to help her. She smiles when she sees me and leans against my arm —a gesture so familiar that I have the impression, just for a second, that everything is going to rewind and we will once again be what we used to be. Then the sheet slips and I discover that all of her hair has been removed. She follows my glance, shrugs, and murmurs in a voice thickened by neuroleptics, "Be careful where you place your fingers; an anesthetic cream has been applied wherever the connections will be placed."

She shivers, mechanically, as the carts leave, clicking on the rails embedded in the tiles.

"I didn't have the courage to talk to you about this before," she added, walking over to the bubble reserved for her. "It's better like this."

"For you or for me?"

She stands still and looks at me, really looks at me. Under the cap that encases her skull, her hair has disappeared, replaced by protruding, high-speed trodes through which the simulation will seep into her mind, until it reaches the drowning point.

"I really like the way you always looked me in the eye, you know?" (She raises her hand in slow motion, placing it along my cheek.) "It made me feel like I was a unique being. At the same time... It makes the world too vast. Our realities don't coexist well. Nothing I start gets completed, everything unravels." (She shivers again and leans against the tank without taking her eyes from mine.) "There are holes in every sequence. I see them, you don't."

"It's that stuff you're taking..."

"They've created a smooth world for me," she continues, without listening to me. "I'll do a tour of the world in a day and then I'll start over again every morning. There won't be anyone but me."

"Why did you ask me to come?"

"Oh that?" (She looks away.) "I have to be covered

with a nano-active substrate before they connect me. Everywhere, even the most intimate places that I have trouble reaching. I thought you could help me. Say farewell in this way."

"You don't want me to wait for you?"

"I don't know if I'll be coming back…" (She says this quietly, her voice as low as a growl, but I feel as if she's bitten me to the point of drawing blood.) "I'm going for a long time and I'm not leaving anything behind."

The nurse hands me a transparent container filled with a grayish-green goop, with the consistency of whipped cream and the odor of machine oil. Moira stands on a tiny electrical pedestal, against the edge of the tank. She smiles at me distantly and raises her arms, legs spread slightly. She turns slowly toward me, as Loekhen looks on with a clinical expression.

"Start wherever you want," he says, turning away. "The important thing is that every inch gets coated. Do you want us to leave you?"

"Please."

"The room is monitored. If you need anything at all, ask for it out loud. I'll come back once you've finished."

He walks off without looking back and the nurse follows, pushing the cart. The container is as light as a feather in my hand. Moira turns her back to me; the inscrutable curve of her hips makes me want to tear her away from there, and carry her off to my apartment and further beyond, to the stars. But I feel that she is forever beyond my reach now. The only ritual that remains is saying our farewells.

I won't rush anything.

I plunge my hand into the pot and, with a fingertip, I draw a circle that starts from her hip and encircles her waist. Then I place my palm on her shoulder, slide it down to her breast, which I envelop with a clinical caress, before smearing it with the greenish goop. There are so many trajectories, so many shared roads that gradually stop being our secret when the nanos cover her. Indifferent, Moira turns in on herself, eyes half closed. I'll close her eyelids last.

As I paint her, I see her disappear, as if my clumsy brushstrokes are erasing her reality, transferring her into a virtual reality, beyond my reach. All of her rough edges melt in the uniform layer of the substrate; my palms flatten her relief and fill the wrinkles and crevices I've mapped so many times. I'd like to hurt her but my fingers slide within her, and she doesn't even shiver; docilely, she spreads her lips so that I can smear them, allowing me to force her one last time, without granting me a cry. When paint her cheeks with a backhand swipe, her face finally grows simple. My vision transforms it into an assembly of toy cubes, a doll like all the others.

With a fingertip, I try to remove the layer, which feels like greasy, oily smoke to the touch. The nanos multiply under my fingertips, dissimulating it.

"I can't see you any more…"

The greenish gray statue opens her eyes and stares at me. Then she stretches out a foot so that I can complete coating her sole and the tips of her toes before she dips it in the tank. I paint the other with painstaking care, but Moira escapes from me and huddles down in her gel bubble, face turned toward the door.

"They'll come to connect me," she murmurs. "I don't want you to see that. Will you leave, please?"

I nod and say out loud, "You can come in, we've finished." Then I bend over Moira and cover her eyelids with one final green tear before backing toward the other tanks.

I can make out bodies, vague shapes, stretched out in the middle of a cluster of multicolored hoses. They're still, barely a shiver from time to time. Almost not there.

A drop of icy water falls from the ceiling onto my cheek. I place the empty pot on the floor and automatically rub my hands, anesthetized by the nanos. The substrate peels off my skin easily; it must be packed with markers specific to Moira's biochemistry and refuses to adhere to me.

"The technical team will take care of the rest," Loekhen announces, behind me. "Let's leave them to their work. You can see your friend one last time when we seal the tank. Meanwhile, I'll show you how our facilities work. It's quite impressive. You'll see."

Mind numb, I leave the room, resisting the temptation to turn back. One short word from Moira would be more than enough to break the bubble of silence surrounding us. A sigh, a hint of regret. But all I hear is the noise of our footsteps on the chalky tile and the tireless purr of the generators. When the door closes behind us, I realize that our farewells are over and I carry nothing from her with me, not even a trace of her scent on my fingers.

The control room is a functional ovoid, filled with flat screens and monitoring tapes. The floor is warm underfoot; somewhere in the basements, supercomputers are busy inflating the digital bubbles that enclose the sleepers in their private cosmos. If I wanted it, Jo-Andra would send me all of the data I'd need to thread my way through the system and take a glance at the world Moira has chosen. He's waiting for me to ask him, and I'm still looking for a reason to do so.

"We upgraded all of our systems five weeks ago," Loekhen states proudly, motioning me to select one of the bubble chairs in the room. We can supply any cerebral interface with a realism coefficient equal to one, or almost."

"Or almost?"

He shrugs. Around us, the data flows like swarms of insects, murmuring on almost inaudible frequencies.

"What do you know of reality?" Loekhen asks, falling into a chair that groans under his weight before enveloping him in its protective embrace. "Do you know that what you take for a stable, continuous universe is in actual fact made up of discrete states in your brain, separated by chasms of inexistence lasting several nanoseconds? We function like the data processing machines of the past century, supplied by the sensors of our nerves and nourished by the illusion that everything around us exists outside our minds. For some, like your friend, that is no longer enough."

"Here, at *Simplex,* we create digital realities that are as solid as real life; our machines can saturate your cerebral areas with continuous data that is so realistic you could never distinguish it from the information provided by your own senses. It would quickly drive you mad, as well." (Loekhen clasps his hands in front of his face, a studied pose that my vision immediately breaks down.) "We've discovered that there must be intervals between the states of consciousness in order to prevent the psyche from collapsing. But we have, nevertheless, been able to reduce them, to reset your internal clock so that you can live otherwise. More intensely. Faster. Carried by the flows, do you really think you'd want to examine the world around you under a microscope?"

"Moira had the means to opt for all this?"

I smile as I say this, but Loekhen looks away before getting up from his chair. Suddenly, he seems eager to see me go.

"As I said, she took out an insurance policy and you're the beneficiary…" (He waves his hand in front of the closest screen and a document is displayed on the wall in front of me. I make a copy in my digital antememory.) "In the event of an accident, everything she leaves behind will go to you. Take the time to read the contract. We need your approval. You have the right to refuse, if you wish."

The last bits of the substrate peel away from my fingers and fall to the floor where they decompose as quickly as my dreams. I feel empty, unable to imagine what Moira's reality will be like, that simplified world where she will leave no trace of her passage. I transfer the document to a pool of specialized Artificial Intelligences, which return their verdict at the speed of light. *Nothing to report…* I sign automatically, placing my thumbs on the ID scanner. The substrate has numbed my nerves; I no longer feel anything, not even the warmth of the digitization plate.

Loekhen nods and stands up with a determined air. He looks as eager to get rid of me as I am to leave his cemetery. The stench of anti-stress chemical cocktails replaces the odor of his sweat.

"Your friend gave us very clear instructions: She has not authorized either visits or digital intrusions. I don't think we'll have the pleasure of seeing you again, however… WHAT THE FUCK!"

I turn around, alarmed. On the screen behind me, ruby icons are flashing above the image of a room filled with immersion tanks. The camera zooms in on one of them, but the frosted walls reveal nothing. Loekhen rushes toward the exit. I follow without thinking. Behind us, the control room gradually fills with strident chirps, as if a flight of destructive crickets has come in to disturb the digital orderliness of the place.

At the entrance to a new storage room, at the other end of the tiled corridor, punctuated with metal doors and circular, frosted glass lamps, Loekhen pounds his fist on a security plate. The blow short-circuits the test procedures. With a clack, a panel slides open and a dart gun is thrust into his hand. The look Loekhen gives me is impenetrable.

The interior of one of the coffins is alive with unctuous wavelets that crash against the walls. Chaotic lines crisscross the control monitor. Loekhen types in a code with his left hand, turning to hide it from me. Slowly, the lid of the sarcophagus lifts. In the bottom of the tank, an emaciated silhouette, bristling with catheters, writhes with spasms, hurtling from one side of the tank to the other. Milky liquid splatters about our feet.

"Get out of here," Loekhen yells, "This is none of your business!"

"Do these types of emergencies happen often?" I ask, ignoring his order.

Without replying, he bends over the sarcophagus, its lid still moving, plunges his hand into the liquid and immobilizes the sleeper by pressing on his chest. The dart gun points at the emaciated body, and wavers a moment before locking in on the target. With a discreet hiss, one dart is ejected and then another. I can't make out where they hit, but the sleeper suddenly arches and then remains suspended for a second in the middle of the liquid, before falling gently to the bottom.

Loekhen removes his hand from the liquid and shakes it over the sarcophagus. A white sheathe envelopes his fingers. He looks at it in disgust before handing me the weapon.

"Hold this for me," he growls. "I have to type the closing code without getting this gunk everywhere. And don't get any ideas; it's just a tranquilizer. Nothing to get upset about."

The lid of the sarcophagus slowly closes. I weigh the still warm gun. It's incredibly light. Its steel butt, which can be unfolded, has been sawn down to the folding mechanism. The stump is barely large enough to grip it.

"It's completely legal," Loekhen says defensively, when his eyes cross mine. "I bought it at the zoo; they used guns like this to treat the last elephant. The doses are calculated for a person of average weight. There's no risk for the sleepers."

"I suppose if you had wanted them to know about this, you would have told them?"

The barrel of the gun is pointed at his knee.

He gulps.

"Don't play with that!"

"Weapons are designed so that any imbecile can use them. That's why so many imbeciles use them."

Behind us, the lid closes with an oily hiss. The sleeper is curled up in fetal position; the monitor displays neutral green lines. The puddle of whitish slobber at our feet is the only trace of the incident.

"You still haven't explained how Moira could have afforded your rates," I say, while caressing the end of the trigger. "I don't like what's going on here and, as the beneficiary of one of your patients, I can initiate an investigation just by talking about what I've seen. Publicly and on all of the information channels I can afford."

"You think you're pretty clever, don't you." (Loekhen is gauging me and I guess that he's going to talk, not because he's afraid, but because he knows the truth will hurt.) "Your friend signed a somewhat special contract with a third party that agreed to finance her. Do you really want that to be known?"

"What do you mean?" (Now, the weapon is aimed as his lower belly.) "Are you going to exploit her in a virtual brothel?"

"Sex? Don't make me laugh. After three weeks, the sleepers all look like white worms. There aren't enough perverts in the world to develop a real business. I'm not saying that there is no market, just that it's marginal. And it would barely cover a slow immersion in a simplified universe. Besides, we don't do that kind of thing here…"

He shrugs ostentatiously; the weapon wavers in my grip. It no longer serves any purpose. Even if I do hand it over, Loekhen will tell me what I want to know.

"Your friend found financing on her own. A four-week-old fetus was implanted in her uterus five days ago. She spent her final hours undergoing examinations to make sure that the future baby had settled in properly. According to her contract, she will only carry it eight months; after that the new incubators are safer and can be used to monitor the genetic adjustments on a continuous basis."

"Plus, everything's just right for a pregnancy in long-term immersion: a pregnant woman secretes more endorphins than normally; the fetus is like a patch specifically tailored for the carrier's metabolism. And your friend could care less about post-partum blues—returning to reality will be enough of a downer. It's a win-win situation!"

Loekhen reaches out and gently takes the gun from me. I don't even think of resisting. I suppose he knows just how thoroughly his words have destroyed me. Yet, he feels the need to go on.

"We would have told you eventually. As the

194

beneficiary of your friend's life insurance policy, you're responsible for all of her possessions... That includes the baby. If anything happens to Moira over the next seven months, you'll have to ensure that gestation continues, using any means suitable, until the baby is delivered to the clients. But don't worry," he says, placing the weapon back in its compartment and closing it with a punch, "As you've seen, everything is under control!"

I take the elevator to the facility's reception area alone and leave, taking care not to disturb the receptionist, whose eyes flicker without seeing me. Outside, the taxi I ordered is parked near the payment terminal. Leaning against the hood, Jo-Andra waits for me patiently, enveloped in a light drizzle that makes the body as shiny as a mirror. He shivers as he sees me and walks around the vehicle without a word.

When the doors close after us and we start to slide along the sidewalk, as if letting go, he scratches his nose and, without looking at me, asks, "We're going back up?"

"We are. As soon as possible."

At the top of the space elevator, the view is blocked by a jumble of beams and holo panels displaying the rates for raw materials. I note a few figures before receiving a prospecting pop-up for two: rare soils are at a level record, as is germanium, and boosted nebular diamonds are always a sure thing. Around the anchor asteroid, a vast rosary of orbiters floats in geostationary mode, connected by flexible, pressurized corridors that people can travel through by foot. Jo-Andra whistles under his breath, a toneless ditty that betrays his inner tension. He detests the artificial gravity of the orbiters, their subtly dysfunctional odor, similar to that of machines about to shut down. And he absolutely hates the busy crowd that envelopes us without touching. Here there are no longer tribes, practically no longer a society. Just individual trajectories and a world that functions only so-so on automatic pilot, waiting for the crash.

I'm spinning in circles inside. I miss Moira so much it terrifies me. When I mentioned the fetus to Jo-Andra, he didn't even look surprised. His eyes glazed, just long enough for his altered brain to generate a handful of digital agents that he released with the blink of an eye.

Then, before getting out of the taxi, he simply said, "It's a girl. She doesn't look anything like you."

I made a major dent in my credit reserves to pay for the interminable trip into orbit, lease the bubble craft and the prospecting equipment, and obtain an operating permit covering a quarter of the Jovian trojan asteroids located around L4. It's a region I know like the back of my hand; I've amassed several fortunes there, large and small, since my neural graft. Jupiter has captured all sorts of celestial bodies in its orbit and some are just exotic enough to contain something other than the traditional carbonaceous chondrites. Several thousands have been charted and the official databases provide the make-up of about half of them—the largest ones. Prospectors like me are more interested in the medium-sized ones, hidden in the middle of the swarm of pebbles from the view of anyone who isn't right on top of them. You can make some good finds there if you have luck and good detection tools.

Usually, I have both.

But above all, when you look up, the Jovian sky looks like a red eye staring down at you. You feel as if you're caught on the wrong end of a microscope, as insignificant as a paramecium in God's eyes. That's exactly what I need right now.

As we enter the prospecting bubble, as tiny as the orbital elevator cabin we've just spent two days in, I experience the familiar sensation of claustrophobia and I eagerly accept the long list of items to be checked before we take off. Even the kick of the orbital canon that catapults us tangentially in the direction of Mars is a welcome diversion. The oppressive feeling in my chest is quite real and my heart skips a beat or two, as if Moira were leaving me a second time. The effect is ruined by Jo-Andra's roars. He prospects for the fun of it—that's what he told me the first time and he's never mentioned the subject again. During the interminable acceleration loop, I try to breathe while he screams in excitement over all the audio channels. It's like surviving a hangover in the midst of a fanfare.

"Do you think this will be enough to get your mind off things?" Jo-Andra asks, unbuckling his harness.

He has the bad habit of asking that type of thing at exactly the wrong time. I'd love to be able to get into it with him, but the acceleration has left me glued to the back of my seat, an unpleasant taste in my mouth.

"And you, why did you come?"

He utters a furtive sigh, which slices his face into two unequal parts.

"Because it's all the same everywhere, captain. And you're paying."

The remainder of the trip is predictable and boring: a double acceleration loop around Mars, a brief thrust from the scramjets every time the collector's field has gathered enough election mass, and gravity of $1/10$ g for the rest of the time in order to save fuel. I remember what Moira told me, the only time I'd managed to convince her to accompany me into space (we were watching the spurts of plasma beam particles stretching in our wake): the particles are like us, they need to go somewhere or they'll be alone. All this energy spent trying to bump into one another. What a waste!

As the Earth shrinks behind us, I make an effort to stop thinking about her, knowing full well I won't succeed—even the wishes that I could express out loud would betray me. The distance that separates us is already so great that I can't get any further from her. She has slipped on board like a stowaway, in collusion with the captain. So, I spend my time on watch connected to the on-board systems, supervising processes one thousand times more intelligent than I am, while Jo-Andra spins in his sleeping bag at the other end of the cabin.

The ventilator that moves the air around his face pushes his hair back, exposing the double neural connectors on his temples. The skin is discolored around the porcelain and bone needles, but the ends of the contacts, covered with a mono-molecular platinum film, are immaculate. Under the bluish light of the plasma arcs, the particular polish of the digital jewels sparkles like ice. When he dreams, I have the impression that northern lights flash on the screen of his eyelids.

Before, taking off, we stuffed ourselves with hormone inhibitors that prevent us from giving off pheromones. The only scent that wafts off our bodies is that of the antibacterial gel we coat ourselves with ritually twice in every 24-hour period. Deprived of olfactory messages, the presence of the other person is easily bearable, a vague background noise at the edge of awareness. In this way, we can share a space that is far too small for several weeks, each viewing the other like a piece of furniture.

Any interaction between us is a conscious act. But Jo-Andra and I have known one another for so long that we can interact blindly, with the superficial courtesy of people who take the same subway every evening, without ever speaking.

As we approach the asteroid field, we synchronize our sleeping rhythms, which means we have to spend more waking time together. We start to speak again, as if configuring servers: a long test phase, simple sentences, redundant protocols then, gradually, the routine appearance of confidence.

It's been a long time since I simplified Jo-Andra, and the features of his face no longer have anything to teach me. I've often had the impression that I'm decoding his feelings as they take form, like a network of cracks on the surface of a porcelain tea cup that is about to shatter. That's why Moira was so precious to me: she abandoned her expressions behind her, like so many useless masks, replacing them immediately with new, inscrutable ones. It was irritating, like a splinter under your fingernail. Moving as well, in a way I can't describe. It would, no doubt, be terribly dangerous if I ever had to pilot a Waldo in tandem with her.

Jo-Andra, on the other hand, is as predictable as my own voice. Traveling with him is like talking to a mirror.

Every time I close my eyes, I dream of Moira.

"Reality is intimate…" (We were eating, looking out at the ocean. Moira was choosing her words carefully, stringing them together like pearls from a broken necklace.) "It's just what we need at a given time, a local function with as few variables as possible. Something personal, you know? I can't share that."

"We could choose to live in the same one?"

"You're too complicated…"

Fruit peels were piling up on the table and the wind smelled of salt. I was watching the sea and its reassuring rhythm, impossible to disturb, asking myself what we were lacking.

"Do you feel like making love," I murmured.

I wake up before I hear her answer.

Inasmuch as possible, we avoid looking outside. Black comes in very few varieties and the celestial bodies don't look terribly different from their virtual images. No doubt, that's why few people prospect metallic asteroids. It's as tedious as underwater treasure hunts, backgrounds completely devoid of surprise, marked by the links of the location network that encircles the world. Automatic bathyscaphs sow and harvest, dig and bury, and the few rare human divers slip through their midst like excited children picking up fossils in the furrows left by agricultural equipment, without daring to approach.

There are more and more automatic processes on Earth, ghosts of ideas and envies, their finality long since forgotten. They are neither our slaves, nor our descendants, yet possibly the species that will replace us if they manage to make their own dreams.

Moira is already prepared to make way for them.

"We're going back to one-third g, Captain," Jo-Andra announces. "Time to put away your dirty socks!"

The first swarms of asteroids loom out of the back of the sky like anomalies. We bypass them as we regain speed. Given the abundance of local material, the reactors kick back in and our return to a semblance of gravity means we have to stow everything that floats. Jo-Andra settles into the cockpit, rubbing his fingers with a pumice stone, a ritual that helps him shed his *Id*. When his conscience is nothing more than an interface, he gains a few precious microseconds that make navigation exciting for him.

"You have a course for me, Captain?"

I uploaded everything I had on the L4 Trojan heaps into the ship's memory, along with the updates exchanged with other nutcases like me. I could base my decision on the latest raw material prices, on the recent prospecting maps—our reactors leave traces in space, like long crystallized ribbons, and the solar system is looking more and more like a blanket of snow filled with the footsteps of mankind—but I don't feel like choosing.

"What would you say about getting lost, Master Pilot?"

"Anywhere, as long as it's off the grid?"

"That's the idea."

"Well then, you're doing the cooking for the next shift. Hang on!"

The first heap is disappointing. The next four are too. Jo-Andra navigates like someone in a rush to reach the end of the horizon, using trajectories with a minimal amount of elegance and wasting a phenomenal amount of energy. When we reach the end of the grid that marks the border of the explored territories, the space buoy sends us a dire warning and asks us to keep our cartographic data for a future operation. At that particular moment, I'm hunkered down near the access panel for the secondary reserves, trying to slip my head through an opening with greasy edges. Jo-Andra's cry of excitement is drowned in the white noise as I make a painstaking exploration of our tin can.

In all leased craft, there is always graffiti left by the previous prospectors in the most unlikely places: under the trap door for the hydraulic systems, inside the boxes of survival rations, even along the waste evacuation pipelines. You have to be a contortionist to read them, nose touching the letters with a dull light. Some can only be seen in ultraviolet light; others only appear in the dark, their weak luminosity clouded by the security lights.

We find everything: treasure maps, improvised Zen koan, drawings painstakingly engraved on hypertrophied genital organs. Rarely names, even less often curses. The ships have always come back. But when you're adrift in deep space, while the automatic systems scan the darkness looking for a promising pebble, the predigested books available from the control panel lose their interest. There always comes a time when you set out to find the traces of the others who came before, while thinking about those we would leave behind.

"Did you see that?"

Jo-Andra's voice tears me from my exploration. I drop the ultraviolet lamp and kick off toward the second pilot's chair. I brush the crumbs that have accumulated against the back of the chair, stuck there by the almost continuous thrust of the scramjets, and I buckle up quickly. Jo's excitement is almost palpable.

The screens fill almost the entire cone at the front of our ship, covering it like a silvery film. We can toggle them in reflection mode, creating the illusion that we're floating in space, or select images based on the flow from the various scanners. Jo-Andra has programmed a composite view including densimetric elements and a scale of colors ranging into the ultraviolet. The result is as appetizing as an explosion in a tomato sauce plant, but he claims that it helps him relax.

"Quadrant four, at 11 o'clock. The thing that looks like the neck of a beer bottle," he says to me, tapping on the navigation pad, which plunges us into the heart of the bloody maelstrom. "There are irregularities in density."

"You interrupted me for this?"

"I was starting to lose my patience, Captain. Plus, I have a good feeling about this thing... Metal—I'd swear on the head of my firstborn—and heavy!"

"Fine, we'll take a look at it, Master pilot. Take us in, and take care not to make me hurl, like you usually do. Can we use normal vision?"

"You wouldn't like that. We're really very close to the swarm, you know."

I glance at the LEDs for the proximity detectors, flashing frantically. Jo-Andra has cut off the sound alarms—he claims they make him lose his concentration—and has plunged into the hypnotic parade of images with falsified colors. The scramjet turbulence is making the double hull vibrate; nanometric particles slip over the surface of the ship with a silky sound. It is strangely calm, as if it were raining outside and we were driving on an endless highway, encountering no one along the way.

Jo-Andra pilots like a guitarist lost in his solo, prepared to spiral out with the slightest incorrect note. I don't even have the time to decode the sensors' indications. Since reality is a succession of discrete states, or so it appears, I close my eyes and feel Moira's ghost slip in and glance over my shoulder.

"We're there, Captain. And I was right!"

I nodded off without noticing—a defense mechanism Jo-Andra has learned not to make fun of. He's cut off the supply to the motors and we're floating, prisoners of a zero point barely a few dozen meters above the irregular surface of the asteroid.

All of the screens in the nose cone display a realistic view of the exterior. We're surrounded by a strange light, ash-colored, streaked with orange ripples. Rocky masses with dirty gray undersides hang in balance all around us. Jupiter's multicolored sphere is for the most part hidden by the swarm into which we've wended our way. It looks like a three-dimensional shot, a frozen eruption. Instinctively, Jo and I lower our voices, as if we might accidentally set a stellar mechanism that could well crush us into motion. Yet, the pile is stable, sculpted by gravity and the infinite patience of time.

"This one isn't like the others."

The asteroid we're orbiting has a vaguely cylindrical shape, flattened at both ends. It has cracked during some accidental collision and is surrounded by a corona of debris that will eventually fall back to the surface, in a few thousand years. On one side, its surface is rounded like that of a pebble; on the other, a deep crevice with sharp angles zigzags from one pole to the other. It is several meters wide and it's hard to gauge the depth, even using radar. The echoes bounce off the metal veins that streak its walls.

The density meters go wild as we fly over the fault. I gather as much data as possible before switching to unfiltered vision mode and activating the zoom. My eyes fall on the black abyss that stretches into the heart of the rock. Even the headlight on the prow is unable to dissipate the shadows.

"Shall we make a tour, Captain?"

"First, we'll send the Waldos in to scrape up a few samples." (Given his disappointed look, I shake my head, making an effort to smile.) "I agree it looks promising, but I don't want to jump in blindly. Maybe the traces are just carbonaceous dendrites and ferronickel."

"You don't believe that!"

"True. And I feel it in my gut that this is something big, too. But, after several weeks in space, everything out of the ordinary looks like Eldorado and I don't feel up to being disappointed. So, we follow the manual like perfect little space prospectors and send in the automatic equipment to do our work for us, while I prepare the meal and you upload the toponometric surveys. If we're going to stake a claim for this thing, I want to know everything about it, including its family history right back to the Big Bang. Pronto!"

"What do you want to call it?"

"I'll leave you the honor…"

I've rarely seen Jo-Andra as excited as this. For him, looking cool in this type of situation is more than an attitude—it's almost a religion. In this case, it's as if he's found an additional engine stowed in the hold and he's waiting to crank the speed up a notch.

I pour a small amount of liquid into two pouches of protein rations and start preheating them. Then I carefully select the spice mixture that will flavor the resulting gruel. Living in a vacuum, we've drunk, filtered and reused all of the water available on board. This makes Jo-Andra and me members of a particular species—piss brothers.

"Just look at our baby!"

He's modeled the structure of the asteroid in 3D wrapped, based on the sensor surveys. It's a type S, with a rather high albedo for its category, close to 0.21. Dark metallic veins branch out, like axons, threading through all of the cracks in the rock up to the pitted surface of the craters.

From above, the fault looks like a dagger wound.

"Too bad it's cracked," Jo-Andra murmurs dreamily.

I would have set it aside for my older years. It looks nice."

"It's not like we have a clear view, is it?"

"Oh, I don't know… When you display only the simulated gravity currents, you feel like you're looking at the ocean." (He fiddles with the controls on the screens and the view becomes terrifying.) "It quickly grows boring, in fact."

"Moira didn't like to look at the ocean, either…"

"The hell with her! Moira is a universe in the process of collapsing, turned in on herself, and you're following her."

In response, the screens display a series of composite incrustations similar to an MRI of a brain in crisis. Alright already, I get the message.

Jo-Andra shakes his head and the view gradually returns to normal. It's still blocked. The orange stripes of Jupiter, which provide a backdrop for the setting wave with a lazy storm moving from east to west. Jo and I drift around one another like the debris from an explosion, avoiding contact.

The greasy odor of the meal has invaded the cockpit. We know from experience that we have to eat while the food is still hot; as it cools, the mixture sticks to the pouch and hardens. An aborted meal takes on an obscene shape after 30 minutes and becomes too large to be handled easily by the waste ejector.

"If you want to hit your head against something," Jo-Andra starts in, catching his pouch, "Let's go outside and explore this pebble. Even its faults look promising. Not like your girlfriend."

Jo-Andra speaks likes he pilots, getting in as close as possible and ignoring the alarms. I wait until my mouth is full, then nod.

The gruel is tasteless.

Ten hours later, I'm strapped into my Waldo, pinned against the wall in the tiny airlock. Jo-Andra has taken charge of the security checks, humming a three-note melody, over and over. I feel like a diver about to leap into the water, so I test the taste of the air in my tank, looking for some alteration. Bits of stew are stuck between my teeth and I don't notice anything in particular, just the pressure difference that is kicking up a rumpus with my inner ear. The sensation of vertigo gradually fades. My finger is resting on the control to open the outer wall, but I wait until my heartbeat returns to normal before facing the void.

I go out first; Jo will accompany me through telepresence, with the second Waldo. He's improvised a crown of optical sensors above my visor, which enables him to share what I see. I hear his breathing in the helmet's audio system, but nothing else.

And, finally, I'm alone, no ghost looking over my shoulder. I press the button and plunge outside of the matrix, toward the ashy light of the asteroid.

I instinctively correct the thrust of the tiny ejection nozzles as I fall head first toward the pebble. The Waldo unfolds around me, multiple arms equipped with sampling tools deployed in a crown around my body. The control banners scroll inside my helmet. Head up display, not intrusive. I murmur, "Green, green, green" like a mantra, even though I know that Jo-Andra is sharing my data and will detect any problem at the same time as I do. But that's the routine and I stick to it. Practice and training don't help us attain perfection. They merely serve to make a certain number of actions instinctive, freeing up the conscious portions of our brains for nobler tasks:

contemplating the majestic beauty of Jupiter in the background behind the asteroids, or resolving a problem before it kills us.

When I finally decide to look, the rock is spinning slowly beneath my feet, barely a few yards away. Close up, I can see that it is pockmarked with tiny impact points, its surface covered with wrinkles. As a result of my modified vision, I can read its history in the pattern of its craters, like a piece of sheet music punctuated with long, silent intermissions. That's one thing I've always liked about asteroids: they look old, worn by eternities that are inconceivable on our scale and yet they create the impression of reassuring solidity.

When the fault appears on the horizon, I point my head down and make my way gently over to it. Jo-Andra's whistling increases and I can't help but smile. I know that he's dying to be in my place; he let me go out first because I needed to.

The Waldo's exterior arms reel out polymer threads that harden instantly on contact with the vacuum. At the ends, microcapsules filled with adhesive gel explode when they strike the rock, sealing the spider web. I patiently weave a security net for a distance of a few yards, over the fault, and equip it with sliding handholds. Then I unroll phosphorescent ribbons over the gray stone lips. A yellowish light gradually spreads inside the crevice. It will only last two days, but that is more than enough for what we have to do.

Sitting back in my control seat, I allow the images of the walls to print on my retina while the sensors scan the entire frequency spectrum, with quick impulses. The hissing of the breathing apparatus floods my consciousness; the prospector's trance gradually swallows me up.

That's when I see them, superimposed on the rock

like anomalies, details that my enhanced vision has no problem isolating from everything else. I aim the frontal spectroscope at the farthest wall and launch a non-destructive infrared scan, in the vicinity of the 21-micron band. Fleeting flickers, like constellations, appear on the dark velvet of the rock. My brain rearranges the pixels projected inside my visor; I zoom with a movement of my chin.

"Jo," I say, trying to control the excitement in my voice. "I think I'm coming in after all."

"It's negative, captain?"

"No, but it's your pebble, so I'll let you play with your shovel and pail while I take care of the paperwork."

"Oh?" (I know that he's trying to decipher the images relayed from my helmet, but he doesn't have the appropriate neural cabling.) "How many tons do you figure, all in all?"

"We'll have to count in carats." (I smile, thinking about the expression on his face.) "And the answer is 'a lot'. They're large enough for me to see them from here…"

To stake out an asteroid, you simply pepper it with self-drilling metal pitons, engraved with a unique code. You can buy them in packages of 20 in the prospecting supply stores. Then you file the reference code with the claims office, along with the position coordinates of the last known location. No one provides the exact figures, of course, but a difference of a few decimals doesn't invalidate the registration. Space is vast and the pebbles in the uncharted zone are hard to track when you only have an approximate address. All you have to do is install a narrow band passive transponder and security code and you can head straight for it, without running the risk of being cut off by a competitor. Space pirates are rare, mostly the stuff of myth, but no one becomes a prospector of the void without a good dose of romanticism and paranoia.

Jo-Andra and I are no exception to the rule. While he finishes up tattooing the asteroid, I heave our waste to the other side of the fault and watch as it softly crashes. It's one way of marking our territory and it increases the payload we can take back. Prospecting ships are small and their holds are essentially used to carry the mass of ejectate needed to accelerate for the return to terrestrial orbit. We can't pick up more than a quarter ton of samples, which isn't much for ferronickel but more than sufficient for diamonds.

"You happy?" I ask over the radio, mechanically caressing my chin. "I'll be overhead in ten minutes."

"Don't cause a shadow as you pass by, Captain. I have two more stakes to install and then I'll slip into the fault."

"Let me know when you want me to replace you."

"Don't worry." (I know him and he'll be there for hours.) "Can you send me a slave Waldo?"

"Getting bored all on your own? I'm coming."

He sniffs in irritation and I smile as I imagine his grimace. There are some crazy crews who go out to prospect a promising rock without leaving anyone behind on board, relying solely on the automatic processes to manage the imponderables. Six years ago or so, I heard about three brothers who were found floating a few yards from their ship, which was locked up tight as a drum. The collision alarm had sounded and the ship's AI had refused to release the airlock controls. They died in their suits, hugging one another in an inextricable embrace, after trying in vain to force the airlock screws by hammering them with their helmets.

That's the kind of story you trade in hushed voices in the vacuum miners' bar, but the guy who told it to us had films to back up his tale. Since then, Jo and I alternate our outings, making jokes out loud to keep the ghosts at bay.

I unfold the second Waldo in the airlock and slip on a remote piloting suit, so fine that it feels like liquid flowing over my skin. Working in puppet mode is exhausting. We have to be very close as a result of the speed of light and it's as boring as a video game. But that doesn't bother Jo; his re-cabled brain is capable of managing several simultaneous neural flows. Once he told me that it made him feel as if he had several extra limbs, like an extraterrestrial arachnid.

I send the Waldo over to the asteroid, lock the 3D immersion helmet and allow myself to float in the weightlessness in the middle of the cockpit. When the data submerges me, I shake myself to get my bearings and then shift the machine's trajectory toward the rock, along a regular spiral. It really has to be very close to Jo so that he can control it with a data jack. Planning a rendezvous between two such clumsy and cumbersome objects requires a certain amount of elegance and a hint of luck. That's another reason I stretched a web from one side of the fault to the other. It reduces the risk of head-on collisions.

"Relax, honey," Jo-Andra murmurs in my earphone. "You can get in closer…"

"I'm afraid of your big claws, moron. I'm on my final approach. Have you taken samples?"

"A dozen or so cores of carboniferous chondrites, of no particular interest, but there are diamond veins that can be mined easily from inside the fault. After our rendezvous, I'll go down to the bottom. That's where the largest ones are."

"Don't go where you don't have a good footing."

"Yes, mother." (His laughter sounds like a squall of SETI signals). "I see you, you're above me. Reduce your speed and you'll fall bang into the net."

When he couples to the second Waldo, the connection is scrambled. I stretch lazily, then remove the immersion helmet before peeling the suit off and rolling it into a ball in a pouch. Once naked, I strap myself into the pilot's chair to wait for Jo-Andra to come back. The real work—slow and painstaking—will start as soon as we can subject the nebular diamond samples to thorough testing. If they even are diamonds.

When I open my eyes, the screens are displaying the images shot by the Waldos' cameras. Jo has headed into the darkness of the fault and is spinning lazily as his front lamp projects a yellowish beam that brushes along the walls without resting. If I hadn't dozed off, I suppose I would have been the one to see the first Trojan flower and things would certainly have turned out differently. But it was my first real moment of peace since Moira left and I allowed myself to get bogged down in its deceitful security.

"Nothing new?" I murmur in the mike.

"No, you snore as loudly as ever! While you were snoozing, I harvested one or two nice little gems…" (Jo places his right claw in front of his helmet and I see a translucent block as large as my fist.) "According to the infrared analyzer, it's the real thing."

Nebular diamonds are sometimes polluted with rare bodies. Morphological singularities appear in their crystalline structure where certain atoms are missing. Their spectroscopic characteristics are highly recognizable and the telecommunications industry is willing to pay a fortune for a microcrystal weighing a few carats that can be used in the heart of the electro-optical modulators it so desperately needs. The specific cutting angle of meteoritic diamonds makes it easy to interface them with silicon semi-conductors as long as the surfaces are micro-machined. This produces very high-frequency signal modulators that are virtually undetectable. Obviously, this is of great interest to governments and criminal organizations alike. If the block Jo-Andra is holding is really what I think it is, he's already collected enough to pay for the trip.

"Given my luck at this time, we've found a glassy meteorite and what you're holding is just a glass ball for tourists. Shake it... I'm sure we'll see snow!"

In response, the claws of both Waldos start to wave obscenely, in a perfectly synchronized sequence. Jo is just the kind of guy who trains so he can give someone a finger in weightlessness for situations such as this. He releases the pebble, which floats in front of his helmet, and I hear him snigger.

"You missed something strange," he announces. There are complex crystalline concretions at the bottom at the end of one of the main veins. I've never seen anything like it. Want me to show it to you?"

He makes a perfect rotation around his navel and dives head first toward to bottom of the fault, followed by the second Waldo, which clings to his back. Intertwined, arms outstretched in a crown, they thrust into the middle of the shadows like Kali returning to Hell. The beams of the headlights paint fantastic mandalas on the grayish walls. Clusters of points of light appear and then disappear, as if Jo is diving along a reef peopled with ghosts. This is the first time we've discovered an asteroid that has been so damaged and the sensation is troubling.

The fault quickly shrinks. The arms of the Waldos

brush against the walls on each side and then retract. Jo has gone very deep. He'll find it hard to turn around and he knows this, but the things that interest him are always hidden in the most inaccessible nooks and crannies.

"Here they are…"

The bottom of the fault is a messy heap of micro-cracks and debris floating in weightlessness. The raw light projected by the headlights highlights the many shadows and scars; this is where the impact must have been the most violent. In the middle of the chaos, struc-tured concretions flourish. They're as wide as my hand and appear to be formed by the intertwining of dissimilar crystals in a pattern and with a geometry that my vision can't decode. The fractal patterns are lost in one another, folded in petrified waves that appear to be on the verge of unfurling in gray foam. When the light catches them, they sparkle in iridescent arabesques that weave a hypnotic fabric I could lose myself in. Regretfully, I turn away from the screens while Jo entertains himself, raising dust ghosts above them.

"Nickel and rare elements, a touch of gallium," he announces. "I don't recommend the densitometric view, it's a crystallography nightmare. My head still hurts. That said, from close up, they look like flowers."

"It's time to go home, you're getting romantic…"

"You want me to pick you a bouquet?"

I don't even have time to agree. The Waldo's arm stretches out toward to end of the fault, the tips of the claws approaching one of the concretions. Through the micro-sensors that extend their reach, I can make out a landscape of folded wrinkles that opens into asymmet-rical, silvery petals. Then the claw closes and pulls.

That's when the attack occurs.

The Waldos' anti-intrusion security systems are not all that great. It's the triple redundancy band that prevents eventual radio signals from disturbing the servomotors. But what rushes into the receptors is a tsunami of malicious, auto-adaptive data, a lather of effervescent information that invades all available space. I lose the voice-data connection within two-tenths of a second, and the Waldo's principal control unit gives out at the same time. Fortunately, the emergency system is robust and, above all, isolated. It triggers the removal retrorockets and Jo-Andra is ejected from the fault, spinning. The second Waldo swings at the end of its servo-cable like a spider swept away by a hurricane.

A portion of the invading data flow has managed to establish a bridgehead in the local antememories of the spacesuit, by the sensors. Emissions spurt from the depths of the fault like kinetic projectiles. For a second or two, the universe disappears, hidden by the digital reality that smears undecipherable information. Jo-Andra attempts to stabilize his rockets, but his Waldo's systems are paralyzed by the aggressive bombardment. His trajectory curves once again toward the fault.

I react instinctively and start the engines. Although prospecting ships are not armed, they aren't exactly defenseless either. The ejectate reservoirs are almost full and I can waste a fair amount to transform the scramjets into blinding torches. The only problem is that Jo is between the asteroid and me.

"Get you fat ass out of the way if you can hear me!" I scream, while guiding the ship onto a tight elliptical trajectory, without wasting a moment's thought on the micro-impacts of the dust on the shield. "I'm going to torch that thing the next time I pass over."

The answer, if there is one, is drowned in a flow of

static. I launch a flurry of commands toward the second Waldo, which seems to respond almost normally. Its claws grasp the lip of the fault and it folds out to make a quarter turn. The cable connecting it to Jo-Andra pulls tight and the slingshot effect turns their trajectory toward space. That's all I see before the ship plunges over the horizon line, toward the other side of the pebble.

Forty seconds later I'm back. Both Waldos are floating in the middle of my path and I spiral at the last minute, cutting the engines. I feel as if I have even more arms than they do. *Jo should have been in my place, he would have considered it a hoot.* Another revolution for nothing… I start the propulsion back up, praying that the scramjets will start without any problems. There are two or three hiccups and then the turbulence calms; the thrust pushes me against the back of my seat. During the second orbit, I can gradually crank up the speed until a blinding white torch is formed in my wake.

As I fly over the fault, I pivot brutally and send all of the power of the ejection mass into the heart of the asteroid. For a handful of seconds, nothing happens and I start to move off, but then the fault seems to grow. Warning lights flash all over the control panel and I once again toggle into a tight orbit that will allow me to repeat the maneuver.

After my 12th revolution, the asteroid splits.

After the 15th, the two main blocks explode in turn and the local collisions shoot debris out. I bombard them with burning plasma to eradicate the last traces of the flowers, but the spinning shards complicate my work. Despite the ear-shattering alarms, I stubbornly burn the digital rapist, just as I should have done with the data flows that kidnapped Moira and dragged her into a world where I don't exist.

After the 30th revolution, I almost hit one of the pebbles in the heap I'm trying to fly around in an effort to return to the site of the carnage. The automatic systems cut everything off in the event of a catastrophe and I have time to see a sooty, pockmarked surface before the thrust stops. Held by my harness, I sigh, then sob. Rivers of sweat pour into my eyes.

Where is Jo-Andra?

The transponders in his suit are mute, but the second Waldo responds to queries. I let the automatic pilot system take me to the source of the signal, tacking about among the debris. *As long as the servo-connection is still intact and they're still together.*

The beautiful orderliness of the pile has been ravaged by the asteroid's explosion. The sector is a nightmare of dust that interferes with my radar equipment, but the signal is growing stronger. When I pinpoint them visually, I turn on the exterior diodes, and flash dot-dash-dash-dot. I don't know if Jo is still conscious but, if he is, the signal will reassure him.

He's floating, curled up in a ball, in a fog of debris. I use the second Waldo to release him from his exoskeleton and guide its clumsy efforts until Jo's entire suit is in the airlock. When I close the outer wall, cutting clear through the cable that connects them, I feel as if I'm committing some terrible act. The masterless Waldo moves off, spinning gently, claws raised in a strange parody of benediction. Jupiter lights it for a second, with orange and rust reflections, then I turn my head away and it disappears. The airlock pressurizes with a hiss and I force myself to assess Jo's condition.

At first glance, his suit is intact. There is no trace of bloody foam on his visor or at the ends of his gloves. Yet, he's not moving. I connect the medical plugs located under the storage pouch at his sternum, which is strangely swollen, then I launch the auto-diagnosis while hauling him inside the ship. We've performed this type of drill dozens of times in zero gravity, but I've never felt so clumsy before.

At the back of the cockpit, the pharmaceutical unit unlocks, displaying its carefully organized racks. Pre-calculated doses of cardiac stimulants, tranquilizers and neuroactivators shine in the bluish light. The color codes on the labels sparkle in electroluminescent flashes like fishes from the depths of the ocean. I make a choice instinctively—in case of emergency, trust your engrams. At the end of the syringe with its homing device, a teardrop pearls on the beveled needle. When I stick it into the space suit's treatment, a green light winks at me reassuringly. The plunger descends with a hiss that echoes like a hurricane in the silent cockpit.

Jo-Andra's space suit is floating near the racks. Stowed to one of the ceiling harnesses, I turn around him, looking for signs of a break in the integrity chain. No noticeable cracks, and the autodiagnostics haven't detected a thing. A fresh, sterile scent rises from the nanofiber plates that envelope it. *Space purifies us.* His dorsal nozzles closed automatically when he entered the airlock and the various system components are on standby.

I place the palm of my hand on the activation plate between his shoulder blades and type in the emergency unlock code.

A splutter of static, followed by a beep, rises from the control panel. Jupiter's magnetic field fluctuates on a regular basis and the positioning algorithms of the navigation systems occasionally find it hard to keep up. While the articulated segments of the spacesuit break apart with a deceptive slowness, I realize that I'm alone, locked up in a tin can barely larger than a bedroom, drifting with the only other human being within reach of the instruments. And I still don't know if he's alive.

The dorsal plate comes off; I see a shard of white flesh. I undress Jo-Andra carefully, circling around him like a shark attacking a diver. His skin is supple, dry, and reassuringly warm. There are no obvious bruises, no lividity. I can unfold his limbs easily, in order to extract him from the suit.

The helmet comes off last. Through the antireflective visor, I can barely make out his features. His eyes are closed; the shadow of a smile plays across his lips, as if he finds something ironic about the situation that has escaped me. I clench my fists while the helmet's other survival units analyze the environment one last time before agreeing to release him.

The pressurized straps give way with a weary bang. The block system shuts down and opens at the same time as the cervical support band. A tiny scratch zigzags along his chin like the trace of a kiss. I try to move his jaw with my thumb; it gives way easily. A thread of inky saliva slides into the palm of my hand. Jo most likely bit his tongue, but that's not serious. There's no sign of wounds on his nose and his eyes are closed. He breathes gently, deeply. It's easy to believe that he'll wake soon under the influence of the cocktail of drugs I injected into him. But, under his lids, his eyes are rolled up and laced with blood.

When the back of the helmet comes off, I notice two twisted wires floating around his temples. Jo-Andra had improvised a link to shunt the system to his neural plugs and he's still connected. *The sneaky imbecile…*

I don't risk tearing out the wires. We've repeated this

exercise often enough that I know what to expect in the case of one false move on my part. Instead, I start the final procedure to shut the suit down and completely purge the antememories. This takes less than two minutes, twelve breaths for Jo-Andra. Then the characteristic shutdown beep, the separation of the now inert helmet and the digital silence of the survival indicators.

I brush the neural plugs with the tip of my fingernail, then grasp the tiny transmission bulb, turn it a notch and pull on it sharply, without thinking. Jo-Andra's body shivers; reddish pearls escape from his nostrils before slowly dispersing around his head.

"Idiot," I murmur, looking away. "You wanted to be the smart guy with the Waldos, and play along the edge of the cliff like a big boy who isn't afraid of anything. You have to wake up now because we're stuck in a cube of space as empty as our lives and I don't feel like going back home alone. I'm tired of being dumped. Say something, why don't you!"

His eyes remain stubbornly closed. I caress his forehead, warm and damp, I pinch his ear lobes, I even try to rinse his nose, without provoking any notable reaction. When his features are completely relaxed, his face is a crazy quilt of unrelated elements. Nothing sticks... Yet, with willpower and nonchalance, he has managed to build an appearance and use it as an interface. Even though the real world interests him less than the digital steppes which he can straddle at will, I suspect that he has created an avatar faithful to what he is, an image of himself he has developed patiently so that he no longer needs to worry about it.

With a sigh, I stow him in the sleeping net, then pick up a second syringe from medical rack and look for a vein in the hollow of his neck.

I program the return route as quickly as possible and try to think of something else. Jo-Andra's body smells like shit. I've washed him with the daily water ration and coated him with antibacterial gel, but his odor is noxious. He shivers; his fingers, and sometimes his toes, tap away, as if he's trying to convince himself of their presence. But his eyes remain obstinately closed.

I've hooked him up to the IV; I've placed sensors everywhere it's possible, using a portion of our prospecting equipment. That kept me busy for two days. Then I go back to my exploration of the ship's nooks and crannies, looking for reassuring graffiti. I never manage to find any. Every four hours, the scramjets flare for the few seconds of acceleration that constitute the only variations in our daily routine.

Finally, I tie up next to Jo-Andra and start to talk to him, eyes riveted on his face, which I know by heart. The echoes of my voice mingle with the gurgle from the piloting systems, air recycling pipes and the medical rack. When I close my eyes, it feels like a dialogue.

On board a prospecting ship, silence is a useless luxury. Everything cracks under the constraints generated by the surrounding void. It is possible—although it costs a fortune—to soundproof an area the size of a cupboard, but the result quickly becomes unbearable. Your inner ear perceives the ship's movement, the vibrations of the floor, the fluctuations in the gravitational currents. The outer ear hears nothing. After 15 minutes, you'll need a good supply of sealed bags, if you don't want to spend your time cleaning up the balls of sticky vomit that cling to the most inaccessible places.

Silence is highly overrated in any case. Sounds carry information and information can save your life if you know how to interpret it in time. I know that the medical rack will wake me if Jo-Andra's vital signs start to decline; I've learned to keep an eye out for the strident whistles of the anti-collision alarm. I've reached the point where I want something, anything, to happen.

That's when Jo-Andra's face starts to change.

I wouldn't have noticed a thing if my modified vision hadn't stubbornly kept on breaking it down into elementary volumes, as it does with everything around me. Two days earlier, we had reached the charted zone of deep space, with the reassuring murmur of the guiding system radio beacons wafting from the audio systems. It's been a long time since I've had anything new to tell him so I talk to him about Moira and me, of the sense of loss that my outing into the void hasn't managed to heal.

When I come back to float near Jo, after making a detour to the pilot's seat, I look at his relaxed face, each feature as familiar to me as my own. More and more often, my vision blurs for a second before once again adjusting to his image. Initially, I blamed it on fatigue—an insidious threat in space where weightlessness reduces the sensation of effort. But it only happens with him. It takes me a second to recognize him, to readjust the parameters of his appearance. I realize that he is changing, that under his usual appearance, a new version is emerging.

A version I don't know.

At the beginning, I was too submerged in my self-pity to realize what this meant. My mind filled with Moira, I would talk to him, without looking at him, eyes staring off in the distance. The world was collapsing around me and Jo-Andra's transformation was only one of the symptoms. Now, the change has become so quick that I can see the traces between two blinks of an eye.

222

During the final hours before we reached terrestrial orbit, I would doze off for a second next to Jo, my hand on the IV drip valve, and wake up next to a grossly disguised stranger who gradually takes on his familiar appearance, until the next time.

"I've got you," announces the mooring station.

The impersonal voice destroys my last remnant of calm. Swearing, I return to my seat to complete the approach formalities. I could bring Jo-Andra over to me, haul him in by his catheters like a beached fish, but in space we learn to leave things float where they are. And the odor is easier to bear from a distance.

While trying to change the viewing mode, I accidentally display the 3D view of the asteroid. The hologram appears above the control table; colored zones surround the impact structures, dark threads indicate the presence of mineral veins. The shape of the crystalline life it houses is beautiful in its own way, completely inoffensive at a first glance, but it contains a trap, a species humankind has never encountered before.

I enlarge the image until it fills half the width of the cockpit, and I plunge my hands into the fault to close my fist around the spot where the flowers are encrusted. I reduced that junk to dust just as they did with Jo-Andra's mind. A tight quarantine will have to be established in that sector of space—if the authorities believe me. I don't have any evidence to back my claims, with the exception of the mission's visual recordings. I erased everything else out of fear of contamination.

"You see, Jo…" (I speak without looking at him, over my shoulder; it's easier this way). "The people who fall apart into little pieces take refuge in small boxes, closed rooms where the dust of their pain falls in layers that eventually engulf them. I know where there's a bit of space, where the solar wind sweeps the shards away, leaving only naked rock. I was wrong to bring you along and you were wrong to follow me."

The transmission unit emits an approving click as I wiggle my fingers in the heart of the asteroid. The locations of our self-drilling pitons are highlighted in blue, like electrodes embedded in a gigantic frontal lobe. I think about what Moira said to me during the sole flight we took together.

Before I die, I want them to encode my brain in the axons and densities of an asteroid in the outer belt and then send it into the dark of deep space, toward the middle of the galaxy. My mind will gradually colonize all of the rock and will live in rhythm with the slow, cold pace of the carbon. It will observe the universe rotating until a star attracts it and warms it within her breast before engulfing it.

All that remains of the killer asteroid is an image frozen in time, a simple appearance devoid of substance. Like what remains of me since Moira left, like what Jo-Andra has become, like what the world of humans is changing into. Lines, trajectories, soulless agitation sprayed with a little sugar water.

I let the auto pilot connect to the guide beam and I automatically push my hair from my temples. It hasn't had time to grow much, but I feel as if I've been gone for an eternity. Moira's fetus is five months old. I wonder if her personal universe has collapsed, how many times Loekhen has had to calm her with his phallic gun.

Above all, I wonder what I'll do afterwards.

The first orbital stations fill the screen and we slip smoothly into the mooring zone. I see the Earth, intermittently, but my mind is too numb to react. I recognize it automatically, but the reflection of Jo-Andra's face is superimposed over it and everything blurs. I bend over when I see his eyes wide open, unrecognizable.

That's what saves my life.

When I wake up, all of the screens in the bubble have been deactivated. The back of my head hurts—I lift my hands up to touch it and bring them back down covered with blood, but the wound isn't too deep. The airlock open light is flashing and the air is saturated with the odor of a particularly violent disinfectant that almost makes me sneeze.

Shit…

I lean back in my chair, cautiously. According to indications on the control panel, we are moored in the peripheral docks, where places are reserved for lessees. Jo-Andra must have handled the final maneuvers. I have no idea what he hit me with or what he did following that. He has left the ship, that's for sure. By this time, he must have made it through the decontamination zone and lost himself in the station.

Who left the ship, in fact? Jo-Andra is no longer here. It's the filth that ate him up from within.

The 3D image of the asteroid is floating overhead. At a closer look, the dark wound of the fault resembles the wound that has split my head open. I have to get moving. I drag myself on all fours to the overturned medical rack on the side and I select a syringe packed with stimulants.

The effect is like being kicked to the stars. In just a few seconds, the fog dissipates. My fingertips are alive with icy pins and needles and I can get up on my knees and then stand.

Get out. Catch Jo-Andra. Settle this shit for once and for all.

I can track him through his links. A cautious query

returns a location ping, accompanied by a brief map. He's closer than I thought, trapped in a sanitary cabinet. The automatic systems in the quarantine zone must have decided that his odor was incompatible with the station's hygiene standards and recommended a thorough scrub. The process takes more than 20 minutes and can't be stopped once started.

I stumble over to the airlock, without bothering to get dressed. They'll give me sterile clothing, made of recycled paper, when I leave the quarantine zone and between now and then, I'll be sprayed with antibiotic liquids almost every step of the way. Might as well make their job easy.

Pieces of Jo-Andra's space suit lie on the ground—I thought I'd stuffed them in one of the cupboards. My vision blurs for an instant and I lean against the wall to vomit, a thin, almost colorless thread. At my feet, the storage pouch for the central unit has been split open. In the panic that followed my recovery of Jo, I'd failed to examine his effects.

Carried along by the strange lucidity caused by the injection, I feel my thoughts fit together like the parts of a weapon. When Jo picked the Trojan flower, just before the attack, he had been in the process of gathering nebular diamonds in the bottom of the fault. The impure crystalline structure of these diamonds can be used to store complex data along symmetrical planes and the carbon 13 atoms can be used to create a stable and controllable memory mechanism on a quantum level. It's possible that the digital virus duplicated itself there, during the centuries spent in space. With the destruction of the asteroid, the diamonds are the only potential backup of what Jo-Andra has in his head. And he knows that.

A drop of blood rolls down my forehead. I wipe it off

mechanically. The airlock has closed—the thread of air from the station has run dry—but the pressures have been equalized between the exterior and in here. I trigger the opening sequence with a simple movement of my hand. Leaving the ship terrifies me; I feel like curling up in the pilot's chair and waiting for someone to find me. But I take one step and then another and I face the deserted unloading platform.

Halfway to the entrance of the sanitary airlock I decide to call the station authorities.

While a high-pressure water spray strips my skin off, I jump from one anonymous voice to another, trying to rein in my impatience. I'm honorably acknowledged as a prospector—all those who have made fortunes are—and the story I tell them is just credible enough to get me past the administrative barriers. I state that Jo-Andra has suffered a fleeting bout of madness, that he has attacked me (even cleaned, the wound on the back of my head is still convincing) and that he has fled with the geological samples we were bringing back. I don't make any mention of diamonds or Trojan flowers at this point. I end my message with the coordinates for Jo's last known location, as well as his ID code and I add, "Don't hurt him. He just needs to return to his senses."

As I leave the quarantine zone, my skin feeling oily from the antiseptic spray, I slip into the recycled paper coveralls, gray and wrinkled, that they give to everyone returning to the Base. Those who hit pay dirt during their prospecting trips stop at one of the many clothing boutiques that surround the docking area. Others settle for hugging the walls.

A semi-automatic transport board waits for me near

the exit. I climb on and start it with a kick of my foot, then accelerate until it hooks into one of the photoluminescent guide rails. Teeth clenched, I force myself to maintain my balance as the passageways flash past me. I'm no longer bleeding, but the wound on my head is throbbing like a quasar signal. I bite my tongue from the pain and the taste of salt fills my mouth. The effect of the injection is wearing off.

I receive terse messages from the security department. Jo-Andra is heading to the other end of the station, following an erratic and confused route. His identification signal is growing weak—it will die soon. This worries the authorities. Moreover, Jo seems to have discovered a way to bypass the video detectors located at the stations nerve centers: he is bombarding the ATM networks with high priority messages that saturate the bandwidth. During this time, certain frames from the surveillance cameras are not retransmitted and he makes good use of this to erase his image. It's as if the filth that colonized him has learned to use all of the functions of both his body and his implants.

"He's heading over to the elevator," I say, looking at the diagram of his route on the plank, beneath my feet.

Even though there are holes in his route, I can break it down into curves that all converge on one point.

"We've already come to that conclusion…" (The official voice of the comm system is tinged with a little boredom, as if the hunt in progress is devoid of excitement.) "There aren't many places to go in the station. I've warned the security guard on site; he'll intercept him. You'll reach them in four minutes."

"Jo-Andra isn't armed."

"You know nothing about that. He's left our sensors' fields on several occasions. We won't take any risks."

I shake my head but say nothing more. The board

flies over the luminous grid of the ground with the implacable certainty of the angels. Around us, notice boards project the prices of raw materials and announcements for upcoming departures on the steel ceiling. The air smells new, the spots of color provided by the windows are as fresh as the first day. The station is a completely predictable artifact, a place built in keeping with human plans where all routes, even the most unpredictable, intersect. We didn't settle for mapping the space around us; we also filled it with streets and straight walls, so that the curve of the horizon becomes unnoticeable and we are where we are and nowhere else. Elsewhere no longer exists; there is only infinity here.

I've come home.

As I approach the elevator terminal, the crowd grows denser and my board reduces speed. The rumble of the departing convoy is covered by announcements and digital whistles from the loudspeakers. Holographic curtains mark off the access routes to the station, just wide enough for two people. With my paper coveralls, stained with sweat, and my caved in head I attract a few sarcastic looks, but no one pays any particular attention to me.

"Security here, we've found your guy. Is something wrong with him or what?"

"Where is he?"

"He's cutting through the lines, heading for the main access. He's all we see. Square 102-02, heading 102-03. He's holding a bag in front of him."

"Can you stop him gently?"

"Hey, I'm on the job, OK? I'll do what I can, but if he continues to jump the line and jostle everyone, things will go badly for him."

"What's he emitting?"

"The sector is jammed over an area of 80 meters. The electronics in the transit cars are sensitive to uncontrolled emissions. That's it. He's going into 102-03. I'm intercepting him. You should be able to see us."

The board stops and I step off, looking down to chase away the dizziness. When I look back up, Jo is on the other side of a bluish cloth. He's walking up the elevator, in the wrong direction, on the unloading lane. He's wearing the same sort of coveralls as I am, but his are virtually in shreds and he's placed the strap of his bag around his neck. A uniformed guy is running toward him, brandishing an electric billy club in his hand, the tip flashing like a beacon. The sparse crowd parts docilely. Behind Jo-Andra, the guard aims the weapon at his back.

Jo pivots on one foot and reaches for the billy club. He holds a piece of connection cable from the Waldos. The weapon hits the bag with a sizzle, then Jo strikes. The cable wraps around the electrified end and short-circuits it. With a jerk, Jo disarms his adversary, then turns back and runs clumsily toward the arrival airlock.

After hesitating for a moment, the guard runs after him.

The crowd has realized that something unusual is going on. The closest spectators have formed a silent semi-circle; each individual is busy collecting as much data as possible about the event, avoiding all sounds that might interfere with the recording. Others have placed their bags on the ground and are watching their pocket screens for the live retransmission of what's happening before their very eyes.

My arrival provokes a certain fluctuation. I'm moving as quickly as I can, but running is out of the question. Sparks surge before my eyes every time one of my felt shoes strikes the metal floor. Jo has almost reached the transit block and the guard is trotting at a cautious distance, two or three steps behind him. It's as if his warrior instincts disappeared along with his weapon.

The door to the airlock is closing. With all my strength, I scream Jo's name, triggering a few irritated comments from the public. The guard glances over his shoulder and decides to accelerate.

Jo-Andra has not turned back.

Just as he is about to rush into the opening, the guard grabs his shoulder, spinning him around. The bag hanging below his neck opens part way and the scene suddenly decomposes into basic, implacably simple elements: fingers grabbing the strap, Jo stretching and tripping, the bag remaining behind, the airlock door sliding in its track, cutting the plastic just short of the outstretched hand and the diamonds pouring out in a shiny spray and falling all around the guard with dull clinks as the images of the screens focus on us.

On the other side of the wall, Jo-Andra watches me for a second with his unfathomable eyes before turning away and locking the accesses. I didn't even have the time to decode his new face.

"You let him get away," I yell at the guard. "You did it on purpose…"

I'm out of breath; the return to the gravity, even reduced, of the station is an ordeal.

"A capsule is reserved for you in a few minutes," retorts the guard, shrugging. "Your friend won't be going anywhere during the descent and the police will pick him up when he arrives. They have cells, incapacitating weapons. Here, we're just a transfer point."

Around us, the crowd is shuffling about in confusion. No one is looking at us anymore; the recorders have been put away and everyone is continuing with their individual migration as the screens return to their shrill announce-ments. The world is a map focused on itself. I kneel down and pick up a handful of the diamonds scattered on the ground and stuff my pockets. They're so large, it's hard for me to carry them all.

"You should go."

The guard has reached out a hand to help me up. Then he points a remote control in the direction of the hol-ogram walls which open to provide access to the entrance zone. The board has arrived and is waiting docilely at my side for me to step on it. I push it away with a foot; I have to learn to walk again.

The convoy that moves down from the top of the el-evator looks like a row of bullets in a machine gun am-munition belt. Each capsule can hold up to four people and includes rudimentary facilities, sufficient for the four-teen hours the trip takes.

"You'll heal," the guard says.

I look at him for a second as if he's crazy, then raise my hand to my skull and enter the capsule, wondering if the entire world is impossible to understand. Or if it's just me.

A few hundred yards from me, as inaccessible as if he were floating on the other side of the sun, Jo-Andra has started to descend the gravity well.

The pain in my head has changed into a nagging throb and then a simple inconvenience. I sleep two hours —an error, judging by the nausea that overwhelms me every time I move in the narrow compartment. I see my reflection in the polished walls and decode my face with-out thinking. In a capsule there's nothing to do but look at yourself.

My comm implants return to life as I approach the

ground when the ionized gas shield that surrounds the convoy dissipates. The news of Jo-Andra's arrival has been duly recorded by the authorities at the earth terminal. He hasn't been certified dangerous, just "disturbed", which should get him a gentle arrest. I've placed the diamonds in one of the paper pouches used in the event of vomiting. Despite their size, they weigh almost nothing. They've survived the death of a star and traveled along the routes of gravity to wind up in a barf bag. I wonder what Jo was planning to do with them. Nothing, most likely. Regardless of the form of the intelligence that has invaded him, it knows little of our reality.

When the approach messages ring out, accompanied by the inevitable advertising flashes, I buckle up wisely in the vertical alcove that is supposed to protect me. My fatigue is eating away at me like acid, but everything will be over soon.

I close my eyes. It's almost midnight, local time, and I've got nothing left.

A brutal impact, followed by a series of jolts. The straps unlock and roll into the alcove with a dry clack, tearing the neck of my paper overalls on their way. I stand up, collect the pouch of diamonds. Gravity weighs heavily on my shoulders, swells my fingers. Tomorrow I'll have to go through an interminable series of medical tests and spend time in a conditioning tank until I can get back into the swing of things without any risk. There will be a tomorrow, then another, and I'll force myself to survive each of them.

The door to the capsule still hasn't opened.

After 15 minutes, after the hubbub from the rest of the train has died down, I decide to contact the emergency services, using my identification code.

And I learn that I'm no longer there.

"You say that he pirated your code? Just like that?"

The cop questioning me in a tiny room at the terminal's administrative services department has politely let me use the only chair available and is sitting on a corner of the desk, one leg flicking nervously in the air before him.

"He already knew it." (I'm trying to hide the anguish that is overwhelming me.) "Listen, I can prove who I am. You've already checked…" (He nods his head, eyes staring at his shoe as it moves up and down.) "Jo-Andra doctored the system to make it look like my capsule was empty, then he took my identity long enough to get past your men."

"There's no one here but me," says the cop. "Do you think we would send out an entire squad to stop some guy who has just spent four and a half months in space and is barely able to crawl under one g? No one cares about the incident. You got your diamonds back. You're alive. What more do you want?"

"To go back home." (As I say the words, I almost wish they were true.) "But if you have a medical rack nearby, I could use a shot before leaving."

"Sorry, the department is closed for the night. But I can offer you a coffee from the machine. And…" he adds with an apologetic smile, "I can get you a jacket before you leave. Can you manage?"

I nod and stand up clumsily. I use my links to order a vehicle to wait for me at the entrance. It will be there in a few minutes.

The rest will take place between Jo-Andra and me.

I collapse onto the back seat in relief. The soles of

my feet are killing me. The bad coffee has left an overly sweet taste in my mouth and I feel my heart tire as it beats in time with my nervousness. Overhead, the stars are invisible. The mustiness of the city and the sea mingle in an insidious cocktail that attempts to convince me that everything is back to normal. Only one odor is missing: mine. My hormone inhibitors are still active and I'm not completely there. I slide over the surface, carried by an invisible current that brings me back to where it all really started. Where Jo-Andra has gone as well.

The Simplex.

We're all dead ends. Each of us occupies a solitary universe, turned in on itself, which others can never penetrate. The life form that colonized Jo-Andra must have noticed this. In order to reproduce, it needs to duplicate in a blank intelligence, one that can be accessed digitally. As the vehicle travels through deserted streets, swept by the wind, I wonder if I'll arrive in time.

In this world, overrun with digital simulations and duplications, there are fewer and fewer real newborns. Jo-Andra knows about Moira's baby and I suspect that he kept the access codes for Simplex, which he had downloaded to help me. He never sorts through the memories stored in his artificial antememories; he prefers to buy additional memory space when he reaches the saturation point.

The public lighting projects orangish-yellow puddles in front of the entrance, where the ruby light of an alarm flashes. The odor of dead leaves is just as I remember it. I walk toward the entrance and send my identity code to the digital terminal that protects the site. No siren sounds. I push the door with a stealthy smile: Jo-Andra is still using my identity and the system recognizes me as a double of myself. I drag myself along a corridor, ash-gray in the absence of lighting, walk around the deserted desk and wave my fingers in front of the elevator's optical scanner. For a second, I have the impression that everything will stop there. But then the door slides with a discreet clink and I descend into the heart of the system.

To Moira.

My felt shoes slip on the tiled floor. I lean against the wall with almost every step. When I reach the room where Moira is resting, the metal door is already open. Out of breath, I glance in before entering.

Jo-Andra is standing with his back to me. He is partially bent over the mechanism that controls the sarcophagi and I hear a cover lift with a slight squeal that resonates in my very bones. Acting on impulse, I turn and head to the other end of the corridor, where the security plate juts out of the wall. I hit it, but not hard enough, and I have to hit it again, twice more, before the plate gives way.

The pistol falls into my hand. At the same time, an alarm sounds.

I'll never know if I triggered the alarm by picking up the weapon or if Jo-Andra did when he tore the main data injection jack from the sarcophagus. The gloomy wail of the alarm shakes me like a whip lash. When I enter the room, pistol aimed, Jo-Andra is curled up in fetal position on the floor, a cable running from his head to the entrails of the system. The expression on his face is ecstatic. I walk over to him and, in the depths of his wide-open eyes, *I see him drain away.* Then, with a splash of jelly, Moira stands up, breasts and belly absurdly swollen. She opens her mouth, lips stretched to the point of tearing, and the sound that escapes is horribly inhuman.

236

So I shoot her, over and over again, until she falls silent and the security guard tears the weapon from my hand, before I plunge into the blessed unconsciousness provoked by a blow to the back of the head.

The last diamond has disappeared in the burning maw of the incinerator. I stretch, my body so painful that I have to bite my lips to keep from moaning. I have no idea if the Trojan flower has survived in the simplified reality that Moira's mind has become—Moira, who will never come out of her traumatic coma, according to the doctors, and her child who stopped living before even seeing the light of day. I told the authorities everything that had happened, but they didn't believe me. All I had to give them was fossils of explanations, swept away by the chaotic evolution of recent days.

Simplex waived any kind of lawsuit.

Just prior to releasing me, the police psychologist carefully explained that my so-called Trojan flowers were nothing other than the materialization of my fear of being taken over, that my love for Moira, which had so obsessed me, had become an autonomous presence, foreign and yet indispensable—the ultimate form of colonization. Symbols and metaphors, the human manner of mapping the spaces in our souls and folding them like origami flowers.

I'm the last one to agree to that.

So, in a few days, in a few months, after I've had time to reassemble the debris of my fortune and my life, I'll head back out to the Trojan cluster, under Jupiter's indifferent eye. I noted the transponder frequencies of the last Waldo, which is standing guard in the midst of the asteroid fragments. It will guide me straight in.

I have no idea whether there is still an intact flower in the middle of the debris. If I find one, I intend to pick it. The only intelligences we know of are our own, and that limitation keeps us from growing beyond a certain point. Even the AIs are a failure since they're too much like us; the mirror they hold up to us teaches us nothing. But perhaps a flower, with its terrifying desire to survive and reproduce, will be able to people the void I've become.

If that's the case, I'll come back.

LOVE YOUR ENEMY

The helicopter approached the island after a tight turn over the bay. The Tyrrhenian Sea rolled out its usual carpet of sun-crushed greens and violets. It took Cayre's practiced eye to make out the iridescent trace left by a ship in the middle of the proliferating algae. Sighing in exasperation, he took out his tablet and coded a short report.

"Stop that!" (Although the cockpit was sound-proofed, the pilot had spoken over the general communication system so that the intervention would be recorded by the black boxes.) "No interference during landing."

Cayre shrugged. There were no other passengers; flight security was the least of his concerns.

"We'll fly another circle over the seaweed strip. I want to plot the pollution trace. Can you take photos?"

"We have 15 minutes of fuel left. And we're already behind schedule."

"It won't take more than five minutes."

"It's your dime…"

The colorful blanket measured only 200 meters long. Not a true degassing, rather a fuel leak. What intrigued Cayre, though, was the itinerary chosen by the polluting boat. Right in the middle of the algae, where the long stems threated to wrap around the propellers. A smuggler? The Center's surveillance system would have spotted it. He scrawled his questions on the tablet and set it to sleep mode.

With a grumble, the helicopter dove for the island.

Without waiting for the composite blades to come to a stop, Cayre stepped out of the cockpit, back hunched. It

was fine and all knowing that there was no risk of decap-
itation, he still tucked his head down into his shoulders
out of reflex. He forced himself to stand up and walked
over to the end of the concrete field where an electric cart
with an immense sunshade was waiting for him. The
driver saluted him and opened the door.

The Center's buildings covered half the slope of a
hill in the middle of the Island. At the peak, windmills
stretched their skeletal silhouettes, waving their articulated arms, to make the most of the ocean breeze. Plastic
greenhouses, separated from the road by honeycombed
brick walls, stood in tight rows. As they drove farther
away from the sea, the few rare access points were covered with kabalistic prohibitions and symbols that Cayre
was unable to decipher. Overwhelmed by an impulse, he
motioned at the driver to stop, shaking his digital tablet.

Grudgingly, the other man parked the vehicle on the
dust shoulder. Cayre climbed out and walked over to the
closest greenhouse to examine it. The heat stuck to him
like glue.

The plastic shutters were locked by a double security
system: code and handprint. The system remained inert
under his fingers. Through a tiny slit next to a support
beam, he saw rows of plants supported by carbon stakes.
No way to determine what they were. He pretended to
scribble on his tablet. Drops of sweat trickled down between his shoulder plates as he walked back along the
short wall to the cart.

From the corner of his eye, he noticed a brown spot
in the narrow tunnel between two greenhouses. The driver
glanced at him, exasperated. Grimacing, Cayre climbed
over the small wall and walked into the passageway.

He blinked in the heavy shadow that reigned there.
After walking a few meters, he saw a couple of naked

children huddling together, their puny buttocks facing him. No more than five years old, he thought as he came to a stop. He coughed. The little girl turned halfway around and stared at him. Then she tore a flower out of the ground and waved it at him like a talisman.

Cayre had never seen that type of plant before. The fleshy petals formed an irregular corolla, with an unhealthy color: a mixture of chrome and flesh, with iridescent streaks, like garbage oil that has been recycled too often. The flower seemed to twist in the dirt-covered fingers that caressed it. Cayre approached and the sweet odor of rot grabbed him by the throat. Just before he turned, he saw the child tear off a piece of the corolla and chew it with an earnest expression. Her pupils dilated and she turned her back to him, her body shuddering.

The day was already well underway when Cayre entered the meeting room at the Centre. He kept the pleasantries to a minimum. (Yes, he'd eaten at the previous stopover, no coffee thank you, yes he would greet the boss later.) They had him put on oversized sterile overalls and he submitted to the decontamination ritual before entering a series of white-tiled laboratories. The flat screens hanging on the wall displayed segments of genetic code or single-cell colonies magnified thousands of times. However, the DNA sequencers were resting, their control panels turned off. Cayre supposed they had interrupted all of the experiments in progress before his arrival. The usual scientific paranoia.

Close-ups of *Caulerpa Taxifolia* were scattered about the desks, particularly the most recent mutations that grew more than a meter per day and whose toxins attacked everything that moved. The show was familiar to him. At this very moment, hundreds of laboratories around the world were working on cleaning up the planet's pollution and he, Cayre, was responsible for making sure the taxpayers' money was spent wisely.

He listened carefully to the spiel carefully prepared by the two team leads. The Center had two specializations: treating oil derivatives—a remnant from the time when oil was particularly inexpensive in Greece—and controlling the flora in the Mediterranean depths. The situational analyses were detailed, obviously based on data that was updated in real time. The results, on the other hand, seemed fuzzy to him. And the medium-term research strategy could be summed up in a handful of empty sentences, heard thousands of times elsewhere.

Cayre forced himself to listen to the presentations until the very end, without interrupting the speakers. He asked a few routine questions and requested the budget evolution graphs and the hiring curve for each team. The Center was operating at full capacity; the researchers—with impressive pedigrees—seemed both motivated and conscientious. But nothing was coming out of their labs. No revolutionary articles, no original technical solutions. Barely more than a few routine announcements on scientific sites. That was what had caught Cayre's attention and convinced him to come and inspect the island.

He leaned back in the articulated chair in the conference room and opened his tablet with a flick. The sterile overalls squeezed him uncomfortably; despite the air conditioning, he felt damp. Opposite him, the two team leads sat shoulder to shoulder, flanked by a handful of scientists who had joined them.

"Before I forget," Cayre, "I flew over the alga carpet surrounding the island on my way in and I saw something curious."

A reedy but perfectly audible whistle rose from the

group of researchers. One of the leaders turned around, frowning, and silence fell.

Cayre allowed the discomfort to grow, then added, "There were traces of oil in the water. A polluting trail that the satellites should have detected."

"No doubt, a fishing boat. The area isn't really off-limits even if we try to discourage the curious."

"I understand. However… (Cayre smiled ironically) the wake was heading straight for the algae. I believe that the invasive strains of *Taxifolia* produce toxins that prevent them from being nibbled at by the submarine fauna. Not exactly the kind of place where one would expect to find miraculous catches. More likely a place people would avoid if they don't want to twist a propeller. Am I mistaken?"

The oldest scientist shrugged ostensibly and said, "There are always a few imbeciles who go to places they shouldn't. If that's all you saw, I'll send a report to the surveillance department."

"That's all I saw in fact. But I plan to spend a few days on the island and glance here and there. It is possible that I may complete your report with my own observations."

Cayre was assigned a tiny studio apartment in the housing complex next to the Centre. In principle, he should have left the same evening and no arrangements had been made for his stay. The comfort of the room was Spartan, the bed barely large enough for him. But the view from the balcony redeemed everything: beyond the greenhouse zone, the sea sparkled. The water looked unusually clean, as blue and transparent as during the time of Ulysses, despite the presence of algae.

For a second, Cayre considered asking them to loan

him a swimsuit, then thought better of it. He'd wait for the night to swim. He knew he was a good swimmer, even though he wasn't used to salt water. In France, the pools and certain mountain lakes were the last places people could paddle about without fearing skin rashes.

Overhead, a jet streaked the sky with twin furrows. The effect was disturbing. Cayre recalled what his father said to him shortly before his death, "We constantly draw the lines of our own destruction and no one knows how to read them!"

He pulled on a T-shirt with the Center's logo and set out to explore the island.

Behind the wheel of a mini-cart, he turned to the landing zone. A narrow road circled the island, bordered on one side by the sea and on the other by the green-houses. From time to time, an olive tree stood out on the horizon. Cayre was starting to feel hungry. He had seen no one outside the Center. The island was inhabited only by the scientists and the few rare seasonal workers who took turns at harvest time. For a long time, European agriculture had been so mechanized that the peasants had been replaced by agricultural machine programmers or by artificial intelligences that analyzed the satellite data in order to adjust watering sessions in real time. But most of the arable land of the old continent had been polluted by industrial waste that overflowed in wild discharges, impossible to treat. For the time being, the oceans served as garbage cans for the entire world.

Cayre noticed a cloud of dust above the greenhouses, on the other side of the promontory he was driving along. Instinctively, he slowed. The sun was low on the horizon; work must have stopped. As soon as he could, he parked on the shoulder, before plunging into a narrow alley, between two white, plastic tents.

Behind the greenhouses, there was an enormous compost hole filled with dry algae, sand and dirt. A small mechanical shovel buzzed all around it, biting into the soil and spitting out enormous mouthfuls. A man, bare-chested, mouth hidden beneath an enormous mustache, operated the machine by remote control from on top of the rock where he was seated. Another rolled a large can toward the hold, using a motorized dolly. Then, to Cayre's surprise, he simply removed the plug and allowed a thick, black, oily liquid, which smelled all too familiar, to trickle onto the compost.

"What are you doing? Are you crazy?"

Cayre spring out into the light, without thinking. The two men looked up at him and watched him approach, gesticulating, without interrupting their work.

"That's oil! You're polluting the entire zone."

"Ne?"

The man operating the machine glanced at him, eyes questioning, and uttered a long sentence in Greek. Cayre shook his head. The man shrugged, placed the remote control on the ground at his feet and pulled a folded piece of paper with the Center's logo on it from the back pocket of his jeans. It was a list of instructions, in Greek and English. One sentence caught Cayre's eye: *spraying on Zone 4, oil and garbage waste, Tanks 1 to 6.* The current date.

The Greek held out his hand for the paper. Dumb-founded, Cayre folded it back up and returned it to the other man. The mechanical shovel went back to coming and going as a second tank was emptied over the hole, its contents mixed with the dirt. The stench of oil and crushed algae rose from the compost but the laborers seemed un-concerned.

When Cayre headed back to his vehicle, the Greek

saluted him nonchalantly. As he opened the door, the investigator saw his reflection in the rearview mirror. The logo on his T-shirt identified him as a Center scientist. That made him a big enchilada on the island.

His mind filled with questions, he headed back toward the sea.

He had to leave the car under a pine tree, at the end of a road that was barely passable. After ten minutes on foot, he reached a tiny beach, enclosed by two rocky outcroppings covered with algae. The water was incredibly clear, barely hemmed by foam. He got undressed, placed a stone on his clothing to keep it from blowing away, and raced over the burning sand to the fringe of the waves.

All too soon, the water irritated his feet and calves, which were covered with reddish blisters. Swearing, he covered them with sand to relieve the pain. He heard the echo of laughter behind him. A half-dozen children, as naked as he was, were pointing at him from the end of the promontory. One after another, they jumped into the water and raced toward the open sea, shrieking in excitement. When they reached the edge of the algae fields, they dove together, disappearing under the surface, their brown bodies wrapped in filaments like obscene mermaids.

Cayre dressed quickly before limping over to the rocks. *Caulerpa* runners, dried by the sun, cracked under his shoes. He knelt down to examine them, taking care not to touch them.

Most were covered with teeth marks.

He wrapped a few specimens in his T-shirt and headed back to his car.

Lying on the balcony, his legs coated with a fishy-smelling cream the Center's nurse had prescribed, Cayre finished reading the most recent scientific articles published by the island researchers. He had long realized that the convoluted phrases of the official reports were hiding more information than they provided. Laboratories around the world were fighting a fierce war, through espionage and sophisticated data mining techniques. Each patent was a victory, each publication a potential breach that the enemy could exploit. To a certain extent, he understood the phenomena, even though he wasn't sure he approved of it. But the Center's publications were decidedly empty of useful content, as if anything that could provide a trail had been painstakingly peeled away.

Cayre smiled inside. His specialty was filling in the missing zones in the reports, based on clues as tenuous as the absence of a crucial reference in a bibliographic list. When that wasn't enough, he investigated, guided solely by his intuition. And he never gave up without obtaining results.

An iced coffee and the *Taxifolia* runners he picked up on the beach stood on the plastic table next to him. He hastily scribbled on his tablet and shook his head. All of the elements he had gathered were organized in keeping with the missing zones, like a cloud of stars orbiting around black holes.

He glanced at his watch. It was starting to get late, but the Center operated on Greek time. No doubt the researchers were staying behind in the labs. It would cost nothing to check.

The research block was locked. The retinal scanner ignored all of Cayre's attempts to be recognized. He settled for banging on the wall until someone came to open up for him.

Once he was decontaminated, a guard took him directly to the meeting room. He was not surprised to find the two team leads who had met with him in the late morning there. With a nod, he took a seat in the first free chair and turned his tablet on with a flick.

"Let's save a little time," he started. "My purpose in coming here is to understand what the enormous budget that has been allocated to you is really being used for." (He raised his hand to forestall any interruptions.) "I also suspect that additional funding has been given to you by various industries. What we give you is not enough for you to obtain your results. I'm talking, among other things, about new varieties of *Caulerpa* that you've developed, while your mission was specifically to find a means to eradicate those algae."

"You don't understand…" said the youngest of the team leaders.

"I'm all ears. A word of warning, however, I know enough to be able to tell when you're trying to lie to me."

"You've only been here since this morning and you think you understand everything that's going on here?"

"I have a few ideas. I've seen your greenhouses and your compost pit. I've picked up various unusual specimens here and there. In short, I have more than enough evidence to bring a battalion of experts here. If that's what you want, of course."

"How much?"

The hostility in the researcher's voice was so strong that Cayre felt like throwing out a figure, just to watch his reaction.

"Sorry, you're off track. All of the information contained in my tablet is transmitted to my department in real time. I'm under surveillance as well."

"Show him the bins, Franz," murmured the older of

248

the two men. "As soon as you've signed a confidentiality agreement, we'll give you the owner's tour. That should convince our patrons that the money they're sending us is being put to good use. You'll leave your tablet in this room."

A half-dozen scientists in rumpled overalls were gathered in front of their workstations or their microscopes. They never even looked up as the group walked past. For the first time since arriving, Cayre felt that the Center was something more than a fake window for visitors. Whatever research work was going on here, those taking part in it considered it crucial.

"We think we've made a fundamental breakthrough," echoed the oldest of the researchers, pressing his eye against the security scanner. "We came at the problem from the other side, with a new look."

"The *Caulerpa*?"

"The pollution of the planet and particularly the oceans." (The wall slid open with a well-oiled hiss.) "The *Caulerpa* is a means, not a problem. You'll see."

In the middle of a room lit by horticultural neons stood a transparent bin, measuring several cubic meters, filled with water. A mass of algae with clearly recognizable fronds grew on the sandy bottom. The stems were a disgusting color; they shone as if coated in grease.

"Our latest baby," the scientist murmured proudly. "Created through bioengineering in 17 months, despite insane specifications. It's still growing a little too slowly, but we should be able to solve that problem soon. After all, the original strain grows several meters per day, when the conditions are favorable."

Cayre walked over to the bin. The network of clues he had gathered pointed in that direction, but he still found it hard to believe. He could not imagine what had driven an entire team to develop an improved version of the enemy.

As if reading his thoughts, the young scientist opened a metal locker, revealing a row of flasks.

"Choose your poison." (He picked up a bottle randomly and looked at the label.) "Mercury sludge. We also have crude oil, concentrated manure, motor oil… Everything that has been poisoning our planet for decades."

He climbed up a stepladder and tilted the flask over the surface of the bin.

"Are you timing this, Georges?"

As Cayre watched, dumbfounded, he poured the content of the flask into the bin. A brown cloud spread over the algae. The water grew so murky it was almost opaque. An unpleasant odor swept over the room.

"We have about 10 minutes to wait. Would you like a coffee? There's a distributor in the lab."

"Black, no sugar." (Cayre had replied automatically.) "But I'll wait until this is over."

He walked over to the transparent wall and looked through it. The dirty water was gradually clearing. He looked for a pump or some sort of filtering device, but found nothing.

"It's the *Caulerpa* that do the work. This strain feeds off all the substances we consider pollutants. It proliferates in the most affected sites and restores the purity of the water in a few months. We've conducted full-scale tests around the island. The results are spectacular."

"The trail of oil I noticed when I arrived," murmured Cayre.

"An hour later and you wouldn't have been able to locate it."

The water in the tank is almost clear. Seized by an

impulse, Cayre climbed up the stepladder and bent over the surface.

"Be careful! The *Caulerpa* gives off rather aggressive toxins," warned Georges. "Don't dip your fingers in the water!"

"I know…"

The sludge had disappeared, gobbled up by the reddish fronds. The sand at the bottom was once again visible.

"Franz has created another variety of garbage plants, as we call them. These ones are for on land. A poppy mutation, halfway between the common poppy and the Afghan variety. It grows without any problem on public landfills or along highways. In the long run, it will cover all abandoned industrial zones.

"I think I've seen a specimen. It looks rather repulsive."

"To us perhaps. But our descendants will get used to it without any problems. Do you want us to show you how the *Caulerpa* processes the oil slicks?"

"I've seen enough, thank you. I suppose everything you have here is protected by patents?"

"Not yet. Our experts have drafted the applications but we're waiting for the green light from our other sponsors to submit them." (The older scientist shrugged.) "Personally, I don't really care. We're working for all of humanity, to clean up the mess our species has left behind. Thanks to what we've done, pollution will soon be nothing but a bad memory."

Franz and Georges accompanied Cayre back to his room, after making a detour to the cafeteria which served frozen dishes sprinkled with Retzina. Now that the veil of silence had been lifted, the two researchers seemed to be delighted to talk about their results. The three men settled on the balcony with a bottle of wine and plastic glasses. Under the star-studded sky, the sea was as calm as a bed-sheet.

"I'll leave at dawn tomorrow," Cayre said out loud. "What you've accomplished here will change the world."

As he put his glass down on the plastic table, he felt the *Caulerpa* runners he had picked up crumble under his fingers. The image of the chewed stems, teeth marks clearly visible, leaped into his mind.

In a voice that barely changed, he asked, "Your creations, these garbage plants as you call them… It would surprise me if they were a good mix for the human species. Apart from the fact that they're hideous, they must also be toxic for current herbivores. How do you plan to get rid of them, or at least limit their proliferation?"

There was a heavy silence and then Georges cleared his throat, saying "We've already solved that problem. I think you know that."

Cayre recalled the little girl's look, eyes dilated as she chewed the petals of the obscene flower, the color of used oil. Once again, he heard the joyful cries of the flock of naked children setting out to graze the algae fields along the coast.

"I guessed it, in fact," he said while pouring another glass of wine.

WITH A WINK OF THE HERON'S EYE

He saw her stumble, in slow motion, and lean against the flower merchant's window. The shopping gallery at the Schiphol airport had been invaded by the usual hustle and bustle of hurried travelers. No one paid any attention to her. When she stood up, a silver tear slipped from her ear, down her blonde hair before bouncing off her shoulder. He watched it, noting every detail, and headed over toward her at a leisurely pace. When he got to where she had been standing, he bent down and picked the earring up off the ground. Then he stood up and glanced about, looking for her, but she had already disappeared, swallowed up in the crowd.

He closed his fist and felt the piece of metal jewelry dig gently into his palm. The boarding gate for Djakarta was located at the other end of the terminal. Suddenly, it seemed inaccessible to him. He headed toward one of the train station entrances, then changed his mind. With a shrug, he straightened his travel bag with its many pockets and headed for the taxis.

The driver dropped him off near Leidseplein. Workers had started tearing up the small street that led to his usual hotel. Among the heaps of stones on the roadway, he caught a glimpse of a small strip of bone-colored sand. Seized by impulse, he crossed over the protective barrier and took a few steps on the secret beach in the heart of the city. Fossil shells crunched under his polished shoes. Eyes closed, he sniffed toward the east and felt the first drops of rain caress his lips.

As he reached the front steps of the hotel, he heard a

woman's voice swear in French behind him. The contrast between the voice, rich and harmonious, and the curse was striking. He turned around slowly. She was pulling an enormous black canvas suitcase and the wheels kept getting caught between the uneven cobblestones. The storm threatened to transform her blonde hair into something unacceptable. He smiled at her as he reached out his hand.

"Let me help you. Amsterdam is fiercely unsuitable for luggage such as yours."

"I've seen worse," she said, automatically wiping her eyes. "You're staying at this hotel?"

"If they have a room…" (He grabbed the handle of the suitcase and effortlessly carried it to the top of the steps). "They know me and I hope they'll find something for me."

He rolled the suitcase to the reception counter that was stuck in a room built all in length, and then courteously stepped back to allow her to speak with the employee there first. Then he adjusted his bag and discreetly walked off. Things were going faster than expected and he would, in all likelihood, have no need to book a room.

The rain swallowed him up without a sound.

He walked, nose turned to the wind, along the Spiegel Canal. It had stopped raining, but the air remained oily under his tongue, laden with the stench of the port and the memory of cut flowers that had been carried on carts for centuries. On each side of the canal, shops down below offered countless marvels: silverware, works of art, maps and portolan charts. He glanced at them quickly, without lingering. He felt nervous, impatient. At the bottom of his pocket, the earring felt very heavy, weighing his step down more than usual.

He heard a familiar staccato on the slippery sidewalk nearby. An old heron with shiny feathers was moving away from the canal with its high-stepping gait to a destination known only to it. He watched it and stood right in the middle of the street to block the half-dozen bicycles arriving from the museum. The heron crossed slowly, beak down as if looking for a place to plant it between two cobblestones, then the bikes continued on their way with the grinding of metal. A bell rang out joyfully close by and he nodded in return.

The heron looked at him gravely. Its round eyes, filled with liquid light, blinked several times. Then the bird spread its wings and heavily took flight.

When the traveler reached the South American antique store, he felt eyes resting on his shoulders, but did not turn around. In the midst of the reflections on the window, he recognized the woman from the hotel, accompanied by an almost identical version of herself. They stood very close to one another, twin sisters rather than lovers, and were consulting a tourist guide, pages fluttering in the wind.

He allowed his eyes to wander inside the shop filled with parchments and old maps stretched on racks. The sun that played among the clouds drew fleeting trails toward Atlantis, Eldorado, the kingdom of Saba. He would have liked to stand in front of the window forever and learn all of the world's secret roads. But everything in Amsterdam encouraged him to move. He turned around and walked quickly back to the heart of the city.

The aisle at the flower market smelled of fresh humus and mayonnaise. A family walked noisily past him, armed with cones of fries drowned in gravy. Overhead, the off-kilter rooftops formed a ragged skyline against the gray backdrop of the sky. He felt as if he could simply reach up and tear off a ribbon of roughly pinked clouds. Someone bumped into him gently and he felt a hand slip into his bag. He forced himself not to look down when expert fingers searched desperately for something to steal in the heap of multicolored scarves and magic rings. Then he pulled on the strap and walked off, catching sight of tulips with bent necks and bags of all kinds of bulbs stacked in stalls.

His tenderness for the city was gradually awakening. Everything here suited him, from the trompe-l'œil styles of the narrow facades to the claptrap of the strident neons that had colonized the entire center. He walked in the shadow of the belfry, and then headed over to Place Rembrandt. Inevitably.

They were sitting on a terrace, holding hands. He allowed the human tide to carry him to them, noting every detail. When he was close enough, he smiled at them and slowed just enough for his bag to swing over their table, dangerously close to the glasses of gin and tonic standing side by side.

"Were you able to get a room?" the older one asked.

"Still waiting. You?"

"My sister handled the reservations. We saw you with the heron. Quite entertaining. Well, I mean unusual."

"Not for people here. The birds were here before them."

He turned part way to look at the younger one, trying to read the lines of a possible story in her features. She held his gaze distractedly before plunging back into her glass and finishing it with a single gulp. The ice cubes tinkled when she put it back down on the table.

"Excuse me for being indiscreet, but you don't seem

well."

"My sister is trying to forget an unpleasant divorce," interrupted the older one. "Moreover…"

"Don't be ridiculous!" (The younger woman shrugged.) "That was over three years ago and I'd like people to stop reminding me about it every five minutes. No, the truth is that I lost my earring." (With an abrupt tug, she brushed aside a lock of golden hair, streaked with a touch of gray that covered her left ear lobe.) "It's stupid, but my sister gave them to me and we don't see one another often, so I wanted to wear them specifically for this occasion. This is our first vacation together since…I don't even know how long anymore."

"I'll give you others," her sister interrupted. "It's not important."

"I wouldn't say that if I were you." (He bent over the younger one and examined her ear.) "Earrings like this are very indiscreet. They hear everything you say and, generally, they remember it all. It would be better to find it. This happened recently?"

"Yes, but I don't know where and I don't even know if they have a lost and found here. Supposing that someone brings it in, which I doubt. It was gold."

"It's easier than that, fortunately." (He took on a concentrated expression and plunged his hand into his bag before placing it over the empty glass.) But I warn you, this might hurt a little… Ready?"

Without waiting for an answer, he touched the exposed ear lobe with his fingers. The young woman felt a pinch, followed by a cold sensation.

"What are you…" she yelped in indignation.

He opened his hand. An earring sparkled wetly in the palm of his hand. A drop of blood pearled on the stud.

"I wouldn't put it on right away if I were you. It's icy

and you might well lose it again."

Around them, the crowd of tourists appeared to freeze, then flashes burst behind him. A bride, looking like an enormous meringue, was posing in the middle of the tables. He turned back to the older one and winked at her broadly.

"How did you do that?" asked the younger woman. (She grabbed the earring feverishly and held it up to the light.) "This is it. Where did you find it?"

"I'm a magician…"

"And you never reveal your tricks. Is that it?" (The older one clapped her hands, dryly two or three times.) "It was well done in any case. My congratulations."

"You're insulting me, you know. I'm a *real* magician, not an illusionist."

"Tell me all about it. I'm certain your explanation will be more interesting than this little sleight of hand. I'll buy you a drink in return."

"Only if you allow me to invite you both to dinner." (He raised his hands to cut off any protest.) "I know a restaurant that's not in any tourist guide, not far from the hotel. You can get antipasti and pasta there. Neither is particularly good. An extraordinary place."

"Really?" (She smiled and it was as if the sun were rising a second time.) "When you put it like that, it's hard to refuse. Mediocre pasta, hmmm. But we'll pay our own way, my sister and I. And I really want to hear your explanation."

"Simple." (He walked around the table, pulled out a chair and sat down between them. At the other end of the terrace, the bride was spinning about to laughter and applause.) "It goes back centuries, to the time when Amsterdam was just a simple fishing village built on swamps. The geography of the sand banks and the lagoons changed with every tide, or almost. Frequently, the inhabitants had to rebuild their homes when they were swallowed up by sand or the sea. So one man, a little more ambitious than the others, came up with the idea of building a dike in order to mold the currents to his will. In the sand, he planted a gigantic stake made of an entire tree trunk circled with iron, then another, and then yet another, until the soil became stable enough to build a house that would last for centuries.

"That's both the charm and the curse of this city. It's nailed to the ground by thousands of needles. Nothing ever gets lost. I…" (A smile made his eyes sparkle.) "I merely listened to your memories and went to find the lost earring in a recent past when it was still hooked on your ear. I brought back a little pain as well—the past is an icy place—but I didn't need to travel back too far in time. See? It's as simple as that."

The younger sister nodded, never taking her eyes from him. Between her fingers, the earring flashed one final time before she closed her fist over it.

"Well done," said the older sister. "We'll meet in the hotel lobby at seven this evening? I'll leave the reservations to you."

He stood up, nodded, and clasped his bag against his thigh. He felt strangely tired. Recovering the earring had given him a jolt of pure adrenaline, and coming down would take a long time.

"Wait…" The younger woman blushed, then said, "This is our first time in Amsterdam. What do you recommend we see first?"

He smiled briefly and flicked the guide she held out to him closed.

"Learn to get lost instead."

Under the veiled sunset, the city spread in a gray and watery green infinity, highlighted with fleeting streaks of pink. It was time for hesitations. He had spent most of the afternoon changing his airline ticket and had not had enough time to walk on the lumpy skin of the streets as much as he would have liked. Along his way, he purchased a bag of chocolates of many flavors—ginger, pepper, thyme—and had munched on them while standing above a canal, seeking his own tracks in the blurry reflection of the waves. The passersby had respected his solitude, punctuating his thoughts with the tinkle of silvery bells.

The two sisters were waiting for him in the hotel lobby. They stopped talking when he entered and he guessed that they'd been discussing him. The second earring had found its place and the younger sister had lined her eyes with make-up. The other woman's face was bare.

He guided them along Neu Spiegel, toward the heart of the city, listening to their enthusiastic descriptions of sites he knew like the back of his hand. He divided his attention among them, equitably. His fatigue had faded; he felt obscurely ready for what was to come and what he had had no hand in determining. He settled for being there, in the center of the vortex of events that had drawn him up in the airport and spat him back out here.

The restaurant was in the basement and opened onto street level by means of a few steep steps that he walked down cautiously. His knee was starting to bother him again; one day, he would certainly need help crossing the street before being able to take flight.

The room was divided into two: the first part looked onto the kitchens and the second was partially filled by a grand piano with the top up. Clay plates with blue designs filled with Italian hors d'œuvres were arranged on a special shelf over the strings. A pianist was playing quietly. A waitress in dance tights and a sequined top seated them in a corner with a basket of breadsticks, menus in four languages, and a carafe of coarse red wine.

"We start with the antipasti buffet, and then we choose our pasta and a dessert." (He unwrapped a breadstick and bit into it, making it crunch.) "Avoid everything that comes from the oven, it's always overcooked. And don't wait to help yourselves. Soon it will be time."

"Time for what?" asked the older one, folding her menu.

She'd selected what she wanted from the list with a single glance; he imagined she would not take dessert.

He placed a finger on his lips and stood up. The younger one joined him next to the piano. Side by side, they filled their plates. With her fork, she chased a purple artichoke around the plate and blushed when she noticed him watching her. Her perfume mingled with the scent of vinegar and garlic that rose from the hors d'œuvres. Now that she'd found her earring, she seemed drabber.

The pianist allowed his melody to fade and played a series of chords, like a signal.

"Your sister is going to have to wait," he murmured. "I wonder why she doesn't like me."

"She doesn't believe in you."

She seemed to realize what she had just said and looked down at her plate, studded with spots of oil and diced vegetables. He grimaced in resignation.

"Stop looking at those artichokes with regret like that and come and sit down. You can come back later if you're still hungry."

He'd had barely enough time to push back his chair when the young waitress asked for silence. The lights lowered; the pianist started to play again, barely brushing the keys. The music rolled around them. *Strauss*...

The waitress opened her mouth and started to sing.

The marvelously rich voice found the melody effort-lessly and echoed off the walls of the small room. Eyes closed, hands clasped over her bosom, she sang of love and the death of desire with an intensity that made her tremble. It was not the polished interpretation of a diva on a stage covered with velvet, but the song of someone who would come back later to serve wine and remove dirty plates. Hanging at her waist, the notebook she used to take orders shook every time she took a breath.

She bowed when the song came to an end and headed back to the kitchens, followed by the guests' applause. Chairs scraped against the stone floor and a line formed in front of the piano.

"I understand why the pasta is always overcooked," said the older sister. "I owe you an apology. I took you for an ordinary flirt while you're certainly more than that."

"Do you want to share my antipasti?"

"I'm not sure I have much of an appetite after that. I'm a musician, you know. A pianist. You can't imagine what I've just experienced."

He held her gaze for a long moment and murmured, "One day, I wanted to know myself. Girls like her study singing in Concertgebouw and earn barely enough here to pay their teachers. They generally don't stay for more than a few months. It's very hard-working until midnight six days a week while singing all day long. There's a con-stant turnover in voices…"

"I preferred your previous explanation," said the younger woman. (She touched her earring, flirting.) "How did you discover this place?"

"That's a secret."

He trapped a tomato confit with his fork and added,

"But you don't have to believe me."

There was another recital during dessert, then the traditional round of grappa offered by the boss. He paid the bill while they took their time in the washroom and held their raincoats for them at the foot of the steps.

"Do you want to go back to the hotel right away?" he asked. "It's not raining and I'm sure we might even be able to catch sight of a star or two. For Amsterdam, this is as close as it gets to good weather."

"We're supposed to go to bed early," said the younger sister, voice tinged with regret. "We're leaving for Rotterdam tomorrow."

"So, allow me to show you a place I like a lot. It's on the way, next to the large casino, quite close to the hotel. You may have walked past it without seeing it."

He pulled up the collar of his leather jacket and headed down the street, one step ahead of her. In the sleeping shops on each side, pale blue nightlights outlined the potbellied shapes of Dutch furniture. In the distance, he heard the hoarse croak of a heron and the clank of a tram. He felt melancholy wash over him without knowing why. The sensation was pleasant, as long as it was shared.

"It's here. Wait a bit and you'll see them appear."

The tiny square was actually a triangle, surrounded by a wood barrier a few centimeters high. In the absence of light, the grass was dark, dotted with tiny puddles that shone like eyes.

Gray shapes, as large as rats, gradually emerged from the grass. As their eyes grew used to the darkness, the details grew clearer. They were metal statues, possibly twenty or so, carefully engraved.

"I present to you the varans of Amsterdam. They

don't look like much like that, but when they're covered with snow, they're quite fascinating."

"Can I go closer to them?"

"That's prohibited. And most likely disappointing. I've never wanted to get close to them. It's all a question of lighting, in fact."

"Like many things that concern you, Mr. Magician." (The older woman firmly took her sister by the arm and prevented her from stepping over the wooden barrier.) "You said that the hotel was nearby?"

"On the other side of Leidseplein."

Almost all of the cobblestones had been removed from the alley. The sandbank shone like a shard of bone under the white neons of the hotel. The older sister had unconsciously slowed her pace, as if unsure of the complicated choreography that would have to be played out at the top of the steps. He allowed her to walk ahead of him and stopped on the bottom step when she blocked his way.

"I'll join you in five minutes," she told her sister. "If they're still serving tea at this late hour, will you order me one?"

Then she took him by the arm and pulled him along a few meters, her heels sunk in the sand like tiny nails.

"How did you do it?" she said after a long silence that he didn't bother to break. "I designed those earrings myself; they're unique pieces."

"My story didn't convince you?"

A veil of darkness flitted briefly over his face. He dispelled it with a broad smile.

"I don't need magic to find an explanation," she argued.

"Let's see if I can give you one you find more acceptable."

He bent down and stacked a few cobblestones to make a miniature table and pointed at it.

"Your sister was there. I bent over her and looked straight into her eyes to keep her from taking an interest in what I was doing. I took an ice cube from her glass, then pinched her ear between my thumb and index finger while pressing the ice cube with the palm of my hand. Pain, followed by cold."

"And the earring?"

"Your sister lost it at the airport. I was a few meters away and I picked it up, but she had disappeared by the time I stood back up. When I saw her with you, I recognized her and I wanted...I don't know what I wanted. To play, perhaps."

He picked up a handful of sand and let it slip through his fingers. A tiny shell stuck to his fingertip.

"There's no such thing as magic," she murmured.

"Magic doesn't exist. That's true. But it can be created. It takes a great deal of energy and time for a result that varies from one person to the next." (His eyes clouded over, growing as dark as the water in the canal in an instant.) "If I give you this shell that I've just picked up, will you have the courage to wear it on your ear? It will tell you what you need to hear, whether that pleases you or not." (She moved imperceptibly back.) "Magic is choosing the dream in which you want to wake up. It's something you can learn."

"I've never needed magic. Or wanted it."

"I know.... Are you going to tell your sister what I've told you?"

"I've always tried to protect her from liars and people who make up lovely stories for her. I failed with her rotten husband, but that won't happen again!"

She frowned, disenchantment ruining the polished

perfection of her features. At that moment, he found her touching. Not beautiful, but attractive, desirable like people who truly exist are. He felt like embracing her, knowing that it was already too late for that.

"In any case," she concluded, "What I decide to tell my sister is none of your business."

"True. Do you want to go in? I believe that I'll walk for a bit…"

She nodded reluctantly and turned away.

"Thank you for the restaurant," she said before walking off. "Whether you believe it or not, I've had an unforgettable evening."

He watched her walk into the hotel and disappear behind the glass door. With a sigh, he raised the shell to his ear and listened, eyes half closed. Determined footsteps, the clinking of cups against saucers, then the voice of the young woman, questioning, and that of her sister, answering.

"I have something to tell you…"

The moisture-laden wind caressed her cheeks as she faithfully repeated everything he had just told her, concluding with, "I know that he's disturbing, for an illusionist, but…"

"I didn't come from the airport," the younger one interrupted. "I took the train."

"How?"

"I was in Brussels. I came by the TGV and I thought I might have lost my earring last evening. What he told you is a lie!"

"That's what I wanted to tell you, but…"

They started to quarrel, two opposing visions of the world that would never in all likelihood ever be reconciled. Yet, perhaps the older one would learn to doubt.

That was the best he could hope for, the reason he had gone out of his way to come here. He cautiously placed the shell back in the sand and walked off calmly, his bag hitting his flanks with every step.

He walked toward the casino's lights without turning back. There were still some taxis stopped at the corner of the boulevard and his plane took off in two hours. When he slipped his hand into his pocket, he felt the silver earring he had picked up that morning at the airport. With a melancholy smile, he brandished it in front of his eyes and watched how it caught the light from the passing headlights. Then he walked over to the canal and slipped it into a crevice in the stone guardrail. One day, when the sun struck it at the right angle, someone would find it. Someone who would know how to look at it, what to do with it. The story no longer belonged to him.

Sources

About the Author

Jean-Claude Dunyach, born in 1957, has a Ph.D. in applied mathematics and supercomputing. He was an aeronautical engineer at Airbus (in Toulouse) until 2019.

He has been writing science fiction since the early 1980s, and has published eleven novels and ten collections of short stories, garnering the French SF Award in 1983, four Rosny aîné Awards in 1992, 1998 and 2008, as well as the Grand Prix de l'Imaginaire in 1998 and the Prix Ozone in 1997.

His short story *Déchiffrer la trame* [Unravelling the thread] was voted Best Story of the Year by *Interzone*'s readers.

His novel, *Etoiles Mourantes* [Dying Stars], co-written with French author Ayerdhal, won the Grand Prix de la Tour Eiffel in 1999, as well as the Prix Ozone.

His works have been translated and published in Hungary, Italy, Australia, England, Canada and the United States.

Dunyach is also a successful lyricist for several French music artists, some of whom have served as an inspiration for his novel *Roll over, Amundsen*.

About the Translator

With undergraduate and graduate degrees in translation and a Ph.D. in Interdisciplinary Studies (Management, Communication Studies, Translation Studies), Sheryl Curtis has spent the past few decades working as a corporate, freelance and literary translator. Her English translations of French, Swiss, Canadian and Québec authors have appeared in numerous collections, anthologies and magazines published in Canada, England, the US and Australia, including at Black Coat Press. In her spare time, she aspires to become a textile artist. She lives in Montréal with her husband and two rescue cats.

Bibliography

Autoportrait [*Self-Portrait*] (collection) (Présence du Futur No. 415, Denoël, Paris, 1986)

Le Temple de Chair (*Le Jeu des Sabliers*, Tome 1) [*The Temple of Flesh— The Game of the Hourglasses*, Vol. 1] (Anticipation No. 1592, Fleuve Noir, Paris, 1987)

Le Temple d'Os (*Le Jeu des Sabliers*, Tome 2) [*The Temple of Bones— The Game of the Hourglasses*, Vol. 2] (Anticipation No. 1609, Fleuve Noir, Paris, 1988)

Nivôse (*Étoiles Mortes*, Tome1) [*Nivose—Dead Stars*, Vol. 1] (Anticipation No. 1837, Fleuve Noir, Paris, 1991)

Aigue-Marine (*Étoiles Mortes*, Tome 2) [*Aigue-Marine— Dead Stars,* Vol. 2] (Anticipation No. 1838, Fleuve Noir, Paris, 1991)

Voleurs de Silence (*Étoiles Mortes*, Tome 3) (*The Thieves of Silence—Dead Stars*, Vol. 3] (Anticipation No. 1858, Fleuve Noir, Paris, 1992)

Roll Over, Amundsen (Anticipation No. 1912, Fleuve Noir, Paris, 1993)

La Guerre des Cercles [*The War of the Circles*] (Anticipation No. 1963, Fleuve Noir, Paris, 1995)

Étoiles Mourantes [*Dying Stars*] (with Ayerdhal) (J'ai Lu Millénaire, Paris, 1999)

La Station de l'Agnelle [*The Station of the Lamb*) (collection) (L'Atalante, Nantes, 2000)

Dix Jours Sans Voir la Mer [*Ten Days Without Looking at the Sea*] (collection) (L'Atalante, Nantes, 2000)

Étoiles Mortes [*Dead Stars*] (J'ai Lu, Paris, 2000)

Déchiffrer la Trame [*Unraveling the Thread*] (collection) (L'Atalante, Nantes, 2001)

Le Jeu des Sabliers [*The Game of the Hourglasses*] (ISF, Paris, 2003)

Les Nageurs de Sable [*The Sand Swimmers*] (collection) (L'Atalante, Nantes, 2003)

Le Temps, en s'évaporant... [*Time, as it evaporates...*] (collection) (L'Atalante, Nantes, 2005)

Séparations (collection) (L'Atalante, Nantes, 2007)

Les Harmoniques Célestes [*The Celestial Harmonics*] (collection) (L'Atalante, Nantes, 2011)

L'Instinct du Troll [*Troll's Instinct*] (L'Atalante, Nantes, 2015)

Le Clin d'œil du Héron [*With a Wink of the Heron's Eye*] (collection) (L'Atalante, Nantes, 2016)

L'Enfer du Troll [*Troll's Hell*] (L'Atalante, Nantes, *2017)*

Trois hourras pour Lady Evangeline [*Three Hurrahs for Lady Evangeline*] (L'Atalante, Nantes, *2019)*

L'Empire du Troll [*Troll's Empire*] (L'Atalante, Nantes, 2021)

In English:

Collections:
The Night Orchid: Conan Doyle in Toulouse (Black Coat Press, Encino, 2004)
The Thieves of Silence (Black Coat Press, Encino, 2009)

Short Stories:
In Medicis Gardens, in *Full Spectrum* 4, Bantam Spectra, New York, 1993
The Dead Eye of the Camera, in *Full Spectrum* 5, Bantam Spectra, New York, 1995
Unraveling the Thread, in *Interzone* 133, Brighton, UK, July 1998; reprinted in *Year's Best SF* 4, HarperPrism, New York, 1999

Come Into My Parlor, in *Altair* 1, Blackwood, SA, Australia, 1998

Footprints in the Snow, in *Interzone* 150, Brighton, UK, December 1999

Station of the Lamb, in *Altair* 6, Blackwood, SA, Australia, 2000

All the Roads to Heaven, in *Interzone* 156, Brighton, UK, June 2000

Orchids in the Night, in *Interzone* 160, Brighton, UK, October 2000

Watch Me When I Sleep, in *Interzone* 168, Brighton, UK, June 2001; reprinted in *Year's Best Fantasy and Horror*, Tor Books, New York, 2002

Enter the Worms, in *On Spec*, Volume 14, Number 2, Edmonton, Canada, 2002

What the Dead Know in *On Spec*, Volume 16, Number 1, Edmonton, Canada, 2004

Separations in *The SFWA European Hall of Fame,* Tor Books, New York, 2007

Birds in *Fantasy Magazine*, March 2009

God, seen from the inside in *Galaxy's Edge* 6, January 2014

Landscape with intruders in *Blind Spot*, May 2016

Love your enemy in *Galaxy's Edge* 20, May 2016

Paranamanco in *The Big Book of Science Fiction*, July 2016

With a Wink of the Heron's Eye in *Galaxy's Edge* 29, November 2017

Queen Robot's Sacrifice (with Mike Resnick) in *Galaxy's Edge* 47, November 2020